THE SNIPER

Nicholas Rhea

Constable • London

First published in Great Britain 2001
by Constable, an imprint of Constable & Robinson Ltd
3 The Lanchesters, 162 Fulham Palace Road,
London, W6 9ER
www.constablerobinson.com

ISBN 1–84119–336–4

Printed and bound in Great Britain

A CIP catalogue record for this book is available from the
British Library

Chapter One

'Who is he?' Detective Superintendent Mark Pemberton stood in the church porch very close to the body but refrained from touching anything at this early stage. The white-haired victim was curled in what looked rather like the foetal position; he was on his right side and a small quantity of blood from a chest wound had seeped from his body to stain the stone floor. That suggested he'd been killed in this place and that he'd lived very very briefly after the injury. That he was dead was beyond doubt. He'd been shot, so it seemed from this early assessment, hit in the chest when either going into or emerging from the church. Like the outer door, the inner door of the porch was standing open, Pemberton noted.

Waiting against a backcloth of tombstones was the village constable, uniformed and anxious to help. It was probably the first murder in rural Roberthorpe's long history; certainly it was a first for young PC Simon Holbeck. 'His name's Flint, sir. Ken, Kenneth. He's retired, a former photographer.'

'A local, was he? Lived in the village?'

'Yes, sir. He lived alone. There's no known family.'

'That might cause problems, he'll need to be formally identified. Any idea why he'd be here?'

'He was one of the helpers, sir, he came to wind the clock every Saturday. He's a keyholder, he unlocked the church every morning, and locked it at night. He did other chores – handed out hymn books on Sundays, took the collection, helped with the choir, that sort of thing.'

'An upright and worthy citizen, then? I wonder if he disturbed some raiders? Surprised an intruder perhaps? Is the church troubled with raiders? Or vandals? This seems a very odd killing, not many church raiders go armed and it's a bit drastic to shoot somebody when only the meagre contents of the offertory box might be at stake. And not many villains go around raiding or vandalising churches at this time of day.'

'We've not had any real trouble of that kind, sir, although the offertory box was raided about two years ago, before I was posted here. A bit of cash went, a few pounds I understand. Nothing more, there's nothing of value left on display. The church is still left open during the daytime, I've had no other reports of trouble.'

'The likelihood of cash, though. A temptation to some perhaps? So who found him?'

'The vicar, sir. Reverend Middleton, Stanley.'

'I'll need to talk to him. Where is he now?'

'At the vicarage, in a state of shock. I got the local nurse to have a look at him, he was deeply upset.'

'Well done. And what time was Flint found?'

'Half-past nine, sir. He usually got to the church at nine or thereabouts to do his chores, you could almost set your clock by Ken Flint.'

'So what happened next?'

'The vicar called the doctor, he thought Ken had had an accident of some kind but when the doctor saw the chest wound, he called me straight away. He thought it looked like a bullet wound.'

'So we're saying he probably died between nine and half-past this morning?'

'If today's routine followed his usual pattern, that's very likely, sir.'

'Right, we can check that. At that time of day, you'd

think someone must have seen something, the village will have come to life, surely? People on the move, going about their daily routine. Would a stranger be noticed? Or a local person behaving oddly, or even a vehicle doing something out of the ordinary?'

'I think so, sir, but I've not had a chance to ask around the village yet.'

'Sure, you can leave that to us. We'll arrange the house-to-house enquiries, but your local knowledge will be important. We'll keep in touch. So people will have come to this porch since his death, will they? The crime scene will have been disturbed, even just a little?'

'Very little, sir. I tried to contain it. The vicar was here, then the doctor and me. No-one else has been, I'm sure. The church was empty too, I checked. No-one else has reported finding Ken. Then I locked the outer door before radioing for assistance. I'm sure no-one else has been inside.'

'Except the killer? Unless this chap was shot from a long distance, in which case the churchyard and even beyond becomes very relevant,' mused Pemberton. 'But well done. You've done all the right things.'

'I've never been involved in a murder enquiry, sir.'

'You're bound to learn from this one. Now, the next thing is to arrange for Forensics to examine the scene, the porch, the church both inside and out, and to have a look at the body. We'll need the entire churchyard and the immediate surrounds sealed off, then fingertip-searched by the Task Force. The pathologist will want to see the body *in situ* too and I need to know the trajectory of the fatal bullet. We need to find the spot from which it was fired, that's vital.'

'I've a radio in my car, sir. Shall I call Control?'

'No need, I've a mobile phone. Did the doctor hint about the cause of death?'

'Not really, although he said it didn't look like a stab wound, sir, more like a bullet wound or even wounds, he thought, although he couldn't be sure. He didn't want to disturb things, not when he realised Ken had died in suspicious circumstances.'

'Sensible man, we'll talk to him later.'

'He did tell me his examination was very brief, but he thought the wound wasn't done with a shotgun, too clean, he felt, and too concentrated in one small area. He said something about a cluster of wounds. All he could do was confirm that Ken was dead and that, in his view, it wasn't accidental or self-inflicted. There was no gun at the scene, not when I arrived or when the vicar found him.'

'I hope no-one's moved it!' sighed Pemberton. Sometimes well-meaning people did move guns, especially when people used them to commit suicide – and thus they unwittingly generated a murder investigation.

'I asked the vicar and the doctor, sir, both said there was no gun near the body.'

'Good. Even if it was fired from a distance, the chances are we'll find the spent cartridge or cartridges. It's murder so far as I'm concerned and that means a full call-out. Is there a village hall? Somewhere we can turn into an Incident Room?'

'There's the parish room, sir. Ken, the deceased, would have a key.'

'I don't want to search the body or his home just yet, Forensic will need to examine him first. The vicar will have a key, won't he?'

'I expect so, sir.'

'Right, you stay here and protect the scene until the experts arrive. Instead of hanging around kicking my heels, I'll go and talk to the vicar, then I'll come back.'

'Right, sir.'

'Keep everyone out except our own people, but don't let them trample in that porch until I get back. Once word gets around the village, the ghouls will find an excuse to take a walk in the churchyard – keep the public away from the scene, but if you do get the chance to talk to any of them, you could ask whether Flint was keeping to his usual timetable, whether he got here about nine as usual, whether he was with anyone, and if anyone was seen around the church or churchyard in the moments before or after Flint was killed. And were any shots heard? If so, what time? And we need to know about Flint's background. Family and so on if any can be found. People aren't usually killed without reason. You can be thinking about all that while I go and chat to the Reverend Middleton.'

'Understood, sir.'

'Now I'll call out my troops, it'll take a while for them to get here, but in the meantime, where do I find the vicarage?'

Pemberton's knock was answered by a uniformed district nurse who admitted him upon proof of his identity. She told Pemberton her name was Jenny Archer, and that she lived in Roberthorpe, at No. 12 Main Street. 'He's very shaken,' she said. 'I've resisted pills, I told him to have a good stiff brandy instead.'

'Good advice I'm sure. Is he fit enough to talk to me?'

'It'll do him good to talk, Superintendent, he's in the lounge, the door on the right.'

Stanley Middleton, not yet dressed in his dog collar and clerical suit but wearing a white tee-shirt and jeans, was a small, round and bearded gentleman with a pale and haunted look about him. In his early fifties, he was sitting on the settee with a brandy glass on a side table, but he rose to his feet as Pemberton entered.

'It's Detective Superintendent Pemberton from Rainesbury CID,' the nurse announced, adding, 'He'd like a word with you, Stan. I'll go now.'

'No need,' Pemberton assured her. 'I must talk to as

9

many people as I can, either now or later. You might be able to help us.'

'I never saw anything . . .' she began.

'Please stay,' the vicar pleaded, and so she settled in one of the armchairs as Pemberton remained on his feet. The vicar sank into his settee with a large sigh.

'I'm sorry, I've not gathered my wits yet,' he shook his head in his anguish. 'It was so dreadful . . . finding him like that . . .'

'Tell me about it,' Pemberton spoke softly, his concern was genuine but he couldn't overlook the fact that the person who reports finding a murder victim is very often the culprit.

'There's not a lot I can tell,' the vicar breathed deeply then expelled his breath in one long sigh. 'I just went round to the church as usual, a thing I do every morning just to check that Ken had opened up, and there he was, lying in the porch . . . I saw the blood, he didn't respond when I touched him or called his name, so I ran home to ring for the doctor. We have one here, fortunately, in the village, he has a surgery at nine on Saturdays, just down the road.'

'Very convenient,' nodded Pemberton.

'Yes, very. He got there very quickly but there was nothing he could do for Ken, he was dead by then. Dr Cochrane said it looked ominous and would call the police.'

'Had Ken – Mr Flint – been inside the church?' asked Pemberton.

'Yes, I'm sure he had, the inner door was standing open, it has to be unlocked too. Either he or I open up daily, we leave both doors standing open to encourage visitors. So, yes, I'm sure he'd already been inside. He would go in to see to the clock this morning.'

'I wonder if anyone followed him in?' considered Pemberton.

'I'm sure the place was empty when I got there.'

10

'Did you look inside? Search the church?'

'Oh, no, I never gave that a thought, I just rushed off to get the doctor . . .'

'But at night, both the outer porch door, and that inner door are locked? No-one can get in? No-one could be waiting inside for Ken to open up? Unless they'd been locked in the previous night.'

'That's right. We used to lock just the inner door and leave the outer one closed but not locked, then youngsters realised they had a place to meet and they began to congregate in the porch. They made a dreadful mess, leaving drink bottles behind and worse, so we decided to lock the outer door as well. Ken had keys, and so have I. Ken might have got there a bit earlier this morning but he was usually there about nine, it takes about twenty minutes to wind the clock and means climbing the tower.'

'So his normal routine would be to arrive at the church at nine or thereabouts, unlock both doors, go inside, climb the tower, wind the clock and then emerge?'

'Yes. He might lay out the books too – we sell copies of the church history and other leaflets to visitors, people put their money in safe boxes built into the walls. He looked after all that sort of thing. I think he would check that our merchandise was ready for the day's visitors – not that we get many but he always made sure our presentation table was neat and tidy, and well stocked. It does generate a small income which goes towards the upkeep.'

'So someone could have sneaked into the church while he was up the tower? He could have surprised them?'

'Well, yes, I suppose so.'

'So how long would he be in the church, generally speaking?'

'Half-an-hour I'd say. Something in that region.'

'And you found him at what time?'

'I can't be too precise, Superintendent, but it was about nine-thirty. I just turned the corner and there he was . . . oh, God, this is dreadful . . . it really is . . . such a dreadful shock,' and as the memory was revived, he buried his head in his hands.

'Would you like a coffee?' asked the nurse of Pemberton.

'No thanks,' he shook his head, thinking she must be familiar with the vicarage – or the vicar – if she could make that offer on behalf of the incumbent. 'I'm sorry to quiz you like this, Mr Middleton, but early information is very important to us.'

Middleton took another deep breath and nodded, 'Sorry, yes, I know you have a job to do and do ask me. You must ask.'

'Was anyone else around? In the church? The church-yard? The village street?'

'I haven't been into the village street yet, I don't need to. I go straight from here to the church, but I never saw anyone, no-one, not even any of the local people around the church. The churchyard was deserted when I arrived, no-one was visiting graves . . . I just walked in and there he was . . .'

'You touched him, you said?' Pemberton was gentle with him now. ,

'Yes, I called out first, something like Ken, Ken, what is it? And when he didn't reply I bent down and touched him . . . he wasn't cold . . . then I saw the blood on the stones . . . I moved him, just a fraction, to have a look . . .' and there he paused.

Pemberton waited as the vicar regained his com-posure, then he continued,

'His eyes were closed . . . and I saw the ghastly wound in his chest, all that blood staining his shirt . . . I just ran, Mr Pemberton, for the doctor. I'm no good at first aid . . .

12

I ran home and called the surgery. Dr Cochrane arrived in seconds, well, it seemed like seconds . . .'

'You went with the doctor? To see Mr Flint?'

'Yes, I waited outside the porch, to shield anyone else from the sight if they happened to arrive. Doctor Cochrane examined Ken and shook his head, saying he was dead and that it looked very suspicious. He said we shouldn't touch him or have him moved. He would ring the police on his mobile and would wait until PC Holbeck arrived.'

'Thanks,' Pemberton said. 'We'll need to talk to you and the doctor in depth later, to go over those first moments in greater detail, and we'd like to know more about Ken Flint, especially his work for the church.'

'I don't know what we'll do without him,' Middleton sighed. 'He was so helpful, always available, always willing to help and anxious to do things.'

'And Mrs Middleton? Could she help?' It was a probing question. Pemberton noticed the vicar had not mentioned his wife.

'She's at work, Superintendent, a vicar's stipend is not really sufficient to live on, she works for the Rainesbury Building Society, on the counter. She left home for work at quarter to eight this morning. She doesn't know about this yet, I'd better call her next but she'll be there all day if you need to talk to her.'

'She might be able to help us with the background of Kenneth Flint,' Pemberton said. 'I understand he has no wife, no family?'

'No, no-one, well, not that we're aware of. He's retired, he said he was a commercial photographer in Lincolnshire before retiring to live here. But there is no Mrs Flint and no children. I've never pried, Superintendent, his private life is his own affair but he never seems to have had visitors, no grandchildren or nephews or such. He is, er was, a very quiet man who kept himself to himself. The church is his only real interest. Was his only interest.'

'We'll have to search his house later, we might find some addresses or contact numbers,' said Pemberton. 'We need to inform relatives if we can find any, and we have to arrange a positive identification. Then there's the funeral to think about.'

'I'll help in any way I can, of course, you only have to ask,' Middleton looked a little more at ease now. 'But it seems so odd and inexplicable . . . I mean, why kill a harmless man like Ken Flint? He's always been so helpful and generous . , .'

'There might be a possibility he disturbed someone who was up to no good, but if you can think of anyone or anything else which could have prompted this, I would appreciate it,' smiled Pemberton. 'Has he upset someone perhaps? Made an enemy? If anything does come to mind, however slight, please let me know. My officers and I will be around for some time, I shall be setting up an Incident Room in the village.'

'Yes, of course. I'll do all I can.'

'Talking of the Incident Room, I will need to hire some spacious premises, Mr Middleton. Is there somewhere in Roberthorpe suitable – the village hall, perhaps?'

'I'm afraid the village hall is usually very busy and booked up well in advance but we have a parish room. I have the keys in my bureau. Use it with my blessing. It's available for at least a month, not as grand as the hall, but serviceable nonetheless.'

'We will pay rental,' Pemberton offered as the vicar rose from his chair to get the key.

'I wouldn't hear of it,' he said. 'This is something we can do for poor Ken, our contribution to the investigation . . .'

As Middleton went to obtain the key, Pemberton turned to Nurse Archer. In her late forties, she was a stout lady with dark hair containing just a hint of grey,

14

and she was in her uniform complete with black low-heeled shoes.

'You live in the main street, you told me?' he began. 'So did you see Mr Flint this morning? Did he have to pass your house to get to the church?'

'Yes he did, he lives, lived, at the far end but I didn't see him this morning,' she shook her head. 'I have several bed-patients to deal with each morning and I was at the other end of the village, the west end, at the time he'd be passing.'

'You know him well? Kenneth Flint, I mean?'

'Not really. I doubt if anyone knew him very well, he was such a loner, very quiet and shy I suppose. I've never been to his house, he's never called the doctor so far as I know. He didn't take part in village activities and I don't think he even went to the pub for a drink. Like most others, I was on speaking terms, but little more.'

'Enemies? Would he have enemies?'

'I would think not, Superintendent. He never got involved with people, the church was his only interest outside the house. He was a good volunteer worker, and I doubt if he'd upset anyone doing that, not to the extent of getting himself shot! He'll be missed, as Stanley said.'

'You're on good terms with the vicar?' Pemberton put to her.

'Yes, with his wife really, she and I are good friends, I'm a regular caller, to see her, I mean, she's a friend, not a patient.'

'Thanks. I may want to talk to you again,' he said, realising she had recognised the drift of those final questions.

'I'll help in any way I can,' she assured him, and then the Reverend Middleton returned. Five minutes later, Pemberton was leaving with the parish room key in his hand. Nurse Archer remained to comfort the vicar.

* * *

15

By mid-day that Saturday in summer, the church of All Saints, Roberthorpe, had been sealed by detectives, along with the churchyard and an access lane which ran behind the burial ground. From some points along its route, the lane, wide enough to accommodate a motor vehicle with room to spare, provided both a good view of the churchyard and the porch. Fences of blue plastic tape marked POLICE – DO NOT ENTER surrounded the area of operations, access to which was restricted to those directly involved in the investigation. The forensic pathologist had expressed his opinion that Flint had been shot from a point either within the churchyard or just outside its boundary, that is, from somewhere along the green lane.

The post mortem had yet to be conducted and further tests made but his initial assessment was that the wounds – and there were at least four – appeared to have come from an automatic weapon – or semi-automatic – which had been fired from a considerable distance into the porch. Calculations based on the position of the body suggested the shots had not come from within the church which, in turn, indicated the killer had not been in either the church or the porch. If that was the case, there would be no traces of his presence in either of those places. The fact that Flint lay near the inner door, however, also meant that the angle of fire was necessarily restricted. By standing where the body had fallen, only a limited expanse of graveyard wall, shrubbery, burial ground and boundary of green lane could be seen. The shot must have come from somewhere within that limited range or, of course, it might have come from a firing point closer to the porch, albeit within the same restricted arena.

A dozen Task Force officers had been summoned urgently and before midday were on their hands and knees searching every inch of the relevant undergrowth, churchyard grassland and the green lane. The body of

Flint had been examined, videoed and photographed *in situ*; there were no other injuries apart from the chest wounds. The post mortem, arranged for that afternoon, would determine the cause of death; by mid-afternoon, therefore, the body had been removed to the mortuary in Rainesbury.

Forensic experts continued to examine, in considerable detail, the area around the porch as well as the interior of the church and the clock tower.

The fully-wound clock supported the belief that Flint had been leaving the church when he had been shot.

As the afternoon progressed, teams of detectives from all corners of the huge county continued to arrive at the parish room where Detective Inspector Paul Larkin was establishing the Incident Room, along with its telephones, range of computers, filing systems and all the other paraphernalia of a busy office as well as the sophisticated equipment vital to the Incident Room of a major investigation. Already, a preliminary briefing had occurred – upon arrival, detectives had been provided with background information and despatched around the village to begin local enquiries. Some teams concentrated on house-to-house enquiries while others tried to locate people who had seen Kenneth Flint this morning or who had been in the vicinity of the church between eight-thirty and nine-thirty this morning. Dr Cochrane would be interviewed, as would Nurse Archer, along with people going for their newspapers, the shopkeeper, the pub landlord, people walking or driving to the surgery, drivers of vehicles delivering to a building site and to the pub, the butcher's delivery driver, the postman with the mail van, people going to work both in the village and further afield. No-one would be omitted, for it was surprising how busy was the centre of this small community on a Saturday morning.

But in addition to all those people going about their normal daily routine, there had been a killer in

Roberthorpe this morning. He'd been able to watch Kenneth Flint prior to his murder so was he – or she – a local person whose presence might not be considered unusual? Someone unnoticed among the locals?

Or had a stranger managed to arrive without attracting attention? And if so, had he or she then slipped away unnoticed? Or had some vehicle or person been seen leaving in a terrible hurry? And as the victim had been shot, had anyone heard the sound of gunfire? And what sort of gun would fire four shots in quick succession? They must have been fired very rapidly for all to reach their target before Flint sank to the ground. And, like most murders, it had probably all been done without witnesses.

As the routine duties of the enquiry got underway, Pemberton took Detective Inspector Larkin into his tiny office, an anteroom at the far end of the parish hall.

'You need to put a good team on to Kenneth Flint,' he told Paul. 'We've not been in his house yet, the keys are still with the body but I'll get the pathologist to release them as soon as possible. That's where we'll get our personal information about him, but we do need to delve into his association with the villagers and the church. Whether that will provide us with a motive remains to be seen, but this is an odd death, Paul, distinctly odd, it's almost like an execution. So what was Flint involved in? Was he really a harmless old church-worker – he looks to be in his late sixties or early seventies – or has he got some kind of hidden past?'

'We've already run his name through criminal records, there's nothing there,' confirmed Larkin. 'He does seem to have been a Mister Nobody, but everyone has a past. I'll put DS Williams and Lorraine on to it, sir, they work well together, they're astute and sensitive, and if there is any sinister background to Flint, they'll find it.'

'And don't forget to check all holders of firearms

certificates, we might even turn up a few who are in illegal possession of guns.'

'I've a couple of teams doing that already, sir.'

'Thanks, Paul. Now, there is another thought to consider. If Flint had four bullets in his chest, the shooting was no accident. This was no stray shot, no one-off attempt, it was a deliberate act of murder. It suggests it was done by someone who *knew* Flint would be in that church porch this morning. I think the killer knew his movements and was waiting for him. And that begs the question – why? Why execute a harmless old chap like Kenneth Flint?'

The sniper had left the scene of the killing with the confidence of one whose actions would remain undetected. His plans, particularly his advance preparations, had been very carefully arranged and the fulfilment of his mission had been masterly. He had left no evidence at the scene, other than the bullets in the body. They were four out of untold millions throughout the world and would not lead to him. And his departure from the scene had been done in such a way that the police were bound to follow the false trail he had established.

More important was the fact that he had rid the world of an extremely unpleasant person and, in his own mind, the death of Kenneth Bourne, alias Flint, was perfectly justified. He congratulated himself upon a brilliantly planned and proficient execution, the first in his campaign.

Chapter Two

The post mortem examination confirmed that four well-placed bullets had lodged in Kenneth Flint's chest. With lethal accuracy, two had penetrated the heart. Dr Paul Lewis, the forensic pathologist, expressed an opinion that the placing of the shots in an area smaller than the palm of a child's hand was the work of a professional or very skilled gunman. That information was relayed immediately to Pemberton in the Incident Room, who was then told the recovered bullets were already en route to the Home Office Forensic Science Laboratory at Nottingham. The lab, which specialised in ballistics, had promised attention immediately they arrived and Lewis had intimated the bullets were especially interesting – he said they were all from a 7.62mm weapon, almost certainly a semi-automatic rifle.

Following the post mortem, Flint's clothing, and the few personal belongings found among them, had been preserved for forensic examination but the senior scientific officer allowed the police to remove the key to Flint's house so that the necessary search could begin. The mortice key was easily identified. It bore a plastic key-ring containing a piece of white card upon which was the legend K. Flint, Ivy Cottage, Roberthorpe, and Pemberton's next task was to examine the house. He wanted someone to accompany him, preferably an officer experienced in the investigation of scenes of crime and soon spotted the right man. At the far side of the Incident Room he could see Detective Sergeant Daniels, a member of the Scenes of Crime department.

'Ah, George,' he approached Daniels. 'Can you spare a few minutes?'

'Yes, sir, of course.' Daniels, in his early forties, was sturdily built but had a permanent expression of solemnity upon his heavy and rather grey face. Some said he looked like a bloodhound and in fact he was a very sound and efficient detective.

'I'm going to make a cursory search of Flint's house. I need to know more about him as soon as possible, to get a feeling for his way of life. I'd appreciate someone on hand to tell me what I can touch.'

'Glad to help, sir, I'll fetch a camera, we might need one.' And so they made their way along the main street towards Flint's house. It was at the western end of a short row of six terrace houses; a two-bedroomed brick-built house with a green painted wooden garage leaning against the end wall, and thick ivy covering the south-facing aspect. A uniformed constable stood guard outside. As Pemberton approached, he could see the outer paintwork needed attention and the windows had not been cleaned for weeks, although the tiny garden was well-kept and the patch of lawn neatly trimmed.

'Any callers?' Pemberton asked after identifying himself to the constable.

'No, sir, no-one.'

'Good. We'll be here for a while, don't let anyone inside. If anyone's looking for me, I'll come out to them.'

'Right, sir.'

The dark green outer door, with paint flaking from it, opened directly into a small living room whose dull white emulsioned walls had not seen a fresh covering in years.

With a fireplace on the right, there was no room for a three-piece suite and the seating comprised of two small

21

armchairs. There was a small knot of brown envelopes on the mantelpiece, tucked behind a biscuit tin; they looked like bills awaiting payment. A small drop-leaf table stood against the inner wall, there was a cupboard full of knick-knacks built into the wall, a television set on a table in the corner between the fireplace and the tiny bow window, but little else. The fire was not burning, but it was laid ready and a few items of household rubbish had been thrown on top of the coal – some orange peel, an apple core and Kitkat wrapper. They were all ready for the flames if and when it was lit. Both detectives stood in the doorway, looking at the plain room before them, not touching anything at this stage; the room was tidy and dusted but the whole place looked as if it had not seen a lick of new paint for years.

'No sign of a forced entry,' noted Pemberton as Daniels took several photographs.

They now stepped further into the room. Pemberton lifted the envelopes from the mantelpiece and found they were bills, some paid and others awaiting settlement. All were in the name of Kenneth Flint at Ivy Cottage. There were no personal letters, no birthday cards or greetings of any kind. Just formal mail. Standing next to them was a mug with a handle missing and it contained spare cash comprising pound coins, silver and small change. There was nothing else of note on the mantel shelf.

Beyond was the kitchen, even smaller than the living room, but also in need of decoration.

It was surprisingly clean and tidy, with crockery on wall racks, cutlery in drawers, pans hidden in cupboards and a 1950s-style wooden kitchen unit containing cans of food, cereals, vegetables and a bowl of apples. No oranges or other fruit, noted Pemberton. As he opened and closed every conceivable place of storage to study their contents without finding any personal papers or other things of particular interest, Daniels took lots of photographs.

'No breakfast pots in the sink,' said Pemberton. 'It seems he washed up before going out. A tidy chap.'

An open flight of wooden steps led upstairs from the kitchen and a back door opened into a small yard. That door was locked on the inside with a mortice key and two bolts, a very simple but secure arrangement. Pemberton opened it and peered on to a back lane which was clearly used for access to this house and those adjoining. A dustbin stood outside; he lifted the lid and peered in to see a few open tins, some discarded food, three or four apple cores, some Kitkat wrappers and a single white-wine bottle, empty.

'An ordinary little house occupied by an ordinary little man, by the look of it,' he remarked. 'No sign of wealth or extravagance, a plain and simple-living sort of chap so it would seem. No sign of feminine presence, no flowers. Now for the bedrooms. We need to find his personal papers, birth certificate and whatever, if they're not kept down here, they must be upstairs.'

There were two bedrooms; the largest, overlooking the front of the house, was clearly the one in regular use, and the door stood partially open.

The room contained a single bed, neatly made, a mahogany chest of drawers with a mirror on top, an old wardrobe full of a man's clothes, many of them years out of date, and some Victorian samplers on the walls. There was a small bookcase containing paperbacks, crime novels in the main, along with a few family sagas and some non-fiction titles, including a book about the North York Moors and reference books about birds, animals, insects and wild flowers. Like the sitting room, it was very plain and in need of some paint; in many respects, it was almost monastic in appearance and lacked any hint of comfort or luxury. A pair of thin brown curtains hung at the window but there was noth-

23

ing in the room which could be described as pretty. Pemberton made a quick search of the drawers and the wardrobe, then looked under the mattress and pillows before shaking his head. Daniels had taken photographs but was now searching a bedside cabinet comprising a small drawer and a modest cupboard. The drawer contained indigestion tablets, cough sweets, paper tissues and a small torch, and when Daniels moved them aside he found a key lying beneath. A door key, judging by its size, but not for this room; its key was in the lock. The little cupboard contained handkerchiefs, socks and underwear, but nothing else. Daniels photographed everything in its place.

'Nothing exciting here,' Pemberton said. 'Old clothes, well-worn shoes, nothing fashionable, nothing expensive. Hardly the sort of stuff that would attract a professional killer. No money lying about . . . no hidden cash, no personal papers. Nothing in fact . . .'

Next door was the bathroom with a plain white bath in need of a thorough cleansing and a washbasin with a dripping tap which had stained the sink. A tiny toilet was next door. Both very simple, neither containing anything of undue interest. Across the landing from the toilet was the second bedroom; Pemberton went to open the door but it was locked.

'Hello!' he muttered. 'Now we might have something . . . where's the key, I wonder? Why would the chap lock the door to this room? A shrine to his mother, perhaps?'

'There was a key in the bedside cabinet,' and Daniels went to retrieve it. Moments later, he inserted the key and the door swung open easily.

'Good God, sir . . .' Daniels went no further than the doorway where he halted abruptly. Pemberton moved forward to peer over his shoulder into the heavily curtained room. Thick net curtains covered the single window; dark heavy curtains hung at each side.

'So this is our nice Mr Flint,' whispered Pemberton as he looked at the photographs on the bedroom walls. There was row after row of black-and-white prints, some enlarged; there were colour prints too, masses of them. And all of very young children – girls – posing in scenes of obscenity and nakedness, some with men and others alone. There was a desk in one corner of the room; that seemed to be his working area. Was it where he wrote his letters and dealt with paperwork? His study, his most private of places.

'I think we have discovered a motive for Flint's death,' Pemberton whispered. 'This one's for your team, George, it needs a thorough going-over. So we have a murdered paedophile, eh? Why didn't we know about him? We should have known about this man, how's he slipped through our net? And who are those children? Some of those pictures look rather old, don't they? Very dated. Can we get these girls identified? We need to talk to their parents or the girls themselves if we can find them. Lock the room when you've got what you want, George, then bring your teams back with all their gear. Go through this lot with a fine-tooth comb, including that desk, get names and addresses, venues, as much as you can. And his personal papers, passport if he has one, birth certificate and so on. Every scrap of paper in that desk needs to be examined. Now we've seen this, we've got something to go on, but we need to search the house and the out-buildings with extra care – loft, garage, any secret hiding places. Has he a car, for example? If so, where is it? You know the drill.'

'Yes, sir,' and so the door was closed and locked, with George Daniels retaining the key.

As they left, Pemberton instructed the guardian constable not to allow anyone other than Daniels and his team to enter until he gave his express permission.

'Make your search as soon as you can, George, we need to dig deeply into this man's background. I'm

25

going for another word with that vicar, he must have suspected this!'

When Pemberton returned to the vicarage, the district nurse had left and Pemberton was admitted by the vicar who looked rather less careworn than earlier. This time, he offered Pemberton a coffee and he accepted before being shown into the lounge, a beautiful room which overlooked the dale. He was surprised to find that Detective Sergeant Andy Williams and Detective Constable Lorraine Cashmore were already installed with mugs of coffee in their hands. Williams, a dapper individual in his country tweeds and brogues, rose to greet his boss while Lorraine resembled a business executive rather than a police officer. The vicar ushered Pemberton towards a chair. 'Sit down, Mr Pemberton, your colleagues have just arrived. I'll only be a moment, the kettle has boiled.'

As the vicar left to go about his chore, Pemberton waited until he was out of ear-shot, then said quietly to the others, 'I've just come from Flint's house, he was a paedophile. We've found a room full of pornographic photographs. Young girls. Background for a motive perhaps? Some angry parent? You'd better arrange to see them, and the rest of his house. Have a word with Daniels. I'll explain more later but we'll keep this to ourselves for the time being, it's not for the public or the press. That's why I'm here now, to see if any hint of it has come to light.'

'From what we've established so far, it seems he kept himself very much to himself,' Williams said. 'He was a very reserved character, no-one knows much about him, not even the local bobby. He's not a native, he's an incomer who arrived about five years ago, he came from south Lincolnshire, so he told one or two people. He told them he'd been a commercial photographer and that he'd retired. He's in his late sixties or early seventies. He's always lived alone, there's been no Mrs Flint or children, and apart from his church work, he took little part in village activities.'

'Has he been involved with children since he arrived?' Pemberton asked.

'There've been hints of that, sir, according to our enquiries. He's involved with the church choir,' Lorraine said. 'We learned that, which is why we are here, sir' – she called him 'sir' because this was a work situation. 'We've just got here, we came as soon as we discovered that so we've not had a chance for an in-depth talk with the vicar.'

'This morning, though, did anyone see Flint heading for the church?' interrupted Pemberton, who wondered if Flint had been away from home last night.

'Yes, we found a newspaper delivery woman who saw him coming along the village street, just before nine. He was alone but heading this way, his usual route and timing.'

'Right, a valuable sighting, it establishes the time-scale. Now, his paedophilia. You said there were hints, so do we know if there've been any complaints about him? Have you come across any hint of concern so far? Among the villagers.'

'No-one has made any direct reference to complaints or worries, but several people have mentioned things that could be suspicious. Getting involved with the choir, trying to take photographs of youngsters, wanting to advise the Brownies on woodcraft or birds and wild flowers, asking to take their photos, that sort of thing. It's one area we were going to mention to the vicar before we expand our enquiries.'

'Good work. So his secret wasn't so secret after all. We'll need names of any children he's approached or been in contact with, and we need to talk to their parents and families, and people like the Brownie leader. Not a pleasant task . . . ah! Vicar!'

Middleton had returned bearing a tray containing a

full percolator, a jug of milk, mugs and biscuits. He smiled and set it upon a small table and poured a cup for Pemberton, then offered to top up the others.

'I have to do my own catering while my wife's at work,' he apologised. 'So, Superintendent, how can I be of further help?'

'I didn't know my officers had arrived,' Pemberton explained. 'But we can all benefit from a chat with you. We need to know more about Kenneth Flint; I understand there has been some concern about his relationship with young girls. You didn't mention this when we last spoke?'

Middleton took a long drink from his mug. 'There has been concern, yes, I would be lying if I said otherwise. It came to my notice from a girl, now in her late teens, who had been in the choir when she was younger. Flint could be overfamiliar, that was the term she used. Brushing her arms, asking if he could photograph her in the woods, that sort of thing. I treat such unsupported stories with some caution.'

'Just the one girl?'

'No, she told me he'd been the same with other girls, they talked about it among themselves, they said he was a dirty old man but I don't think any of them told their parents. I believe they helped one another, you know the sort of thing – always making sure they were in pairs when he was around, never being alone with him, not going to his house or to the woods with him. The girl who talked to me thought I should know, she'd left the choir and has left school now, she's sixteen or seventeen, and got a job in a Rainesbury department store I think.'

'You should have told us,' chided Lorraine. 'Now we'd like to talk to her.'

'I'm sorry, it never occurred to me it might be relevant. Her name is Sandra Ingram. The council houses, number twelve. She lives there with her parents.'

'I'll see her later, and I shall exercise discretion, vicar. So what was your reaction when you first heard about this?'

'I must admit I was reluctant to believe it at first, Ken seemed such a nice man, so helpful and supportive, especially in his church work. But when I looked at his behaviour, in the light of what I had learned, I did see that he could be rather overfamiliar. There are times when it's hard to know if a man is behaving criminally or just being very friendly. I know some of the girls didn't like him too near them! I heard one say he was creepy. After learning that, I did my best to make sure that whenever Ken was involved with the choir, or any other church event featuring young girls, there was always another adult present, myself where possible, or my wife.'

'And were his activities reported to the police?' Pemberton put to him.

'Not to my knowledge, I don't think any of the parents considered things were at a dangerous stage, or that there was any real risk. I know I didn't. People can be rather familiar with one another without there being any sinister motives.'

'There's always a risk with people like him,' Pemberton stated. 'And have you any children?'

'A boy and a girl,' Middleton confirmed. 'But he didn't interfere with them, if that's what you are suggesting. They're older than those that interested him. Mine are in their twenties now, they were in their late teens when he arrived, he seemed to prefer them at the pre-puberty stage.'

'Thanks for being so co-operative, Mr Middleton. Detectives Williams and Cashmore will pursue that line of enquiry, from people in the village whose children might have been approached by Flint. They will talk to you at length when I've gone. I came to ask how much you know of Flint's personal background. Where he came from, for example, whether he had any contacts or friends you know about. We need to trace his relatives, if he has any, and I have to find a motive for his death. Had he any enemies for example? Did he confide in you?'

'He never confided in me, no, and he rarely spoke about his past, other than to mention his photographic career. He did say he'd worked in Lincolnshire and on one occasion I heard him refer to working in Norfolk, but he was never very specific about such things. I got the impression he was deliberately being vague – perhaps now I can understand why.'

'His interest in children, you mean?'

'Well, yes, I mean, he's an old man now. When he was younger, he might have been more active, if that's the right word. These things happen, sadly often among church choir members and those in a similar position.'

'You mean you think he might have been hiding some guilty secret?' Pemberton asked.

'I must admit there were times I did have worries about his past. It bothered me when I saw him trying to befriend little girls. In fact, Superintendent, I did try to find out for myself, by trying to ring colleagues in the areas where he said had worked, but I could never discover anything. He was always too vague about precise locations; I never did know exactly where he had lived.'

'It all adds up,' agreed Pemberton.

'Even so, Mr Pemberton, his conduct never reached the point of someone involving the police and no-one made a formal complaint to me. It was just talk . . . perhaps I should have been more assertive, more suspicious of him but one never thinks of involving the police, not for what could be based on mere gossip.'

'Gossip does often have some basis in truth,' smiled Pemberton. 'So the information you gained about him, the snippets you followed up, they all came from himself, did they? Without any confirmation from else-where? Like working in Norfolk and Lincolnshire?'

'Yes, I had to rely on what he'd let slip during in-formal chats.'

'You think he was being deliberately vague,' Pember-ton reminded him. 'So do you think he was laying a false trail?'

'That thought did not occur to me in the first instance, not when I first met him. I trusted him and he seemed a nice man, but as I became more worried, I did wonder if his avoidance of background detail was because he'd left under some kind of cloud and didn't want his past to be known.'

'As you said, these things do happen!' smiled Pemberton.

'If I'd known precisely where he'd come from, I could have had discreet words with the local vicar, but I daren't make too much of a fuss – after all, there was no firm evidence against him, just innuendo. In my profession, one has to be so careful about making allega-tions – even suggesting irregularities – without sound evidence.'

'Don't we know it!' grimaced Pemberton.

'But there was enough innuendo to cause you genuine concern?' Lorraine said to him.

'Well, yes, I suppose there was, and I must admit I did feel a bit helpless.'

Pemberton said, 'We'll examine the rumours, Mr Middleton, and we'll speak to the children and their parents who might have been in contact with him. You can understand our concern, can't you? We need to determine whether anyone had sufficiently strong a motive to kill Kenneth Flint.'

'Oh, that's a dreadful thought, that someone here, in this village, one of our parents, would do such a thing. I can't imagine anyone going to those lengths . . .'

31

'Has anyone expressed a deep hatred of him, or shown sufficient anger to do this?' asked Pemberton.

The vicar shook his head. 'No, everyone's been very discreet and sensible. Those with deep concerns just kept their children away from him.'

'I can sympathise with them, but it does help if we are fully informed.' .

'I can understand that now, in hindsight you should have been told, but I can also see that few parents would wish their children to be interrogated on such a sensitive issue. I do not wish to be judge and jury, I must exercise Christian charity.'

'I couldn't agree more. So what we are really saying, Mr Middleton, is that no-one really knows anything about the man now lying in our mortuary?'

'I'm afraid that is true. In my work I must accept people at face value, Superintendent, sinners and all. Unlike you, I suppose, you can delve much deeper.'

'There are times we have to delve very deep. This looks like being one of those times! I must go now, but Sergeant Williams and DC Cashmore will remain with you. I hope you can add more to this. Goodbye, Mr Middleton.'

Pemberton's immediate task was to return to the Incident Room, just around the corner from the vicarage, and there he sought Detective Inspector Paul Larkin.

'Paul,' he led his deputy into the ante-room and closed the door. 'I've had a look at Flint's house and I've been to see the vicar. He's a paedophile – Flint, I mean, not the vicar. His house has a room full of indecent photographs of children – there might be more hidden around the place. DS Daniels is going to give it a thorough search with his team.'

'Any hint of this in the village?'

'The vicar now admits he's had concerns. Andy Williams and Lorraine are quizzing him now. Flint seems to have been rather guarded about his background, he came to Roberthorpe after retiring from Lincolnshire so he said, and he's also mentioned Norfolk. He's been deliberately vague, it seems, not telling anyone precisely where he came from, and that kind of thing makes me smell a rat, it stinks of a cover-up for a murky past if my instinct is true. So can we run another check in Criminal Records Office? Try the Suspected and Wanted files too, do a thorough search. If he's changed his name for any reason, we might learn through a fingerprint check and we'll need DNA samples from his body. While you're seeing to all that, I'll have words with my oppo in Lincoln, to see if Flint was known to the local police.'

Larkin departed to comply with those instructions and Pemberton rang the Headquarters of Lincolnshire Police in Lincoln City and asked to speak to Detective Superintendent Boothby. Boothby was in his office and responded immediately.

'Len, it's Pemberton from Rainesbury,' and the two senior detectives, who knew each other well, exchanged a few moments of inter-force gossip before Pemberton turned to the subject of his call. He explained about the murder and ended by saying, 'Kenneth Flint is the victim, a man in his late sixties or early seventies, a paedophile who's talked about work in Lincolnshire as a photographer. We don't know much about him in this neck of the woods, he moved here about five years ago on retirement and I wondered if he's cropped up in your records?'

Boothby said he would ask his office to search their files and computer records; he'd do so immediately and ring back. Pemberton told Boothby that Flint had also made reference to Norfolk, and said he'd ring Norfolk Constabulary in Norwich with the same query. At Norwich, he spoke to Detective Superintendent Bradwell, whom he'd not met, and presented him with the same information. Bradwell said he would institute the necessary enquiries and call back as soon as possible.

The moment Pemberton concluded those two calls, the phone rang again; it was Larkin. 'It's the press, sir, wanting confirmation there's been a murder.'

'Tell whoever it is that we are investigating a suspicious death in Roberthorpe. You can say the deceased is a man in late middle age who appears to have died from gunshot wounds. We can't reveal his identity until we've got a positive identification. You can say an Incident Room has been established and some forty detectives are engaged on house-to-house enquiries. Then we need to arrange a news conference for later today. How about four o'clock? Have a word with the Press Office, Paul, get them to arrange something.'

'Right away!' confirmed Larkin.

'I know it's early days, Paul, but we might need help from the media on this one. Tell the press officer to be as co-operative as he can.'

While Larkin was busy with that, Pemberton went into the Incident Room where his staff of secretaries, computer operators and statement readers were already hard at work among the noise of telephones, the rattle of computer keyboards and loud buzz of continuing chatter. A large-scale map of the village dominated one wall of the room, while a blackboard contained details of the crime, such as the date and time the deceased was found, the few personal details that were known, and a note that the body had been discovered by the Reverend Stanley Middleton. Some detectives had already filed statements from the early house-to-house enquiries, all negative ones at this stage, and they were being processed. Salient details were highlighted by the statement readers before being entered into the up-dated HOLMES, the acronym for the computer system used for long-running or complex murder investigations.

Pemberton had quiet words of individual encouragement for members of his team, the work of the Incident Room staff being as important as that of the detectives who were now deep into their enquiries in the village and its surrounds. And then Inspector Fowler appeared in the doorway.

'Ah, sir,' he spotted Pemberton. 'Just the fellow.'

'Brian, how's things with the Task Force?' Pemberton asked.

'We've combed the churchyard, sir, concentrating on the area just outside the porch, and we've extended away from the porch for about quarter of a mile, including Green Lane. And we've found nothing that appears relevant – the usual rubbish is plentiful, the sort you find in churchyards – discarded drinks containers, french letters, orange peel, old newspapers, dead flowers . . . but I doubt any of it can be linked to this crime.'

'No ejected bullet shells? Is that what you are saying?'

'Right, sir. Not one. We've combed the grass for them.'

'Would a killer hang around long enough to hunt for and retrieve four spent bullet casings?'

'A professional would.'

'Even if the bullets themselves can be recovered from the body?'

'The bullets tell us what calibre of gun fired them, the shells tell us precisely which gun it was – when we find it. We need to find those shells, sir.'

'And you're saying they're not there?'

'I'm saying we haven't found them in spite of a most careful search.'

'This is looking more like a professional hit as each hour passes! Can we be sure they're not there? Hidden in thick grass? A hedge bottom?'

'My lads have done a fingertip search, sir, of every blade of grass in that churchyard, every flower-pot, behind every gravestone, in long grass, short grass, nettles, briars, the lot. There's nothing, sir, other than the

35

rubbish I've mentioned. The bullet cases are not there, I can guarantee that.'

'This makes it extremely interesting . . .'

'We've kept all the rubbish if you need it – along with a note of the precise spot each item was found.'

'Fine. And footprints?'

'Nothing identifiable. There are traces near some of the gravestones, in places where there are patches of bare earth, but they're old marks, sir, people tending the graves, we think, well weathered. The only recent mark is a fraction of a tyre-mark on that green lane which runs alongside the rear wall of the graveyard. Its name is Green Lane, by the way. It's a fresh tyre-mark, not weathered, but it's a very tiny sample. It might be too small and indistinct to be of evidential value in a court, we can't lift the impression or take a cast, but we have videoed it and photographed it. We'll have a go at trying to identify the make of tyre which made it.'

'Relevant, you think?'

'Very likely. It could lead us to the vehicle which left it, even if the courts won't accept it as evidence. And the lane does extend from the road which runs down the hill past the church; it goes along the rear wall of the churchyard and into some fields at the west of the village. There is a public footpath along there too, it follows the route of the lane which peters out at the fields, and emerges at the far end of the village, on the west. There's a very good view of the church and the porch from Green Lane.'

'It's the sort of place where we'd find dog walkers or horse riders?'

'Absolutely, sir. The path continues through the fields and emerges at the western end of the village, near a stream. A nice round trip for a dog on walkies and ladies on horseback.'

'You think the shots might have come from Green Lane?'

'It's very possible. Chummy could have taken his car along that lane, parked it to fire his shots, and then left immediately. It's quite feasible. And it could explain why no-one was seen in the churchyard.'

'Houses nearby?'

'Just one, sir, on the corner where Green Lane joins the road. Elm Tree Cottage. Even with that house nearby, he could operate virtually unseen, the hedges are tall and the trees overhang very heavily.'

'That sounds an interesting theory, Brian. I'd like you to show me the lane but right now I've got to wait until Norfolk and Lincolnshire ring back . . .'

'Do you want us to do another sweep of the church-yard, sir?'

'I might, when I've seen Green Lane. Those shells have got to be somewhere.'

At that point, the telephone rang. Larkin answered it. 'It's Detective Superintendent Boothby from Lincoln, sir.'

'I'll take it in my office,' Pemberton said. 'Brian, wait here until I've dealt with this call, I might need a further chat. Get yourself a cup of tea or something.' •

Pemberton settled at his desk and his caller began, 'Mark, we've positive news for you. Flint is known to us. He came to live near Boston, he was living in Nor-folk before then. He left us under a cloud. Like your part of the world, he was living in a village and got involved with the church but started interfering with little girls and he left. Drummed out by the locals, we think. He left the area, and until now we had no idea where he'd gone. To be honest, we'd forgotten about him until your call.'

'I've put a call in to Norfolk too,' said Pemberton.

'Good, well, they'll tell you he wasn't called Kenneth Flint when he lived there. He was on our patch for about four years, under the name of Flint. He moved to your part of the world five years ago, you think?'

37

'That's the local gen,' Pemberton said.

'It fits our knowledge, it could be the same man. It means it's nine or ten years since he left Norfolk. He was then called Kenneth Bourne, a single man. He never married. He changed his name to Flint at the time he moved to Lincolnshire, and we were told about his arrival on our manor.'

'So he must have been known to the police at that stage? If Norfolk were keeping tabs on him and they bothered to tell you, they must have been interested in him. So what's the story?'

'A nine-year-old girl was murdered and raped in Norfolk. Bourne, as he was called at the time, was charged with the crime and he appeared at Crown Court, but his defence managed to convince the jury there was doubt about his guilt. This was before the days of DNA, and even though forensic evidence said his blood group matched that of the killer, the defence planted sufficient doubt in the jury's mind for them to produce a not guilty verdict. He claimed he'd been somewhere else at the material time, the witnesses were pretty pathetic when it came to a matter of identification, and those who put him near the scene were not very convincing. Everyone knew he'd done it, he had convictions for indecency with children which were never revealed at the trial. The locals turned nasty at his acquittal, his life was threatened by vigilante-type people and so he fled to Lincolnshire, under his new name. We were told about him, we kept an eye on him, but no-one made any complaints to us about his behaviour. In spite of that, it does seem he started his antics again, interfering with little girls, and the locals dealt with it themselves. He left our part of the world – thankfully – and it seems you inherited him, Mark.'

'But no-one told us about him! No-one told us we had a suspect paedophile on our patch! One who'd been charged with a child murder!'

'He was found not guilty. We had no idea where he'd gone, he did a moonlight flit, he has no car so we couldn't trace him through his registration plate. The truth was, we had no cause to pursue him – he wasn't wanted for any crime. His convictions were fairly minor, indecent assault and so on, and as you know we don't generally notify movements of such minor offenders. Or we didn't at that time.'

'Fair enough, he's our problem now.'

'He wasn't on the Sex Offenders Register, you appreciate, his convictions were all before 1997.'

'OK, but you've a file on him?'

'We have, yes, I'll send you a copy by courier.'

'Thanks, we'll need it. So, Len, the family of the girl he was accused of murdering? Could this be a revenge killing by them?'

'You'll have to ask Norfolk about that, they have details of the family, but it's not impossible. They didn't pursue him into our patch, though, we had no such worries and it's rather a long time to suddenly take revenge. The murder was more than ten years ago. According to our files, though, it's surprising he wasn't lynched in Norfolk at the time of his acquittal. Feelings were running very high.'

'I wonder if something has happened to rekindle that old hatred?'

'That's something only Norfolk can tell you,' said Boothby.

'If it is a revenge killing, it looks as though they've hired a hitman – Flint was executed, I'm sure of that, no bullet casings were found, the shots were all grouped in a small cluster and I'm convinced the killer knew his movements and had been waiting for him. It all smacks of a very well-planned operation.'

'Nothing would surprise me, Mark. And good hunting, as they say!'

'Thanks, Len,' and as Pemberton replaced the telephone, it rang immediately.

'It's Bradwell from Norwich, Mr Pemberton. It seems someone's done the public a useful service, eh? Getting rid of Bourne, or Flint as you know him.'

'What can you tell me? Lincolnshire have just given me some information about him; the murder acquittal and so on.'

'Good, then listen to me. I can tell you more.'

The sniper had tuned in to several radio stations but so far none had made any reference to the killing of Kenneth Flint. He wondered if the story would interest the national networks or whether it would be restricted to a more localised audience; at this early stage, he felt the latter would be the situation.

The curious but violent death of an elderly church helper in a quiet Yorkshire village was hardly the stuff of national headlines, but it would be interesting to see what the press made of the story and whether they suspected the truth about Flint. It would be equally interesting to discover how the unsophisticated police of rural Yorkshire coped with such a skilful killing.

But he had no intention of resting upon that single success. There was more work to do.

Chapter Three

Detective Superintendent Geoff Bradwell confirmed everything said by Boothby of Lincolnshire. He added that the parents of Victoria Robson, the girl murdered by Flint alias Bourne, had been devastated by her death but stressed they were not the revengeful sort. She had been an only child, and following her death they had left the United Kingdom to start a new life in Canada. They had taken the ashes of their daughter with them and in Bradwell's opinion, a revenge attack by either one of them, or any of their relations, was highly unlikely. Today was not an anniversary of any kind so far as that murder was concerned, and they had not expressed any malevolent intentions at any stage of his dealings with them.

Bradwell did say, however, that another Norfolk child had disappeared some eighteen months prior to Victoria's death. She was Laura Steadman, aged nine; she had never been found, dead or alive, but there was evidence to suggest she had been seen with a man answering to the description of Kenneth Bourne. He had been questioned on several occasions, but had always denied any involvement with the girl, something the police did not believe. They were convinced he had taken her into some local woodland where he had sexually assaulted and killed her but they could not prove so. The case had attracted a lot of publicity but had never been resolved.

'You'll be taking DNA samples from his body?' asked Bradwell.

'We shall,' Pemberton confirmed.

'If and when we do find Laura Steadman, it might enable us to close the case,' he said. 'We'd appreciate that. It would help her parents too, to know her fate.'

'I'll make sure you're kept informed,' promised Pemberton. 'And we'll co-operate in any way we can. So are Laura's parents the sort to take revenge like this?'

'I doubt it, not after all this time, but I'll put a team on to it, we'll have them interviewed and their whereabouts ascertained. We can always disguise our real interest by telling them of Bourne's change of lifestyle in Yorkshire and his well-deserved finale. Society is well rid of a man like that. The gunman did us all a favour.'

And so Pemberton's net of enquiries began to spread beyond the tiny moorland village of Roberthorpe but he needed to concentrate upon the scene of the crime and its surrounds. A visit to Elm Tree Cottage, the house at the end of the Green Lane, was a good starting point. He told Paul Larkin of his intended destination and departed with a reminder that he was expected to attend a news conference at four o'clock. It would be in the village hall, not the parish room.

'I'll be there,' he promised.

Elm Tree Cottage was brick-built with a red pantile roof, but it had a look of antiquity and charm so often denied houses constructed of such materials. It had a rustic porch complete with honeysuckle, a cottage-style garden rich with border plants and shrubs, bay windows and creepers clinging to the western end of the roof. The garden gate opened on to Green Lane; Pemberton would walk that route after speaking to the occupants of this house. His knock was answered by a middle-aged and rather plump woman wearing a classic

42

country-style floral apron and with hands covered in flour.

She'd be in her late fifties, he estimated, and after introducing himself, she invited him into the kitchen and offered a cup of tea – she had one in the pot, she told him, and so he accepted. Her name was Mrs Piper, Hilda Piper, and she invited him to sit at the kitchen table while she pummelled a large pile of dough.

'Bread,' she explained. 'I like making my own bread, but if it's my husband you want, he's gone off to the cricket match. Umpiring.'

'A local match, is it?' he asked.

'We're playing Ashfield, a league match. We should win, he reckons. How can I help you, Mr Pemberton?'

'You've heard about Mr Flint?' he put to her.

'I have, in the shop when I went for some baking powder this morning, and a sad affair it is, nobody deserves that, Mr Pemberton. I hope you catch the chap responsible.'

'If we're to do that, we need information from the public, which is why I am here.'

'Well, there's not a lot I can help with, I never saw a thing, not living down here. I can't say I knew Mr Flint very well although I did see him knocking about the village sometimes. He was a good churchman, helping the vicar with all sorts. A nice chap, by all accounts, very decent, and he kept himself to himself.'

'I'm interested in the lane that runs past your house, Mrs Piper. I'll have a walk along it when I leave here, but I understand it goes past the churchyard?'

'It does, Mr Pemberton. It's a farm track really, leading to some fields. Lots of villagers use it for walks, nice for dogs and exercising horses, children go along as well, sometimes, playing or riding bikes, that sort of thing. It keeps children off the road and Jack doesn't mind, he's the farmer who owns it.'

'Did you see anyone using it this morning? After, say,

43

half-past eight or so, until around nine-thirty. Earlier perhaps? Or even on other days? A stranger perhaps?'

'Well, quite a lot of folks use it for walking dogs, Mr Pemberton, early morning and well into the day, or riding,' and she reeled off a list of Roberthorpe residents who might have used Green Lane this morning. In his official notebook, he jotted down the names, with addresses where she could recall them, and assured her his officers would interview every one of them. She knew them all, they were residents of Roberthorpe but not, in her opinion, the sort to go and shoot Mr Flint. She added she hadn't seen any of them this morning but he kept his notebook handy, in case she produced any more gems worthy of permanent record.

'It's the time leading up to half-past nine this morning that particularly interests me,' he stressed. 'I wonder if someone was hanging around there.'

'Only that chap in the motorhome,' she said. 'I went upstairs to make the bed, and happened to peep out. There was a motorhome, one of those mobile home things, a white one, and a chap beside it having his breakfast. He had a primus stove or something similar, had pulled into the lane, off the road, and he was sitting there on a canvas chair, eating sausages and bacon by the look of it.'

'How long was he there?' Pemberton's heart began to pound. Here was a witness saying someone had been in that lane around the material time . . . with a vehicle too, one which might have left a tyre-mark. So could this be the killer or another potential witness?

'He was there quite a time, Mr Pemberton, long enough to get his stove going, his meal cooked and then eaten, I would say. More than half an hour.'

'So what time did you see him? Can you be precise about it?'

'I noticed him about half-past eight, I reckon, but he was already set up by then. Jim, that's my husband, was

44

trying to hear the weather forecast on local radio, because of the cricket match, so yes, it would be half-past eight as near as dammit when I first saw him. He'd got his breakfast cooked by then, so he must have come earlier.'

'Which way was the van facing? Into the lane, or out of it?'

'Out of it, I think he must have backed up from the road, it's not all that far, it's easy enough to reverse up, or maybe he'd gone frontwards into the field at the top, turned around and come back down. I didn't see him actually arrive. When I spotted him he was already parked there.'

'Blocking the lane, then?'

'Not really, there's plenty of room to walk past a vehicle parked there, a horse could get past easily enough but I doubt if a car could. Jack Headlam uses the lane when he's ploughing or haymaking, and gets his machinery up and down without much bother, other-wise not many folk take vehicles up there. It's private really.'

'The farmer doesn't object to people using it?'

'Oh, no, not him, not if folks are reasonable. That chap stayed with his van which meant he'd be around to shift it if he had to. Not like some townies who seem to think they can do as they like in the countryside.'

Pemberton was scribbling down the gist of her infor-mation, then asked, 'The van, Mrs Piper, a motorhome you said. Can you describe it?'

'Well, one motorhome's much like another. It was one of those vans or mobile homes that you see about in summer time, a smallish one. I don't know the make, and if you're going to ask me for its number, I couldn't see it and probably wouldn't have thought to note it anyway. You don't, do you? You don't note things like that when folks are just having a picnic?'

45

'Was there anything distinctive about it?' was his next question.

'No, it was just like those vans you see coming and going from the caravan site, a caravan and car combined. Just like a big van fitted out so you can sleep in it.'

'Where was the door? Could you tell?' Pemberton was wondering by which route the man had disembarked from his van. He might have been hidden from Mrs Piper's view as he'd gone about some of his routine.

'Door? You mean the door into the living part? Not the driver's door?'

'Yes, the door into the living section of the van?'

'At the side, I'll tell you why I know that. The van had a window on the side nearest me . . .'

'The offside,' he muttered, for his own information. 'So the door must have been on the nearside, that's the normal position.'

'Aye, mebbe. Well, the van was facing down the lane towards the road, so that window would be on the side nearest me, the driver's side; the door was on the other, away from me.'

'Right,' he was pleased that had been confirmed. He now had a mental picture of the parked vehicle.

'Well, the door into the living bit was open, it had been slid open I think because I couldn't see it standing wide. In fact, it was a bit close to the hedge at that side to open a door wide. That's why I'm sure it had a sliding door and when it was open, I could see right through the vehicle, on to the hedge at the other side. I couldn't have done that if the door had been shut, could I? That was at half-past eight. He was sat in the middle of the lane, on a canvas stool, having his breakfast. At nine, when I saw it again, the curtains on my side were closed, the curtains of the window nearest me I mean. I thought he might be using the loo, you see, after his breakfast and before setting off. He'd gone from his

46

stool, and it had gone as well. The van was just standing there with nobody around it.'

'So you think he'd gone inside the van by nine o'clock?'

'That's what I thought, yes. Roughly nine o'clock, I can't be too accurate.'

'Thanks. Some models do have sliding doors on the nearside,' Pemberton nodded. 'I can check the range which includes that style. Now, the man you saw. Can you describe him?'

'I didn't take much notice, he had his back to me so I couldn't say whether he was tall or short, or fat or thin, old or young. I couldn't see his face either, Mr Pemberton.'

'How tall?'

'No idea, he was sitting down the whole time I saw him, but he did have very dark hair and he wasn't bald at all, no bald patch. Fortyish, I'd say, at a guess.'

'Alone, was he?'

'Yes, I never saw anybody else around the van, and there was just the one stool. I don't think there was anybody with him.'

'Then, what did he do?'

'Well, I don't know. As I said, when I'd finished upstairs, the van was still there, nine o'clock or thereabouts I'd say, but he'd finished eating and had cleared away his stool and things. Oh, I've just remembered, when he was sitting there, with his breakfast, he was reading a paper. I never saw him leave, Mr Pemberton, I came down and went into the kitchen to see to the washing machine and next time I went upstairs – half-past nine or just after – he'd gone. And the van.'

'Is it unusual to see cars in that lane? Strangers' cars, I mean?'

'Not really, not at weekends, or at times in the summer. Tourists sometimes pull in to have a picnic, they like to get off the road. They can be a nuisance when

Jack wants to be into his fields, they think they've a right to park there, but they haven't and some get very nasty with us locals . . . so when I saw the van, I never thought it was suspicious. There was nothing worrying about that fellow, I mean, he wasn't misbehaving or trying to hide himself or anything like that. So far as I was concerned, he was just a tourist stopping to have his breakfast like some of them do, no more than that. A funny place to do that, I know, so he must have had a reason.'

'Did you hear shots? A gun being fired?'

'While he was there you mean? No, well, I did have the washing machine going full belt, and it makes a lot of noise, rumbles a lot, but I never heard shots, Mr Pemberton, but there's often guns going off in the countryside, you know. Rabbiting, pheasant shooting, that sort of thing. Living here, you tend not to notice guns going off, not that folks would be shooting pheasants at this time of year . . .' she paused suddenly, as if the direction of his questions had now registered in her mind. 'You don't think it was him, do you? The man who shot Mr Flint?'

'We don't know. He'll have to be traced and eliminated from our enquiries, Mrs Piper. And of course, he might have seen something or somebody in the churchyard around that time. He could be a very important witness, that's why we need to talk to him. You said it was a funny place to park, why did you think that?'

'Because of the time of day. We have a caravan site in the village, it's on the outskirts to be precise, but if he'd been staying there, you'd think he would have had his meal before packing up and leaving? Most of them leave on Saturday mornings, you see, but they have breakfast first. I wondered if this chap had been travelling all night, or set off somewhere very early on his way to the site . . . anyway, that's what I saw, Mr Pemberton.'

'He was reading a paper, you said? Any idea which one?'

'One of those with big pages, Mr Pemberton. I thought he must have got it from the shop.'

'The village shop, you mean?'

'Yes, it sells papers and magazines, and it opens early, half-past six most mornings except Sunday.'

'Thanks,' he smiled. 'You've given me a lot to go on. One thing before I go. Can I have a look out of the window you mentioned? You can show me where the van was parked.'

'It was our landing window,' she said. 'Come along, I'll show you.'

She led him up the stairs and halted before a large window with net curtains which overlooked Green Lane – and it also overlooked the churchyard with the porch in sight. A wonderful view, albeit at a slight angle. The church was slightly to the left as one looked out of her landing window, and although the porch was in view, it was impossible to look into it from here, partially due to the angle and partially due to the darkness of the porch.

'So where was the van parked?' he parted the net curtains to gain a better view.

'You see that hawthorn in the corner of our garden? Well, I'd say his tail end would be about level with that.'

'And he was facing the road, down the slope?' he sought confirmation of that. 'And having his breakfast at the rear of his van about half-past eight?'

'Right,' she nodded.

'And when the van was parked there, could you see the churchyard and porch?'

'Oh yes, we've a good view from that landing, Mr Pemberton. But I couldn't see the part of the graveyard very near to the house, the van was in the way, blocking my near view, close to the churchyard wall. But over it, yes, I could see the churchyard and church.'

'Was there anyone else in the churchyard at that time?' he asked gently. 'Or in the lane?'

'Not when I was looking out at the van, no. I can sometimes see folks coming to tend graves or visit the church, and I get a good view of funerals but there was nobody there this morning. Not when I first looked out, not in the churchyard or the lane, except that chap I've told you about.'

'And was the outer porch door closed or open? Would you know that?'

'It was closed when I went upstairs at half-past eight, I remember because we've a Neighbourhood Watch scheme going and I look out for suspicious folks visiting the church. Seeing the van there made me look at the church door. Ken, Mr Flint, comes down to open the church about nine most mornings, and he winds the clock on Saturdays. Well, he used to, poor man, they'll have to find somebody else now.'

'So at half-past eight, you don't think Mr Flint had arrived to open the door? He hadn't arrived early?'

'No, he usually came later, about nine, but as I said, I'd come back downstairs to the kitchen about then, that's when I saw the chap had gone into his van and drawn the curtain, but when I went up again just after half-past nine, the van had gone.'

'So you looked out three times? Half-past eight, nine and half-past nine?'

'Right. And I did see the vicar hurry out of the church that last time, but that's not unusual, he's usually rushing somewhere.'

'The vicar?'

'Yes, he was rushing out in a fluster.'

'Around half-past nine?'

'About then, yes.'

'And did you see Mr Flint?'

'No, I never saw him.'

'He might have been lying in the ground, inside the porch.'

'Well, no, you can't see into the porch from here, can you? Not at floor level anyway. If I had seen anybody lying there I'd have done something about it.'

'Good,' he could see she was right. 'So we know the van was parked in this lane at half-past eight, and it had gone about an hour later?'

'Yes,' she nodded vigorously. 'That's what I'm telling you.'

'That's important to us. Now I'm going to have a look along the lane myself,' he told her as he went downstairs and prepared to leave. 'I might come back for another chat, Mrs Piper, so if you do remember anything else, jot it down.'

'Right, I will.'

'Me or my officers will come back later for another chat, you might remember more.'

'Well, if I can help you catch the chap who killed that nice Mr Flint, I'll be very happy.'

And he left her to her baking as he strolled along Green Lane.

There was a uniformed police officer at each end, preventing public access until the Scenes of Crimes teams had concluded their work. It was a narrow unsurfaced track running between two hedges, which were interspaced with dry stone walls in places, and it climbed steadily from the road, passing Mrs Piper's house which stood on the left as one ascended towards the field. The church, surrounded on all sides by the graveyard, was on his right when slightly further up the lane. He stood near the hawthorn at the edge of her garden and he could see the porch; the door was standing open and there was a uniformed constable on duty outside. The church, as the scene of a murder, had not yet been released; Scenes of Crime might still be working there. But from this point, it was possible to see into the porch – it was made easier because the sun was high in the southern sky and shining directly into the open space of the porch; this morning, when it was in the east, there would be shadows . . . but Pemberton realised that the man in the white van could have fired his rifle from this place – the angle, the distance, the view were all there, and would be hidden from Mrs Piper's view by the vehicle itself or by the closed curtain. Had he actually stood in the doorway of the van? The one she'd seen open?

And had the ejected cartridges been cast into the vehicle and conveniently carried from the scene? But for a man to sit and calmly eat breakfast before murdering someone . . . that was most odd, chilling in fact, and most unrealistic. Pemberton walked the full length of Green Lane, seeing the piece of broken tile which protected the fraction of a tyre-print found by the Task Force; he examined it and realised it was of limited evidential value, but at least his team had found it and recorded it because it was of value to the enquiry, if not the courts.

If the print vanished now, it was not be a disaster, but he replaced the protective cover. Even if the mark could be linked to the white motorhome, it did not prove the breakfasting man was the killer – but it was one important piece of evidence and it might lead to a valuable witness. It could not be denied, however, that the breakfasting man had been in the right place at the right time to commit the murder. Mrs Piper had seen no-one else, except the vicar leaving in a hurry – probably having just discovered the body of Kenneth Flint. From Pemberton's own viewpoint, the killer could have seen the porch from that motorhome's parking place. Beyond all doubt, this was a prime suspect, the first to go in the frame. All Pemberton and his team had to do was find him.

Having examined Green Lane, Pemberton realised there was just time to visit the paper shop before attending the news conference and behind the counter of the village general store, he found a small, freckle-faced lady who smiled a welcome.

'Yes? Can I help?'

He identified himself, then explained the purpose of his visit and even though the news had spread around the community like wildfire, she expressed her horror at the death of Mr Flint. Clearly, she was anxious to help his enquiries.

'I know it's a difficult thing for you to recall, but did a dark-haired man, a visitor to the village, call in this morning and buy a paper? He might have arrived in a motorhome, one of those mobile home type of vehicles, a white one?'

'Yes, he did,' she smiled at him. 'I remember him because of the van, he came in several times during the week, but this morning parked it right outside, just before two buses and two lorries arrived from different directions. He had to move it to let them through.'

'What did he buy?'

'Well, sometimes he bought a *Guardian* and sometimes an *Independent*, then today he picked up a *Telegraph* then changed his mind and swopped it for a *Yorkshire Post*.'

'Did he say anything? Give any idea where he was from or where he was going?'

She shook her head. 'No, not ever. He just smiled and gave me 40p, and told me to put the 2p change in the Lifeboat box. I thought he'd come down from the caravan site, we get quite a lot of them in here, buying papers, food, drink and so on. He did come from that direction. I'm sure he was staying at the site, but he never said much. Sometimes he came without the van, I think he walked down.'

'You'll be able to describe him then?'

'Well, yes, he was always very pleasant but he never

stayed long. He'd be in his early forties, I'd say, quite tall, getting on for six feet I'd guess, with very dark hair, black almost, clean shaven, good teeth, a pleasant voice with no noticeable accent . . . he usually wore casual clothes, tee-shirts and light slacks. There was nothing remarkable about him, Mr Pemberton, he seemed very calm and content, and once or twice he said he was enjoying looking around the district.'

'Did he mention his work or family or where he'd come from?'

'No, nothing like that, although he did look a bit like a policeman, with his smart haircut and upright bearing.'

'Really? And what were his purchases? Anything odd?'

'No, usual things that holidaymakers need – washing-up liquid, food of various kinds, fruit, he bought a lot of oranges, several most times he came in, a bottle or two of wine, newspapers, that sort of thing. He always paid with cash, even if his purchases came to quite a lot. He bought a bottle of whisky on one occasion, with a few bottles of wine, but it was always cash. Some get their credit cards out once the whisky or gin bottles appear. And he never quibbled about prices, always putting any small change into a charity box. He seemed a very nice man, Mr Pemberton.'

'So what time did he call this morning? For the *Yorkshire Post*?'

'Quite early, before eight. Quarter to eight I'd say, something like that.'

'Alone?'

'Oh, yes, quite alone, he always was.'

'Did he buy anything else this morning?'

'Yes, some oranges, half a dozen. After he'd paid for his paper, an afterthought, I suppose.'

'Thanks, and did Mr Flint shop here?' was his next question.

'Yes, he did, regularly. He was always very quiet, a shy man I felt, never wanting to stop for a chat either with me or the other shoppers. But he always paid cash as well, never asking for credit although I must say his purchases were modest, I don't think he bought spirits, for example, but sometimes he'd get a white wine, a cheap one. It was dreadful, him being shot like that, Mr Pemberton, really it was an awful shock for the village, with him being such a quiet man, and so helpful in the church and so good with the children. It hasn't sunk in yet.'

'Did they ever meet?' he asked. 'The camper man and Mr Flint?'

'Just once, Mr Flint came into the shop on Thursday morning, to buy his *Gazette*, the weekly paper that is, and to get some fruit and vegetables. They're in fresh, you see, on Thursday mornings, that's when we get our deliveries, and he did like fresh fruit . . . well, that camper man followed him in and tried to get talking to him, but Mr Flint was very reserved about it, he didn't like talking to strangers, he told me afterwards.'

'Fruit? Mr Flint bought a lot of fruit? Did he buy oranges, like the visitor?'

'Oh, no, not oranges, Mr Pemberton. Mr Flint couldn't stand oranges, he liked apples and pears, with plenty of grapes if they were in good condition.'

'Did the camper man know Mr Flint's name?' he asked.

'I think he did because that morning, when Mr Flint had gone, the man said, "Isn't that Kenny Flint?" I told him it was Ken although I'd never heard him called Kenny, and the man said he would try to look him up to renew acquaintances so I told him where Mr Flint lived, but I've no idea whether he called on him.'

Pemberton emerged from the shop more convinced that Flint had been stalked, that his movements had been monitored by the dark-haired motorhome man,

55

and that his paedophilia or past record had probably been the reason. There did appear to be a motive for his death, so who was the motorhome man and what was his association with Flint? He had been in the right place at the right time to carry out the crime, and it appeared he'd done so in cold blood.

But now Pemberton had to decide how much information he should release to the public because it was time for the first news conference.

The sniper was confident the rifle would never be traced to him. It was held illegally, no-one knew he possessed such a weapon and it did not feature upon any firearm certificate or other documentation. It was one of more than seventy million manufactured for use around the world, and he smiled at the concept of the rustic police of a Yorkshire village trying to trace and account for every one of them! And, of course, he had recovered the four spent cartridge cases. Already, they had been disposed of, tossed into separate waste bins miles away from the scene.

He'd finished with the motorhome too, removing the false tax disc and number plates, and returning the vehicle to the hire company in pristine condition, with a full fuel tank, no excess mileage and no damage. Even if it was traced to this depot, the trail would end there.

As time ticked away, he noted there had still been no mention of the murder on national radio or television. That was normal for such a low-key crime – at least it would be low-key until Flint's past was discovered – and in particular he was delighted the motorhome had never been mentioned. Not that the police would refer to – they would think themselves too clever to refer to it in case he set fire to it or disposed of it in some other way. Even now, it might be in use by another happy camper who'd have no idea of its previous role and who'd leave their fingerprints and debris all over it.

And so the happy sniper settled down to watch the sports coverage on television.

Chapter Four

The recently appointed Press Officer for the Force, Inspector Don Collins, was awaiting Pemberton in the Incident Room. A youthful man, slim, with dark brown wavy hair, he wanted prior discussion about the content of the news conference and some guidance on the content of his news release, so Pemberton invited him into his private office.

'Has there been any press interest in this murder?' Pemberton began.

'It was slow in starting, sir,' the Inspector said. 'I think that was because no-one called the ambulance or dialled 999. The immediate emergency was dealt with very locally, so the press didn't learn about it until some time afterwards. A local correspondent, living in Roberthorpe, alerted a freelance – since then, of course, I've had several enquiries.'

'And what have you told them?'

'I confirmed we're investigating a suspicious death in Roberthorpe and have provided them with the basic background material. I didn't release the victim's name, sir, although the freelance does know it, courtesy of our local informant.'

'Good, well, I've given this a lot of thought, Don, and there's a good deal to keep out of the papers and away from public knowledge, at least for the time being.'

He explained about Flint's background then said, 'I don't want his past, especially his name-change, to be publicised at this stage. If you get any hint of such a story, let me know. If we can talk to the press before they publish, we might be able to explain our side of things and persuade them to exercise caution.'

'It is common talk in the village that Flint was a bit too familiar with little girls, sir, the freelance mentioned it, there's gossip he might have gone too far with some child or other, and that might have led to his death.'

'Clearly, the village correspondent has a nose for a story! I think your response should be that those rumours have not been substantiated. Certainly, no-one has complained to the police about "Flint", as he's known hereabouts. He has no convictions for child abuse under that name either, but that won't stop the speculation. You can't libel a dead person and all that! If the press go to town on the paedophile suggestion, they could describe this as a revenge killing, but in any case public sympathy would shift from Flint. Those who think it's a case of good riddance might not tell us what we want to know, they might shelter his killer or do their best to prevent his capture. So we must be careful with this one, Don. Now, the other thing is the sighting of a suspect. I'll not mention that at the news conference just yet – I don't want the suspect to read about our interest in him or his vehicle, I don't want him setting fire to the vehicle or destroying any other evidence.'

'I understand, sir.'

'Good, so play the cautious line, and if there's a problem, talk it over with me.'

'Got it, sir. You'll chair this conference then?'

'I will. You'd better join the CID conference which follows, I want you to be fully informed, so you know what *not* to release!'

'Right, sir.'

'OK, you go to the village hall and get your journalists settled in, I'll talk to television or radio if necessary. I'll be there in five minutes with Inspector Larkin and

Inspector Fowler. I want a chat with them before we leave.'

He invited the two inspectors into his office, first addressing Larkin, explaining about the suspect man and vehicle. He asked Larkin to make checks in an attempt to find the names of manufacturers of such motorhomes, and then to try, through the Police National Computer, to determine how many were on the road. With some good fortune and a lot of detailed work, the owner might be traced. If such a vehicle had been seen near the scene of any other crime, the 'Suspect' index might provide the relevant details. Larkin nodded and Pemberton turned to Inspector Fowler.

'Brian, your Task Force team did examine Green Lane, didn't they? In considerable detail?'

'Yes, sir, a thorough combing, a fingertip search.'

Pemberton explained his chat with Mrs Piper, adding, she saw the man sitting on a canvas stool having his breakfast about eight-thirty. 'Now, I recall you told me you'd found some orange peel in the churchyard, along with other things.'

'We did.'

'Where was it precisely?'

'Under the yews in the south-west corner of the graveyard.'

'Fresh, was it?'

'No, it wasn't fresh, sir. It looked as if it had been there for days, which is why I felt it was not relevant.'

'I agree anyone could have dropped it, but I've been to the village shop and learned our suspect has been in during the week, buying oranges, lots of them. Maybe he got careless when he was checking out the churchyard? And I did notice some orange peel in the fireplace of Flint's house – yet Flint did not eat oranges. Somebody else must have put it in his fireplace, it seems he'd had a visitor.'

'I get the drift, sir.'

60

'So did you find any orange peel in Green Lane?'

'No, not a scrap.' Fowler's face revealed his thoughts
. . . he began to wonder if he had overlooked some vital
evidence and listened intently as Pemberton continued.

'Right. So the house, Flint's house. Maybe chummy
threw that peel into the fireplace, we think he may have
called on Flint. Those apparently innocuous bits of
orange peel have assumed some importance, Brian. It
might be possible to ascertain whether any came from
the same type of oranges which are sold in the shop.'

'I'll check,' said Fowler.

'And maybe you could find out who bought them,
other than our suspect?'

'I've got the message!'

'But – and this is important – if chummy was blatantly
sitting at his breakfast in Green Lane, minutes before
committing murder, he might have eaten an orange or
two.'

'There was no peel there, sir, not in Green Lane.'

'Exactly. If he was careful enough to pick the ejected
bullet shells, he'd collect his litter as well, orange peel
and the lot. He'd make sure the entire place bore no
traces of his presence. But suppose he had eaten an
orange or two? What would he do with the pips?'

'Spit them out?' suggested Fowler.

'Right,' said Pemberton. 'And if that was a habit, he
might not have realised he was doing it. They might still
be there. So did you find any?'

Fowler shook his head. 'No, sir, no pips.'

Pemberton went on, 'It's an instinctive reaction to spit
out orange pips, especially in the open countryside. So
let's have another look for them, in the churchyard, in
Green Lane and Flint's fireplace.'

'Right, sir.'

'Get on with it now, Brian, while the press are
engaged at the conference. If you want to know exactly
where he sat to have his breakfast, speak to Mrs Piper at

Elm Tree House. If you've not finished by the time our conference is over, I might let the press take a picture of your lads on their knees, from a distance of course.'

'I'll warn them to smile for the cameras and look their best, sir!'

'Put on a good show for the cameras, but we mustn't say what you're looking for! So far as the press is concerned, they're searching the crime scene for evidence.'

Larkin then spoke, 'Sir, with regard to the van in Green Lane, one of our teams has found a dog walker who saw it there at half-past eight. The statement came in a few minutes ago.'

'Good. Did the witness note anything special?'

'No, just a man sitting there eating sausages, he was on a canvas chair, a picnic chair, and he spoke to the dog walker – "Hi, nice morning", but nothing else. No noticeable accent. The timing, and his description fits that given by Mrs Piper.'

'If that man was waiting to shoot his victim from that site, he was taking a hell of a risk, he could have been seen actually firing the gun,' said Fowler.

'Not really,' Pemberton countered. 'If that had been me wanting to take a pot shot from that location, I'd park my camper so that I could operate from the open doorway of the sleeping quarters and I'd position the vehicle as close as possible to the nearside of the lane. Anyone walking past would have to go by the other side of the vehicle, unable to see the man even when holding a gun. And if he fired it while inside the motor-home, he'd not be visible, even at fairly close quarters, not with the curtains closed at one side. Remember, the offside curtains were open at half-past eight, but closed at nine o'clock when Flint was due to arrive at the church. And if he is a professional lining up his victim, firing would only take a matter of seconds.'

'A very risky business nonetheless, sir,' said Larkin. 'He could be seen and heard.'

'This man seems prepared to take risks. It could be the action of a very cool and skilful operator,' remarked Pemberton. 'He might have deliberately put himself into a prominent position. It seems to me he *wanted* witnesses to see him. Not actually firing the gun, of course, but I think he wanted to be seen around the place. He's been in the village for several days, he's been in the shop, he's not exactly been hiding and he's probably been at the caravan site.'

'We've a team up there now, sir,' Larkin confirmed.

'Good. It does look as if the chap made a conscious effort to be noticed.'

'Why would he do that?' asked Fowler.

'To set up a false trail. It's an old device. Suppose he wanted to make people remember the man with the dark hair when in fact he might be a natural blond or brunette or as bald as a coot? It's easy to change the colour of one's hair. And the motorhome. That can be misleading. He might have borrowed it or hired it and been using it under false plates. If this man is a professional killer, gentlemen, he would never allow himself to be put into a position where he might be caught, traced or recognised, and the quality – and daring – of his marksmanship does make him a professional, in my view.'

'Rather like a military operation?' commented Fowler.

'Very like a military operation,' agreed Pemberton. 'His behaviour was far from normal. It smacks of a cold and very calculated plan. My gut feeling is that we've got to creep up behind this character without him realising we're on to him, and then give him an almighty surprise.'

'Those orange pips might clinch it all for us!' grinned Fowler.

'When you find them!' laughed Pemberton.

'I'll get started now.'

'And we'll go and talk to the press,' Pemberton led Inspector Larkin from the room, telling the staff where they were going.

Don Collins had arranged the village hall chairs and a table so that a formal news conference could be held; he had placed just one chair at the table – for Pemberton. Immaculate as ever, even after several hour's work, he took it and the journalists settled down to listen. He noticed a couple of microphones clipped to the table, two journalists had portable tape recorders and others were relying on shorthand. A TV crew waited in the background – they would interview him after the conference. Collins stood in front of the table, called for silence and made the introductions, identifying Pemberton by his rank and role as officer in charge of Rainesbury Divisional CID, Roberthorpe being a village within that police division.

'This is the situation,' Pemberton began. 'The body of an elderly gentleman, a retired man living in Roberthorpe, was found in the porch of the parish church at nine-thirty this morning. He was dead, he had been shot and the weapon was not found beside the body. The death is suspicious, it was not self-inflicted or accidental and so we have launched a murder investigation. An Incident Room has been established in the village and I am in charge of the enquiries. Forty detectives have joined me from the force area, many of them currently engaged in house-to-house enquiries in the district. Scenes of Crime officers have attended and the Task Force is currently undertaking a fingertip search of the graveyard and surrounds. A post mortem examination has been conducted and it confirms that death was from gunshot wounds. We cannot release the identity of the deceased as he has not yet been formally identified and we are currently trying to trace relatives. It does not

64

appear, however, that he was ever married or has any family living locally. I can, however, confirm that he is a local man who was engaged in voluntary work for the church. At the moment, no-one is in custody for this crime and we do not anticipate an imminent charge.'

He included the final sentence because it meant the press could speculate and print the outcome of their researches, something not permitted under the contempt laws if a person was in custody with the likelihood of an imminent charge. Pemberton was aware that the press could sometimes uncover information denied to the police and he did not object to them making their own enquiries – at times, such co-operation was beneficial to both parties. His statement was necessarily bland while providing sufficient information to create interest, and at its conclusion, he asked, 'Any questions?'

'Was he shot in the porch or was the body placed there afterwards?'

'We are confident he was shot where he was found.'

'At short range?'

'That has to be determined, forensic tests are being conducted.'

'What kind of weapon was used?'

'We are in touch with our ballistics experts on that matter. I can say it was not a shotgun. We believe it was a rifle, we've yet to determine its model or make.'

'Who found him?'

'The Reverend Stanley Middleton, the vicar, during a routine visit to the church.'

'Was an ambulance called?'

'No, the vicar reacted quickly and sensibly, he called the doctor who has a surgery nearby, he arrived almost immediately and pronounced the victim dead at the scene.'

'So he had been dead for some time?'

'We think it might not have been longer than half-an-hour. It was the custom of the deceased to open the

65

church doors and, on Saturdays, to wind the clock. He usually did that around nine o'clock, and we have no reason to think he altered his routine on this occasion.'

'So his routine would be well known to other people?'

'To some other people,' smiled Pemberton.

'Right. Has any motive been suggested?'

'Not yet, that is one important focus of our enquiries. We are attempting to determine a motive.'

'I believe there is a suggestion in the village that Mr Flint had an unhealthy interest in little girls?'

'I have not named the victim as Mr Flint, but the police have received no complaints about the behaviour of the deceased. He was not known to us as a paedophile or suspected paedophile, he is not on our records as such. Clearly, however, we are investigating every facet of his background.' Pemberton chose those words with care.

'He came here from Lincolnshire, did he not?' persisted the same voice. 'Upon retirement, as a photographer? Are you liaising with other police forces?'

'We are attempting to establish where he lived before he came here, yes. At the moment, we have no confirmation of any previous address or addresses. Once we can confirm his earlier addresses, we shall seek the assistance of any police forces in whose areas where he lived.'

'To check his background? His reputation?'

'To establish anything we can about him, and to trace relatives,' smiled Pemberton.

'Is this a revenge killing, Mr Pemberton? Some angry parent or relation wanting revenge for what Flint, er, the deceased, had done?'

'That is pure speculation, but we shall be investigating every possibility. At the moment, I have an open mind. I can only base my findings on the evidence which comes to light – evidence, not gossip. As I said, the police have received no complaints about the conduct of the deceased during the five years or so he has been living here.'

'I am told you are interested in a man with a caravan who called at the village shop this morning?'

'There is a caravan site on the edge of Roberthorpe, with some movement in and out at weekends. My officers are checking records with a view to tracing those who may have occupied a pitch there in recent days. We did hear that one man shopped in the village early this morning, but there is no reason to suspect him more than any one else. If we can trace him, it will be for elimination purposes or as a potential witness.'

Quite deliberately, he played down this aspect, hoping the press would print the word 'caravan' rather than mobile home or camper van. It might mislead the killer if he read any account of the enquiry. It was evident from the tenor of the questions that the press had been carrying out their own enquiries in Roberthorpe. It could be only a matter of time before some journalist discovered his previous address in Lincolnshire – his photography work was an easy clue – and then linked him with Kenneth Bourne. Pemberton wanted to trace the killer before such speculation reached the press – and he could always halt speculative reporting by saying a man was in custody and a charge was imminent. He had to bear in mind that the killer could be monitoring progress through news reports.

Following the formal part of the conference, he gave personal interviews for some radio stations, did a television interview with the church in the background and allowed the cameras, from both TV and newspapers, to depict Task Force officers on their knees as they combed the churchyard for any kind of evidence. As Pemberton told them, 'We don't know what we're looking for until we find it.' The photographers would have to be content with a long distance shot because the churchyard remained sealed until search teams and SOCO had concluded their work, including another search of the church.

Pemberton and his team returned to the Incident Room, where many of the detectives were returning to file their first batch of statements. Although they would be working until nine each evening, they were encouraged to bring their work into the Incident Room as soon as possible.

That would enable incoming statements to be processed in stages instead of waiting until the end of the day. Another benefit was that the teams obtained a cup of tea and a cake or biscuit during such visits. The statements would be logged into the system and read by the statement readers, whose job was to extract salient information which would then be entered into the HOLMES computer. Things like names, descriptions and registration numbers of vehicles, sighting and descriptions of unidentified people, unusual noises, gunshots and a whole host of other facts would be entered and cross-referenced by the computer. In charge of the statement readers was Detective Sergeant Ian Kemp, a sharp-faced, fair-haired Scotsman with a keen brain. In his late thirties, he had a delightful sense of humour.

'Anything of interest, Ian?' asked Pemberton.

'It's amazing how many statements include references to caravans!' he chuckled. 'You'd think we've had a caravan rally through the village, the place seems full of the things. The villagers hate them, motorists can't stand them, lorry drivers and deliverymen curse them, but the caravan site loves them if these statements are anything to go by.'

'So is there anything for us among all that?' asked Pemberton.

'The vehicle seen by Mrs Piper, sir, and by the shopkeeper, well, it's been seen around the place on and off during the past week. The descriptions tally – it's a white motorhome, two-berth by the sound of it, make and model unknown at this stage.'

'Registration number?' asked Pemberton.

'The only thing we've got is one witness who thought the letters CUB were on the number plate. I've got the team in question searching the PNC for any such vehicle with that combination of letters.'

'Anything from the caravan site yet?'

'We're hoping their records will come up with CUB; if it was parked up there, we might get a name and address. Our team is still up there.'

'I doubt if our man would leave such details behind. But keep looking. So where has this vehicle been seen? Any particular places?'

'It was parked outside Flint's house, sir, the witness thinks it was last Thursday evening. He didn't see any-one with it; it was there when the witness walked to the pub, and it had gone when he returned. He thought nothing of it until we started asking questions. It was there about eight-thirty and it had gone by eleven.'

'That ties with the information from the shopkeeper. We've no record of anyone speaking to Flint, have we? Outside the shop I mean, or at his house? Or has he ever been heard making reference to the vehicle or its driver? Remember, he had a visitor, somebody left the orange peel in his grate.'

'I'll bear all that in mind, sir, as the statements come in.'

'Good, and keep a beady eye open for references to this motorhome, or any motorhome in fact. I'm not going to tell the press about it, not yet, but it does feature at the top of our list of suspect vehicles.'

Kemp continued, 'The other thing which is emerging is Flint's unhealthy interest in children, sir, girls that is. Several witnesses have referred to that, saying he was a dirty old man and they wouldn't let their children or grandchildren be alone with him.'

'It's good to get that kind of confirmation and we can see that a pattern is beginning to emerge, Ian. Great stuff! And what about Flint? What did he do with himself when he wasn't attending to the church clock?'

'From what's come in so far, he seems to have led a very quiet life, sir, not going out, he wasn't one for having a pint in the pub or joining the domino team, he didn't invite people in for a drink or a chat, he did a bit of gardening, read quite a lot and spent most of time doing things in and around the church. And trying to involve himself with little girls. No-one's stressed his photography, perhaps most of the villagers don't know about that? Except those who said he sometimes offered to take pictures of little girls. He doesn't seem to have carried a camera around with him.'

'Maybe he saw retirement as not having to touch another camera – except on those special occasions when it involved little girls!'

'Could be, sir. It seems he kept his room full of porn locked against all comers. No-one's mentioned that in their statements.'

'Fine. Well, we'll have the usual round-up at half-past eight, we'll have all the teams in to hear what they've turned up. Thanks, Ian.'

Pemberton adjourned to his inner sanctum as the work intensified in the Incident Room and began to read the first file of statements.

That was one of his chores – even though highly experienced and competent statement readers ploughed through each one, he had to do likewise. Most were negative but they were included – they contained short statements like, 'I wasn't in Roberthorpe on the morning of the Saturday in question and cannot help you,' or 'I'm afraid I did not know Mr Flint.'

Sometimes a witness changed his or her mind . . . and

70

it was all on record. As he worked, the clock ticked onwards to five-thirty and then the phone rang. Pemberton lifted his handset and announced himself.

'Lightfoot in Nottingham, Mr Pemberton. Firearms Division, we got your samples mid-afternoon and got cracking immediately. I thought I'd ring with our preliminary findings, we've more work to do on the samples but I thought you'd want to know our initial conclusions.'

'Fire away,' he invited, then wished he hadn't used those words.

'I don't need to tell you that the four bullets all came from the same rifle, that's pretty obvious and I can confirm that, but I can also confirm they're 7.62mm calibre as your pathologist thought. This is interesting, Mr Pemberton because our first conclusion is that they were fired by a Kalashnikov AK47, its rifling is quite distinctive.'

'A Kalashnikov?' he cried.

'We're certain that is the weapon, Mr Pemberton. Now, there is another factor of considerable importance. The calibre of the bullets suggests it is an old weapon; in 1974, the cartridge size of Kalashnikovs was reduced to 5.45mm so your murder weapon is older than that but still capable of firing those four shots in rapid succession into the same tiny target. And it's lethal up to 1350 metres and it's capable of firing 600 rounds a minute. Quite some weapon, Mr Pemberton, in spite of its age.'

'Not the sort you'd find on a conventional firearms certificate?'

'Far from it. In the past, you needed a special licence to hold one of these in private hands, granted by no less a person than the Home Secretary, but semi-automatic weapons of this kind were banned after the Hungerford massacre. They're still around, illegally held of course – more than seventy million were manufactured and they

71

are all around the world, used by terrorists as well as conventional armed forces in both the communist and free countries. It won't be easy tracking this one to its owner. It might help you to know, however, that a lot of former soldiers smuggled these guns into the country, in their kit bags, after wars like the Falklands or Gulf War. Some were allowed to keep them as war trophies providing they had been de-activated but some kept them in their original form. God only knows where they all are, Mr Pemberton, but it seems you've got one of them, or had one of them, on your quiet patch of England.'

'And if chummy smuggled it into the country, in his kitbag or whatever, then he'd fetch some ammunition too?'

'He would have to and remember, one magazine holds thirty rounds. That's enough to kill a lot of people – even at four bullets a time!'

'Thanks, you're right. I did need to know this. Now, have you any other murders which we can link to this one?'

'No, we checked with the National Crime Squad and our own sources. This is the first – and I hope the only one. But if you've got a serial killer at work, he can make a big hole in your murder statistics, if you'll excuse the expression. Like a man-eater, once he's tasted blood, he might take a lot of stopping . . .'

'You'll send the usual written report?'

'I will, and if you find the weapon, get it down to us as soon as you can, then we can confirm it fired those rounds. We'll do some more work on the bullets – we might be able to pin them down to a particular batch of Kalashnikovs, or even a particular date of manufacture. More in due course.'

'Thanks, I appreciate this.'

The sniper cleaned and oiled his precious gun, showing

what amounted almost to affection for it. It had saved him on occasions but now it was helping to bring a new meaning to his life. And tomorrow he would check the research he'd undertaken before he used the gun once more.

Chapter Five

Pemberton did not immediately pass on the information about the Kalashnikov, preferring to announce it during his end-of-day conference of detectives. By imparting this knowledge just before they booked off duty, he hoped it would occupy their minds overnight, and hopefully throw up some useful idea or suggestion for tomorrow's endeavours. It did mean, however, that all former soldiers living locally would have to be checked. If any had had access to Kalashnikovs, their homes and places of work would have to be searched.

Meanwhile, statements were arriving in ever-increasing quantities but most of them continued to be negative, with none producing another likely suspect. No-one had been seen in the vicinity of the churchyard that early in the morning, and apart from Mrs Piper and the dog-walker, no-one had noticed the motorhome in Green Lane. The village constable, PC Simon Holbeck, had been interviewed by detectives and, although he had been able to help with the background of village personalities and facts about the daily routine of some villagers, his efforts had not produced the name of any possible suspect living locally. His input was valuable, however, guiding detectives to likely witnesses, people he knew would be out and about at the material time.

Pemberton had to accept that, at this early but vital stage, he had but a single suspect, although he felt sure that continuing enquiries would reveal more – as he delved into Flint's life within this community, and in previous ones, he felt sure that further suspects would be revealed.

In a few moments of blissful silence in his office, Pemberton contemplated the motorhome suspect's behaviour. He began by assuming the man was indeed the killer, not merely a suspect or possible witness. If he was the killer, therefore, and if he had chosen to let himself be seen so many times, then it was possible he expected, or wanted, to be pursued. Not caught, no criminal wanted that, but merely pursued as a means of wasting police time and resources. Was that his reason for laying a false trail? If he was laying a false trail, then he had probably effected some kind of simple disguise during his time in Roberthorpe. Even a modest change of appearance would be sufficient to misdirect witnesses and frustrate police enquiries. And in allowing his motorhome to be so eminently visible, especially around the time of the murder, it seemed he expected – and wanted – the police to hunt it. If that was the case, it would have been equipped with false number plates and a fake tax disc, all misleading facts designed to conceal the true identity and whereabouts of the real killer.

This deviousness and planning suggested the crime was not spontaneous; no spur-of-the-moment murder, no speculative killing. Someone had deliberately set out to kill – to execute – Kenneth Flint, which elevated the case into more than a routine murder investigation. In addition, although only half-an-hour or so had elapsed between the murder and the body being found, it did allow sufficient time for a vehicle to be some twenty miles or even further from the scene before the crime was discovered. That offered time enough to remove the false plates and documents, and time for disposal of the vehicle.

If he'd driven it over a cliff or set fire to it, however,

it would attract immediate and unwelcome attention, so Pemberton had become convinced the killer had hired or even borrowed it. By now, it would have been returned in its true guise. In spite of all that, the truth was that if the vehicle still existed, it could be traced, given time. And if it could be found after chummy had lived in it for, say, a week, then it would surely carry his DNA, perfect proof that he had used it. DNA that would surely match any orange pips that were found . . .

However, with almost a full day having elapsed since the crime, the suspect had had ample time to dispose of the vehicle completely. Pemberton would ask police forces nationwide for reports of any burnt-out motor-homes, or any which had been driven on to scrap heaps, over cliffs or into the sea or river.

As he pondered these points, Pemberton struggled to get into the mind of a clever and, perhaps, professional, killer. Had the man been paid to carry out this execution, or was it committed for some personal motive? Who would pay for such a killing? And in such a case, what would a killer expect the police to do?

It was almost a hundred percent certain that the killer would be listening to the radio and watching television, or that he would examine any newspaper which featured the crime. He would surely wish to find out what had resulted from his actions and how the police were tackling the investigation. Pemberton knew he was in a Catch 22 position – the killer would know that a simpleton in charge of the investigation would tell the whole world about the motorhome and the man with dark hair.

A simpleton would establish a wide-ranging and time-consuming search which would be an utter waste of time and resources; the police would hunt a man and his van which had both been disguised. Perfect for the killer.

However, an astute investigator would believe the

van and its driver had been deliberately used to establish a false lead and such a detective would *not* make a public song and dance about seeking either of them! But he would still have to find the motorhome, so he'd have to make very discreet enquiries, not letting the criminal know that the police were interested in the vehicle in the hope that it would not be destroyed. Exactly what Pemberton was doing – and exactly what the killer expected him to do! The killer would know that without a splash of national publicity, the chances of finding the van were remote. Ultimately, failure to find it would benefit the killer more than knowing the police were on his trail.

Pemberton was keenly aware that he couldn't underestimate the cunning and intelligence of this man. He needed to find that van and his only option was to publicise the presence of the motorhome and its dark-haired driver. Perhaps the change of tactic would make the suspect nervous. He'd be more comfortable when the police were doing what he expected them to do.

This investigation looked like becoming a battle of wits beyond conventional investigative techniques and Pemberton hoped he could rise to the challenge. He'd begin his new strategy by releasing details of the motorhome at tomorrow's news conference, along with a description of the suspect. He would not, however, tell the press about the Kalashnikov. He could give that matter further thought.

He wondered what the killer was doing right now? This Saturday night? This evening? This minute?

Engrossed in his own thoughts, and with detectives popping in and out of his office with snippets of information, most of them negative, Pemberton found the time passed with bewildering speed and suddenly it was time for the end-of-day conference.

Paul Larkin marshalled the assembled detectives, most of whom had to stand due to a lack of seating and Pemberton moved behind the table to address them.

'Thanks for the efforts you've put in today,' his voice sounded warm and genuine as he brushed back a stray lock of his fair hair. 'It's never easy, settling into the routine of a murder investigation. The first day is often the toughest, but I reckon we've made a good start and you've all done a good job. I'll pass my news to you first, then we can pool the knowledge we've all gathered during the day.'

He paused to allow them to consider whatever they might wish to say, then began, 'First. The firearm, the murder weapon. I've had advance information from Ballistics. It was a Kalashnikov AK47 rifle, semi-automatic, an old one with 7.62mm ammunition instead of the modern 5.45mm. So who would own such a rifle? Or have access to one? When you're checking houses, especially those known to be occupied by firearm certificate holders, or farms with shotguns about the place, or the homes of former service personnel, think Kalashnikov. No private individual should be in possession of such a weapon nowadays but AK47s are still around. Old soldiers – who nowadays are not necessarily old men – sometimes smuggled them into the country, from wars like the Falklands or the Gulf. Have we any people hereabouts who fought in those wars and might have brought home an AK47 as a war trophy? That's an important line of enquiry. Remember, four bullets went into the body, in a neat little cluster. So it's the act of a skilled operator, someone accustomed to using a Kalashnikov. And where did the ammo come from? Have we had any thefts locally, past or present? Raids on army stores? Rifle clubs? Has this kind of weapon been used for any other crime, locally or nationally? We need to know. Bear all that in mind when you are making your enquiries, but don't tell the press. I don't want publicity about this weapon, not yet. We don't want the killer to dispose of it when he discovers we know about it. Now, the most significant piece of information concerns a suspect and a white motorhome type of vehicle.' ❧

He provided a detailed account of the man and his motorhome and although most of the detectives present had been told of this development, it did no harm to reinforce the earlier messages and they all listened carefully. Pemberton concluded by saying, 'He has been seen in and around the village during the past week, he's made no attempt to conceal himself and so I want you all to ask about him. He might not be the killer, but he could be a vital witness. We need to know if he's talked to anyone, at the caravan site, in the shop or the pub, or even the church, anywhere in fact. He must have had meals somewhere, or bought petrol. I'm going to publicise both the man and his van at tomorrow's news conference, I want every amateur detective and *Crimewatch* fan in the country to be on the look-out for that van and its man. Now, the deceased. And here, I demand the utmost confidentiality from you – if anyone gossips and releases to the press or the public what I am now going to tell you, he or she will be disciplined. It is vital to the enquiry that the following information is kept highly confidential.'

He then told them the full story of Kenneth Flint. The place lapsed into a heavy silence as he presented them with the dreadful past of the murder victim. When he had finished, he said, 'There you are. It does seem we have a reason for this man's death, a powerful motive. Is it someone from his past? Norfolk and Lincolnshire are helping us, tracking down relatives of his past victims in an attempt to eliminate them from the enquiry, but we do need to look very closely at his life in this village too. DS Williams and DC Cashmore, you're looking into Flint's life and you're tracing vulnerable young girls in this village, I believe?'

Williams replied. 'We have, sir, we've been in touch with all groups with young girl members, and their parents too – Brownies, a ballet class, school of course, playschool, the church, the choirs – and most of the people in charge were aware of Flint's propensity for touching children and trying to persuade them to allow him to take photographs. But I think the local bush telegraph was successful. He earned a reputation as a dirty old man and didn't get his hands on any of them, not to our knowledge, anyway.'

'Good. And the photographs in his house? George?'

Detective Sergeant Daniels told the conference that he had asked a member of the photographic department to examine the pictures in Flint's bedroom, and he had expressed an opinion the black-and-white prints were all old photographs, probably processed fifteen or twenty years ago. There was nothing to indicate the names of the girls or the venues of the photographic sessions and it had not been possible to link any of the girls depicted in them with anyone living in Roberthorpe.

Some colour prints were more modern, but probably eight years old, or thereabouts. Daniels felt all the pictures were from some long-ago association or associations.

'We've fingerprinted the house too,' he went on. 'There's no sign of a forcible entry and we've got some good images of prints we're sure belong to Flint. We can use them to confirm his identity, he's in the fingerprint records as Kenneth Bourne through earlier samples taken when he was charged.'

'Good. Any luck with personal documents?' asked Pemberton.

'They were all in that desk in the bedroom, sir, we found his birth certificate, pension book, bank accounts, documents relating to his business as a photographer and so on. He is sixty-nine, sir, born in Brighton, and there's details of his name change, he did it by deed poll, so it was all official. I think we've enough to get him formally identified even if we don't trace any relatives.'

'Fair enough. And what about newspaper cuttings of his trials or arrests? Or the murders he's supposed to have committed. Did he keep any of those?'

'No, nothing. He seems to have kept very little in the way of files and correspondence, except necessary personal stuff.'

'Probably because he's had his house searched so many times!' smiled Pemberton. 'And the orange peel thrown into the fireplace?'

'We've recovered that, as an exhibit, and there were some pips among the coal! Other than those two pieces of evidence, sir, the house didn't reveal much.'

'There was an empty wine bottle in the dustbin,' Pemberton reminded him.

'It had come from shop, sir. Flint had bought it a fortnight ago. He did buy a bottle on occasions.'

'Thanks, Sarge.'

'If the killer was in the house at any stage – even by invitation – perhaps he managed to sneak a look into that bedroom?' suggested Paul Larkin as Pemberton concluded his chat with Daniels.

'And become so sick at what he saw that he decided to get rid of Flint?' suggested Pemberton.

'It's a possibility. A sight like that could turn the stomach of a loving parent,' commented Larkin. 'Whoever viewed those pictures might have gone away and thought about it for a long time . . .'

'Depending on the personality we're dealing with, it may not necessarily have taken a long time. It's an idea, Paul, but if that happened, where did chummy get his gun from?' Pemberton asked. 'This killing has the hallmarks of a carefully planned operation, not a sudden whim based on a chance discovery.'

'If chummy was in the village, with his rifle conveniently on hand, he would soon discover Flint's regular movements, it wouldn't take long to discover enough to track him down and bump him off. You could set your clock by Kenneth Flint, so we've been told. Clearly a man of regular habits.'

'You're suggesting the killer might have come to the village for an innocent purpose and then been appalled by what he discovered?' Pemberton put to him.

'It's a theory,' agreed Larkin.

'It's worthy of consideration,' nodded Pemberton. 'But where would he obtain his rifle, if he was an incomer, that is, or a holidaymaker? I feel he's either a local with the gun available on his premises, or he travelled here especially to deal with Flint. If the latter was the case, it suggests he knew Flint – and all about him – long before he got here. I think he came especially to kill him.'

'You can acquire an illegal firearm, sir, quite easily, provided you've got the ready cash. No questions asked. There's a big trade in unlawful weapons, the aftermath of Dunblane solved nothing. Criminals can still get hold of guns.'

'Point taken. I agree we can't rule out a casual visitor who might have stumbled on Flint's dirty secret and been mortified by it. Painter and decorator? Window cleaner? Salesman of some kind? Local authority official of some sort, anyone who might have had legitimate access to his house? When his bedroom was unlocked.'

'Vicar, doctor, nurse, policeman . . .' added Larkin. 'Burglar even. It wouldn't be the first time a burglar's reacted after discovering a paedophile's hoard of child porn.'

'There's no sign of any illegal entry into the house but we've scope for lots of enquiries,' Pemberton remarked to the assembled detectives. Then he said to Larkin, 'You'll allocate teams to those actions? Now, the caravan

82

site?' and again he addressed the gathering. 'Who's been dealing with that?'

Detective Sergeant Brian Johnson and Detective Constable Josie Stevenson had been charged with the task of making enquiries at the caravan park. Johnson acted as their spokesman. He explained how the caravan park allocated pitches to caravans with a separate area for motorhomes, and how there were facilities for advance reservations as well as accommodation for unsolicited arrivals. A large volume of business came from vans which arrived without prior booking and the park's owners did maintain a register. There was a form to complete upon arrival, and visitors were asked to complete the site register – that contained dates of arrival and departure, the name of the person registering, the number of people attending and the registration number of the vehicle. The register, which remained on the counter of the site office, did not contain private addresses – the arrival forms, with the private addresses, were filed separately in secure cabinets. Johnson and Stevenson had examined the register and a motorhome was recorded for the week ending this Saturday – a Renault which had a sliding door on the nearside of the accommodation section. Its number was recorded but a check with the PNC showed it was false. And the name of the man who had completed the register and the arrival form had also been checked – it was false too. He had arrived last Saturday afternoon at 3 p.m., indicating a stay of one week, and had paid cash. His description matched that given by Mrs Piper.

'So,' Pemberton asked. 'Did the site owners have any contact with him?'

'Only to book him in, sir. He arrived on spec last Saturday, said he wanted a pitch for a week, paid the full fee in advance in cash, and completed the necessary paperwork. The CUB letters mentioned by an earlier witnesses were on this van, sir, I'm sure it's the one

83

that's been seen around the place during the last few days. He registered his arrival in the name of David Rushforth and gave an address in Northampton. We've checked, we're sure the name is false, the address most certainly is. It doesn't exist in Northampton. We ran a check with the PNC to see if any David Rushforths are on the Wanted or Suspected lists but they're not. It could be a one-off use of the name, and we're checking to see if there are any genuine addresses anywhere else in the country to match the one he gave.'

'So he didn't make himself known to the site owner, or other campers?'.

'Most of the campers have left, sir, most were like him, there for just the week and they'd booked out by the time we arrived. We can trace them but it'll take time, and some are still touring, we believe, going on from Roberthorpe. We did catch a few who are staying for another week but they couldn't tell us anything about him. There was a social do at the site on the Friday night, a kind of barbecue, but he didn't go to that and didn't seem to want to socialise with the others. Some went to the local pubs in small groups, he was invited, but declined.'

'So he kept a low profile?'

'That's the impression we got. We can have the other campers interviewed, sir, by other forces, we do have access to their names and addresses. We can check if any of them did have more contact with David Rushforth.'

'I think we should do that. How many happy campers are we talking about?'

'A hundred and fifty units, sir, or thereabouts.'

'Right, we've got to do it, spread the load among other forces, get them to do the initial enquiries at this stage. If something turns up, we can always have another word with the witnesses concerned. Rushforth might have talked to some of them and let something slip about himself. So yes, do that, Sergeant. Leave no stone unturned, as they say. It seems he was reluctant to let the public get acquainted with him, but he was happy to put himself on show when the police were likely to become involved. I'm becoming increasingly sure he's baiting us . . . now, Inspector Fowler, what about your second search of Green Lane?'

'We did a very thorough second search of Green Lane, near where the motorhome had parked, and we found a pip. An orange pip, just one!'

'Wonderful!' breathed Pemberton. 'Just what we need! Let's retain it for DNA comparison with the one from the fireplace – and any others we might find. Brilliant!'

Pemberton invited contributions from the other detectives; farmer Jack Headlam, owner of Green Lane, had been interviewed but couldn't help. The vicar's wife had been seen too, and apart from providing her unflattering opinion of Flint's underhand and creepy behaviour, could offer no suggestions about his death. Several detectives engaged on house-to-house enquiries confirmed the general feelings about Flint's character without any specific instances to support the rumours. He did not visit the pub, his social activities seemed restricted to the church, and for transport he relied on the local bus service. He didn't even own a cycle. The village was generally free from crime, the local constable confirmed that and there was no doubt, in Pemberton's mind, that today's incident had been highly unusual, shocking and totally unexpected. As the clock ticked towards nine, he dismissed his teams and asked them to report to the Incident Room tomorrow morning at nine o'clock.

It was time to go home.

Many of the detectives preferred to visit a local pub for a bar snack before going home; it was a means of relaxing but it also enabled to them to discuss their day's work in pleasant surroundings. Great benefit was derived from these informal chats, even if the participants had to be constantly aware that members of the public might overhear their conversations. Care was taken to avoid any confidential aspects and Pemberton was always invited to join his teams, but usually he declined. For one thing, he did not like discussing work outside duty hours and second, his presence could be inhibit his subordinates. Tonight, though, there was another reason. He wanted to be alone with Lorraine, something which had been impossible during his tough and sometimes long working days. Due to their varied duties, he found it increasingly difficult to spend time with her, but today she recognised his wishes and said she would go home with him. She accepted there were times when her loyalties might be construed as divided – by not joining her colleagues she wondered if she was being selfish or whether she might be seen as snobbish, but when one happened to be the live-in companion of the Detective Superintendent, one also had loyalties to him. In any case, she rationalised, when she was off duty, that time was hers, her precious free time when the constraints of work did not apply.

Invariably she and Mark used separate cars in which to travel to work; their individual duty commitments were liable to take them in different directions which again reduced their time together, and so it was that tonight, they drove in convoy back to Rainesbury, a drive of around an hour.

Unable to discuss their thoughts during the drive, Lorraine knew that Mark would want to bounce his theories and worries off another person, preferably a professional like himself. Invariably he wanted Lorraine to be that person. She was his best friend, his counsellor, his guide, his lover. On their way home, therefore, she was following his car and, with the time approaching nine-forty-five, his indicators unexpectedly announced he was going to pull into the car park of the Horse-breakers' Arms. With its olde-worlde exterior, it looked most inviting as she followed and parked beside his Vauxhall.

'I couldn't wait any longer,' he told her as they re-united. 'I need to talk to you.'

'We can't talk here, Mark, too many flapping ears.'

'I couldn't find a moment to be alone with you,' he sounded dejected. 'And now, much as I want to get home as soon as I can, I thought it was getting too late to start fixing a meal . . . and it is Saturday night.'

'So you thought a meal out was a nice idea?'

'You don't mind?'

'Mind? Heavens, Mark, no! I think it's a great idea.'

'Restaurant or bar?' he asked, visibly relieved.

'Oh, the bar, I'm too scruffy for a smart table in the restaurant? she said. 'Work soiled is perhaps the right word! I'm not dressed for dinner. You look fine, but then you always do. You're as smart as you were this morning!'

'I don't feel smart, I feel work-stained and in need of a wash and shave, so the bar it is.'

They found a table in a quiet corner, ordered a steak for Mark and a fish meal for Lorraine, plus a glass of wine apiece, with a sweet and coffee to follow, and settled down to unwind. The bar was dark and inviting, full of oak beams and panelling and it was busy with customers chatting and laughing. There was enough background noise for them to talk without being over-heard – the adjoining table comprised eight people hav-ing some kind of family celebration and that party was already fizzing with happiness and joyful with alcohol. Their noise filled the room.

'Come on,' she encouraged him. 'You want to talk . . . it's not been an easy day, l could sense that when I saw you at the conference.'

'I don't want to talk shop, I just wanted a few moments alone with you before we get home too shattered to do anything but sleep . . .'

'You're sure you don't want to talk about work?' she interrupted.

'No, I don't! It's one of my rules, not to talk about work in our private moments.'

'Rules are for the obedience of fools and the guidance of wise men,' she smiled. 'That's what you are always telling me! So break your own rule. I don't mind, honestly I don't. If you need to talk about it, Mark, do so, you mustn't bottle things up. Something's worrying you, isn't it? I can sense it.'

''You're right, as always. You read me like a book! Yes, it's work,' he admitted after a long silence. 'That's why I wanted to talk here, home's for relaxing.'

'I know,' she maintained her gaze. 'So, in your own time . . .'

He sipped at his glass of wine, not wishing to drink a lot because he had to drive home, and it seemed he was wondering how to begin; Lorraine waited.

'This murder,' he kept his voice very low. 'It's unusual, it's not normal.'

'Is there such a thing? As a normal murder, I mean?' she put to him.

'Well,' he struggled to find the right words. 'They do tend to slip into fairly identifiable categories. There are domestics, there are murders in the course of rape, murders by burglars or during bank robberies, gangland killings, drugs killings and others. Those categories are repeated throughout the country. There's almost an identifiable pattern to any murder which is why we detect so many, but this one doesn't fit any of those. I'm sure Flint's sordid background is a factor, it has to be. And this suspect – at one point I thought the vicar might have done it, but I've gone off that idea – but the suspect was around for a week beforehand. He's been noticed several times. Was he planning his crime? Coolly plot-ting his actions, weighing up the risks, selecting the location? Did he come because he knew Flint was here? Did he visit Flint, get to know him, watch his move-ments around the village – then kill him? If so, why? Flint has kept his nose fairly clean since he arrived and that tends to rule out a local killer, so who would take the trouble to find him after such a long time, plot his murder, carry it out in broad daylight, make himself so highly visible and then clean up the crime scene? It doesn't add up, Lorraine. That's what bothers me, there are so many contradictions. Perhaps there's something I've missed? Some obvious piece of evidence I've not recognised?'

'I don't think so,' she reached across the table for his hand. 'I think you've spotted the important evidence, and I think that knowledge is bothering you.'

'What evidence, exactly?' he frowned now.

'The fact that the suspect let himself be seen so openly, then removed evidence from the scene. That's impor-tant, isn't it? In your opinion?'

'I'm sure it is, so what do you make of it?' he put to her.

'I think he expects you to follow the false trail that he's established,' she smiled. 'And you, being you, don't want to do that. Or you don't want him to think you've fallen for his ruse? Is it pride, Mark?'

'Pride, what do you mean? Pride doesn't come into it. It's a fact of life, of criminal investigation, that I must follow his trail, however false it might be. I have to go through all the motions, I have to pretend I've fallen for his ploy because even a false trail can provide valuable clues. We need to find that motorhome, Lorraine – I wonder if he thinks I won't bother to look for it?'

'So when you try to find it, he'll know you've fallen for his ploy?'

'I've decided I'll do that, to let him know I've fallen for it. I'll communicate with him through the press.'

'Then he'll know you're doing that, won't he?'

'Exactly,' he smiled. 'Or he'll think he knows.'

'So what else will you be doing while it seems, to the outside world and to the killer, that you are pursuing that high-profile line of enquiry?'

'What else can I do?'

'We have to concentrate on Flint, haven't we? He is the victim after all, and his past behaviour must yield some kind of clue. That's my task, with Andy Williams. We'll keep digging, Mark, it's early days yet, and we've a long way to go.'

'I know that's important, but let's look at the crime itself. It smacks of some kind of military operation, some well-planned scheme using diversionary tactics. That's what I mean by no ordinary murder.'

'You used the word, Mark!'

'What word?' he puzzled.

'Military,' she said. 'Military operation. You mentioned soldiers at the conference, you said some brought guns home with them, as trophies, and you thought the skill displayed by the killer had the hallmarks of a trained gunman or a soldier. And the Kalashnikov is a soldier's gun, isn't it?'

'Right,' he smiled. 'So all I need to do is find a soldier, or someone with military experience, who has some connection, however remote, with Kenneth Flint, either now or in his previous life as Kenneth Bourne. I hope we find that connection.'

'If the killer is behaving like a soldier,' she spoke softly, 'he might not have any close connection with his victim, might he? Soldiers don't know the people they kill, do they? Their killing isn't personal. They kill people because they're the enemy, for no other reason. It's their job. There's no personal animosity, there're no links between killer and victim, are there? In a war?'

'Are you suggesting there might be no personal link between our killer and Flint? That our research into Flint will produce nothing?'

'I'm not saying that, Mark. What I am saying is that if this is an execution, it's one aspect that has to be considered . . . that it might not be personal.'

'A murder with no personal link between killer and victim, eh? Now that would be unusual.'

'You've already identified this killing as being different from other murders,' she said. 'We don't want to spend hours and hours trying to establish such a personal link when in fact there is none.'

'It's a valid point, but we've nothing else to go on, have we? No starting point? No clues leading to a man who kills because he feels it is his duty, if that's what he is thinking.'

'We have a starting point, Mark, we have the motorhome,' she smiled. 'You know that. Our killer wants us to follow that route, so you believe, but the fact is that it's the only link we have. If the killer *thinks* he's leading us into a cul-de-sac, he might not be. He might not be as clever as he thinks, he might not know about modern investigative techniques and developments. Besides, the motorhome is the only object we know – or strongly suspect – to have been used by the killer – apart from the orange pips! And the rifle. We might have difficulty tracing the rifle, we have no bullet casings, so we *have* to find the motorhome. We know that everything we touch carries a trace of our presence, so if and when we find that van, Mark, it will carry some trace of the killer. Some critical trace. We need that van.'

'So, although he wants us to pursue that line because he's set it up as a waste of our time, we shall do so! You're right, of course, it could be his undoing . . .' he muttered and smiled. 'Ah, here's our meal.'

'You will enjoy it, won't you?' she asked.

91

'I will now,' he said, reaching for the French mustard.

The sniper checked the Saturday news bulletins on television and national radio but there was no reference to the death of the church-helper in Roberthorpe. He realised there was no point in listening to his local radio station because he lived such a long distance from that area of operation – his local news bulletins would never feature a murder in Yorkshire unless it was something of national interest.

At this early stage, the death of Kenneth Bourne, or Flint as he had been known in Yorkshire, was of limited interest to the public beyond that village but he would, nonetheless, check the Sunday papers.

Already, he was planning his next operation. Thanks to the library services, he had photocopies of extracts from several newspapers covering the subject that was his focus at this point. He could read the material at leisure in his own home, then it was really just a case of selecting the right candidate.

Afterwards he could undertake some rather more detailed background research, both in documentary form and on location, and then he would be in a position to carry out another mission, one more of his intended target of eighteen. All with his Kalashnikov.

Chapter Six

Sunday was a normal working day for the teams engaged on the Flint murder investigation, although it was customary, unless there was some dramatic development, to finish at five instead of nine in the evening. It gave the teams some free time if the enquiry threatened to be long-running.

Pemberton and Lorraine left their home in separate vehicles and the Incident Room was humming with activity when they arrived. Paul Larkin was already busy preparing for the influx of detectives; some had arrived and were making tea or coffee, others were studying files. Six copies of a thickening wad of photocopied statements were available for everyone – and the room bore an air of optimism and cheerfulness. Half a dozen keyboard operators arrived – their task was to type the statements into their word processors for later incorporation into HOLMES, and when Larkin noticed the arrival of his boss, he allowed him time to reach the office, take off his coat and settle down.

Lorraine joined the other detectives – her domestic world with Mark Pemberton was suspended during their periods of work; here they were boss and subordinate, two very professional police officers, a Detective Superintendent and a Detective Constable. Difficult though it could be at times, they made it work; Lorraine was acutely aware of the distinction in her professional life and worked that much harder to make their roles acceptable. Then, after some twenty minutes, Larkin tapped on Pemberton's door and walked in.

'Morning, Paul, how's things?' Pemberton greeted him warmly.

'Fine, sir, and we had two deliveries overnight. Those files we asked for, from Lincolnshire and Norfolk. I've not had a chance to study them yet, but I'm sure they'll be useful. There is some feedback from other forces following our general nationwide circulation. Negative most of it, no trace of the motorhome for example, or the suspect. Judging from what we've received so far, Flint, or Bourne, was unknown beyond the areas with which we've already established links, and none of the other forces have any record of shootings with older Kalashnikovs, or thefts of such weapons or ammo. We've the honour of being the first!'

'And the last – I hope!' Pemberton said wryly. 'Can you plough through those Norfolk and Lincolnshire files and see if there's anything we should know about? I'm interested in potential suspects at this point. And, of course, any leads that might show up.'

'I'll give them my undivided attention! Now, do you want a news conference today? It's a Sunday, remember, press attendance tends to be sparse on Sundays and we don't have much new stuff for them since yesterday. To be honest, staff reporters don't often show up, most nationals and regional papers rely on freelances.'

'That's a shame, I want massive coverage of the motorhome, Paul.'

'You're going ahead with that? I thought you were playing that one low key, no publicity.'

'I was, but I've changed my mind.'

'If you want a big headline splash, it might be best left until Monday's news conference.'

'That means waiting another full day. I'd like it in Monday morning's papers as well as TV and radio, something for the journalists to follow up during the

94

week. Do we know a good freelance? One we can invite along today?'

'I'll talk to Don Collins, he'll have his contacts.'

'Good, do that. Tell him to drop hints we've a good story to offer, the description of a suspect and his vehicle. That's always good for a few paragraphs. He's got a couple of hours to pass the word around. Now, what have we for the troops this morning?'

'Nothing new, sir. It's a case of continuing existing enquiries with due emphasis on Flint's contacts and movements around the village. Lorraine and Andy Williams are on that action. We've still a lot of homes to visit on house-to-house, and we're continuing to trace children who've attended groups which attracted Flint. We're looking at their parents and family members, sir, trying to see if any of them could have owned or used that gun. And we're double-checking for ex-soldiers who might be living hereabouts, or people who might have come to Roberthorpe to work, say lorry drivers, builders and such.'

'Good. And the vicar? Are we delving deep into his background?'

'We are. We've turned up nothing of significance so far.'

'I don't think he's in the frame even though he found the body; his story of that rings true. Mrs Piper unwittingly confirmed his story.'

'It was confirmed by Dr Cochrane as well. The doctor never attended Flint, by the way, he didn't frequent the surgery. The doctor knows nothing about him.'

'And Nurse Archer?'

'Not in the frame, sir. She has an alibi for the material time, attending bed patients, and her relationship with the vicar is platonic, no suggestion of a romance. She and the vicar's wife are long-standing friends. We've verified all that. And the nurse can't help with Flint's background. She never attended him.'

'What about other church workers? There must be others who've had contact with Flint?'

'We're checking flower ladies, cleaners, those who keep the graveyard tidy, sidesmen, the organist and so on, we got a list from the vicar, he's been most helpful.'

'And the shop? The purchase of oranges? Was that checked out?'

'It was, sir. George Daniels went along; the owner did remember selling the oranges to the dark-haired man who was quite a regular visitor in the past week, almost daily so far as she can recall, and she's sure the peel came from one of the kind she sells. They have little stickers on them, red and green, they're from South Africa, although the peel in the churchyard was several days old.'

'So we can't prove chummy dumped the peel in the churchyard, but we've got to bear in mind the balance of probabilities, and of course the timing. We do know chummy bought oranges. Perhaps we can match pips to a certain kind of orange, if we have to?'

'I'm sure our forensic fruit experts can do that. Oh, and he bought some yesterday morning, sir, when he got his *Yorkshire Post*.'

'He's keen on them, to be sure, and pips seem more important than peel right now, so we can't ignore the orange link. Now, anything more on motorhomes, camper vans or whatever we call them.'

'No reported sightings from the national search, but I've sent a team round local suppliers to get brochures of every possible make and type, including Renaults.'

'You'll make sure Mrs Piper sees them?'

'Yes, once we've reduced them down to those likely to match the one she saw – I'm sure we'll find something.'

'We'll need some kind of picture or description for the press. Can Mrs Piper be seen before the news conference? To try and identify the one she saw? We need to match it with the one at the caravan site if we can.'

'It will be done first thing, sir, first job this morning.'

'Make sure you catch her, I'll bet most of the villagers go to church this morning, to pray for Kenneth Flint . . . we've finished with the church, haven't we?'

'We have, church and grounds. The vicar's been told he can have them back. The service is at ten-thirty, sir, I checked. I thought someone ought to be there, to represent the police.'

'Well, I shall be attending our news conference then. I'm sure you can find a volunteer, Paul; if you can't you might have to attend yourself. You might chat to parishioners on the way out, get a few names for later interviews and get more background stuff from the vicar. Like the good shepherd, he should know his flock! And you can pray for the repose of the soul of the good and kind Kenneth Flint, eh?'

'Do you think God forgives people like him? Or can anyone forgive people like that? Or, as a matter of debate, should they be forgiven?'

'Don't ask me!' Pemberton grimaced. 'I'm just a policeman. All I know is that the world is full of villains and our job is to bring them to justice on this earth. There are times I think it's a bit like trying to stem an avalanche with a lollipop stick.'

And so the rhythm of the day's investigation began to gather pace. A competent freelance reporter did attend the news conference by which time Mrs Piper had been further questioned about the motorhome. Although she did not find one in the brochures, they did help her to recall more detail. Not being a driver or a car owner, she did not have much idea about makes or models of motor vehicles, but she did say she was sure it was a small mobile home, white in colour, looking higher than a normal van and she was confident it had a sliding door on the nearside. All that confirmed her earlier description. However, she now added she had noticed a spare wheel attached to the outside of the rear of the vehicle, on the passenger side, and remembered that each side of the uppermost part of the roof, towards the rear, bore a design of horizontal blue lines. There were three short lines, she said, about an inch and a half deep and about two feet long, and beneath them was a third blue line which ran from the front to the rear at roof level – the normal roof level, she said. She remembered the lines because she thought they made a nice pattern, rather like the one on her kitchen curtains. In this case, it looked at if the vehicle roof had been raised so that people could stand up and walk about in the rear sec- tion – that part of the roof was higher than that of the driving cab.

It was a noticeably high vehicle, she said, and she'd recognised a skylight on the top of the rear section of roof. She'd seen that from her upstairs window, but she had not noticed any registration number. She had no idea how old the vehicle might be, and could not help with any suggestion about its manufacturer. Nonethe- less, it was a very good description, one which was perfectly suitable for publication because it might pre- sent a challenge for readers, listeners and viewers. Pemberton hoped this description would persuade some members of the public to try and name it.

When Mrs Piper looked through the accumulation of catalogues, with particular attention to those from Renault, she failed to find a single motorhome which matched the one she'd seen. Some were very similar, but she could see nothing which was, as she put it, 'marrow to the one I saw'. Nonetheless, it was felt her description would provide sufficient detail for some vehicles of that kind to be traced or identified; Pemberton felt sure that the name of a likely make and model would be the outcome – and he hoped it matched the vehicle seen at the caravan site. The journalists present said it was a good story and they would endeavour to give it as much publicity as possible in tomorrow's papers, along with the part of the registration number – CUB – and a description of the dark-haired man. Pemberton agreed to a couple of taped radio interviews, but there was no television news crew at the conference. When it was over, he felt satisfied that he'd get his publicity.

Because Lorraine and Andy Williams had dealt with the Flint action and interviewed the vicar along with some of the other churchworkers, Inspector Larkin felt they should attend morning service in the village, and so they did. The theme of the vicar's sermon was one of forgiveness for the killer, and for any sinful behaviour committed by Kenneth Flint; during coffee afterwards, Lorraine and Andy spoke to members of the congregation, but gathered no new relevant information.

There were no useful developments during the rest of Sunday. Sandra Ingram, the girl who'd been pestered by Flint in her younger days, was interviewed but as the events had occurred nearly five years ago with no family repercussions, it was felt they had little bearing on the current enquiry, save to reinforce the knowledge of Flint's personality. Besides, Sandra and her family had alibis too.

For the teams of detectives, it was a case of plodding around asking the same question time and time again, and checking facts gleaned from earlier enquiries, invariably without any positive further result. But that was the essence of detective work – you keep plodding along until something exciting happens. Not even the files from Norfolk and Nottinghamshire produced any real suspects – each of the forces had scrutinised the files prior to despatching copies to Pemberton, and had marked the names of some likely suspects, with small annotations to say that some had already been interviewed. All had alibis, they could explain their presence

99

at the material time and those forces had concluded that none could be seriously considered a major suspect.

By doing this with such speed, they had saved Pemberton's teams much work but, as the chief constable of Norfolk had said in his covering letter, if Pemberton wished to take the matter further in the Norfolk area, the alibis could be checked by Pemberton's own teams in the light of any other developments which might occur. Pemberton decided that was a very wise course of action. He would satisfy himself that no-one on his patch was responsible for the murder before trying to break the alibis of others further afield, others who, it seemed, were not in the frame. Apart from that, the last thing he wanted was to stir up strife, anger and resentment among the relations of those who had been Flint's victims.

He would regard such further enquiries as a final resort. Sadly, the enquiries into Flint's life in Roberthorpe and district were producing very little additional information. He had led a very quiet and unobtrusive life, virtually all within the bounds of this tiny village. Those closely associated with the church, including members of this morning's congregation, could add very little to what was already known about Flint; indeed, most of them commented upon his charm and friendliness. Pemberton ended that Sunday with a feeling he was getting nowhere. He went home wrapped in hope that the publicity about the suspect and his motorhome would produce some new leads. He needed something to provide a new impetus for his investigation.

Monday morning's papers did contain news items about the murder of Kenneth Flint but the nationals had given it very little coverage.

Typical was one report which said, 'Police in North Yorkshire are seeking a white motorhome which was spotted close to the scene of a murder in Roberthorpe, a pretty moorland village near Rainesbury. With blue stripes on the bodywork, it was driven by a dark-haired man in his forties. A police spokesman said, "We would like to talk to this man, he may be an important witness." The name of the dead man has not been released, but he is believed to be a retired photographer who was a keen supporter of Roberthorpe parish church.'

The local papers were more effusive, some linking the name of Kenneth Flint with the reports, even though his name had not been confirmed, and others publishing photographs of mobile homes which they believed to be very similar to Mrs Piper's description. One paper even managed to print a very good pen-and-ink drawing of a motorhome but Mrs Piper said it wasn't very like the one she had seen, and some of the local radio stations did broadcast descriptions of both the vehicle and its driver. Pemberton knew that Monday morning's news conference would be concentrating upon both the suspect and that motorhome, but the publicity did result in calls from the general public, with a range of possible vehicles being mentioned. All would be checked but at this stage, none excited the investigation teams – a matching Renault had not been found.

At the morning conference of detectives, Pemberton told his teams that he would be concentrating on publicising the motorhome and man with black hair, hoping for nationwide coverage.

He realised there was only so much information available within the village but nonetheless stressed that his officers concentrated on Flint's activities and life within the community, and that continuing efforts be made locally to trace the source of the Kalashnikov. So far, none of the soldiers living nearby could be regarded as suspects, all had good alibis. The morning news conference concentrated on the motorhome because Pemberton wanted to trace all vehicles which might fit its description rather than worry about precise makes and models; his real desire was to keep the story running for as long as possible. The dark-haired man had not been traced either and no suggested names had been forthcoming, he told the press. He did not, however, release any information about the Kalashnikov – he simply said the murder weapon had not been traced.

Following the conference, Pemberton felt it would be a good idea to have Flint formally identified so that his name could appear in news releases and publicity; no relatives could be traced and so he decided that he would ask the vicar to look at the body and sign a statement to the effect that this was the man known as Kenneth Flint; scientific support could be given by matching his fingerprints with those found in the house he'd occupied, and his Bourne name, supported by documentary evidence from the house, could be revealed when it was convenient to do so. There was no requirement to reveal his alternative name at this stage, and the formal identification meant the inquest could be opened, then postponed until the enquiries were complete.

At half-past eleven that Monday morning, by the stroke of good fortune that every murder enquiry needs, a secretary in the offices of a caravan and motorhome hire company read the *Daily Express* and saw the piece about the motorhome. Her name was Alison Potter and she alerted her boss, showing him the paper.

'Mr Denton', she said. 'That's like ours, that old one we keep for people who want a bit of nostalgia.'

'Our old passion wagon? The Renault?' he asked, picking up the paper to read the article.

When he had finished, he said, 'I don't think it's ours, the number is different. Ours hasn't CUB in its plate. And I don't think the hirer was heading for Yorkshire, if I remember correctly, he told us he was going to

Cornwall for a few days, for some kind of artists' reunion near St Ives, he said.'

'I know, but there can't be many left on the road as old as ours, and in such good condition. It might be a false number.' There was excitement in her eyes, 'I mean, Mr Denton, if our van had been seen near that murder, it might have been the murderer himself and it was, he might have used false number plates on it . . .'

'Was the hirer a dark-haired man?'

'No, he had fair hair,' she said, 'Quite thin on top as well.'

'Well, there you are. A different man, and a different number. I don't think it's our van, Alison. It was Cornwall, wasn't it? Where he was heading?'

'Yes, he said that. St Ives, he said. There was some kind of artists' gathering, I remember thinking he must be an artist as well, even if he didn't look like one.'

'Well, this murder was in North Yorkshire, that's a long way from Cornwall! But we'll keep that newspaper, Alison, just in case. We'll see what it says tomorrow.'

'You don't think we should tell the police, then?' she put to him.

'I know you're a fan of Crimewatch, Alison, and I don't want to disillusion you, but I think we'd be wasting police time – there's nothing to link our van with the one they're looking for, other than a vague similarity of description. The drivers are different, the van numbers are different and they were in different parts of the country. And on top of that, there must be hundreds of these old campers still on the roads. They're not vintage or unique by any means.'

'It would be exciting, though, wouldn't it?' She was exhilarated now, and her mind was racing along the lines of one who followed Crimewatch and read crime novels. 'If it was our van, I mean. If the murderer had decided to make things look different, they do that, you know. They put false number plates on cars and things, and dress up to look different. I mean, it could be him, Mr Denton. So if it was, what would they do with it, do you think? The police, I mean, if it was that van.'

'Well, they'd examine it, scientifically I expect . . . they'd take it away, Alison, which means we'd not have it available for hire for maybe weeks . . . where is it now?'

'It's gone in for service and valeting.'

'And when it was hired, the name and address given by the hirer was checked against his driving licence, was it?'

'Yes, it was, Mr Denton.'

'So there was nothing suspicious about him, and his cheque didn't bounce?'

'He seemed a very nice man, but he didn't use a cheque, he paid cash in advance, Mr Denton. I remember him saying he wanted to pay cash.'

'Did he?' The tiniest of frowns now appeared on Denton's face, then he said, 'Tell you what, Alison, get the file out, will you? Just in case the police come asking about that van. Let's see what tomorrow's papers say about that murder, if they haven't found the van they're looking for we might change our minds. Now, on Wednesday, we have a couple want to hire a 1969 model of a two-berth caravan for a fortnight. It's to celebrate their silver wedding. Have we anything suitable?'

Because there were no dramatic developments during the investigation that week, Pemberton was able to concentrate on the minutiae of Kenneth Flint's life. Andy Williams and Lorraine had produced a thick dossier of information about him, much of which comprised the trivia of domestic life and his church work. Further assistance from Norfolk and Lincolnshire had emphasised the persistent efforts, many unsuccessful, made by this man throughout his life to infiltrate a range of social activities involving young girls.

The childhood and youthful life of Flint/Bourne was well-documented. His antecedents had been compiled in readiness for his trial for murder, to be read out to the judge when considering sentence but, of course, he had been found not guilty. Thus that information had not been made public although it had been kept on file. What was lacking, of course, was a list of the names of people with whom he had had close contact throughout his life.

For example, Pemberton wished he had the names of Flint's neighbours as a child, details of his school mates, his workmates when he'd first been employed as a photographer in a studio, his customers when he was a commercial photographer in his own right, his friends and contacts when he was living in Norfolk and Lincolnshire, those whose daughters he had attempted to seduce and that whole range of people he would meet on a normal daily basis, like the postman, the shopkeepers and so on. Although much of such information was not contained here, Bourne's early addresses were listed and so, if this enquiry began to pall, then Pemberton must consider despatching Williams and Lorraine to Bourne's former neighbourhoods to fill in the gaps of his life by talking to any people still living there. But that was an expensive and time-consuming task – first, he must scrutinise these files to see if they contained any information, however slight, which would lead to his killer. And as he read, he began to make notes of points which he felt relevant, such as the name of the family who first made a complaint about Flint/Bourne's activities so far as their daughter was concerned. He jotted down the father's name. A visit to that family may be necessary; the girl in question would be a woman now, but her memories might be valuable.

Through carefully digesting the information, Pember-

105

ton slowly began to compile his own mental image of a sickening and very unpleasant character. He began to feel that Kenneth Bourne alias Flint should have been locked away years ago. So how much did his killer know about him? Had Lorraine been right? Maybe the killer knew very little about him – but if so, why kill him?

The sniper was preparing for his next challenge, but he was delighted to see that Detective Superintendent Pemberton, the officer in charge of the Bourne/Flint murder investigation, was spending time and effort in tracing the dark-haired man in the white motorhome. He smiled with pleasure as he read the reports, and he praised himself for his professionalism in bringing about that result. To date, the name of the deceased had not been released and he wondered if the police knew Flint's background and, if so, whether that would be revealed to the public? Not that it really mattered – Flint or Bourne was dead, justice had been done.

The sniper's research into his next enterprise was almost complete. Much had been done in the past, of course, along with other similar projects planned for the forthcoming months and at this stage it was a case of fine tuning now that his choice had been made. Within days, he would undertake that duty. With his Kalashnikov.

Chapter Seven

Steven Abrahams, a wealthy entrepreneur who owned three nightclubs along with other businesses on north Tyneside, turned into the drive of his beautiful, isolated mansion. Dating to the mid-Victorian era, it stood in wooded grounds outside East Creston – a small village, just off the A1 and lying roughly halfway between Morpeth and Alnwick in Northumberland. It was three o'clock on Sunday morning and he was driving his silver Series 7 BMW; he was alone at the time.

He stopped the car and climbed out, leaving his headlights blazing as he opened the gates; further along the drive, there was a second set of gates which, for security reasons, were operated electronically from the car or the house. But Abrahams never regained his vehicle. Someone called his name, he turned to see who it was and was instantly shot dead. He fell to the ground beside the car. He was not found until later that morning, when a passing motorist noticed his body on the drive beside the car. Its lights were still burning and the driver's door stood open as the engine ticked over. The motorist rang the police on his mobile telephone, said the man was beyond medical aid and was asked to remain at the scene until the police arrived. It took the first car a matter of twelve minutes with blue lights flashing; it was then eight-thirty.

On the following Tuesday afternoon, Pemberton, whose own enquiry was now struggling to find new and relevant information, received a telephone call from Nottingham Forensic Science Laboratory.

'It's Chris Lightfoot, Mr Pemberton, from the Firearms Division.'

'Morning,' Pemberton said, recalling the name. 'What can I do for you?'

'Bearing in mind your murder, I thought you might be interested in something that's turned up,' said Lightfoot. 'There's been a shooting in Northumberland, a night-club owner shot in the early hours of Sunday morning as he was turning into his drive. Four shots in the chest. He must have died instantly.'

'Go on,' Pemberton could feel the adrenaline begin-ning to rise.

'The bullets came from a Kalashnikov, Mr Pemberton, we've compared them with those from your weapon. It's the same rifle.'

'Oh, God,' he sighed. 'You're sure about that?'

'I am, Mr Pemberton, they're very distinctive, too distinctive to make an error of that kind. So there you are, your man has struck again – or the gun has. One may presume it's still in the same hands.'

'I'll contact Northumberland immediately,' Mark Pemberton said. 'Do they know about this link?'

'No, I thought you'd better know first. You'll contact them? Detective Superintendent Radcliffe is in charge.'

'Thanks, I know him, I'll call right away,' and he replaced the handset.

'Something wrong?' Paul Larkin saw the expression on Pemberton's face and realised it was bad news.

'Another shooting, Paul, in Northumberland. With that same Kalashnikov.'

Pemberton provided the details as Larkin listened intently, then asked, 'Who's the victim?'

'No idea, except it's a nightclub owner. I'll ring Jack Radcliffe now.'

Detective Superintendent Radcliffe listened to Pemberton's outline of his own case as Paul Larkin remained at his side, and he followed with the salient points of Abrahams' murder.

'What do you know about Abrahams?' Mark Pemberton asked eventually. 'Has he any form?'

'He's generally been on the borderline of the law but overstepped the mark sometimes,' Radcliffe confirmed. 'He was a villain, a clever one who learned to keep one step ahead of the police. We know there's drugs in some of his clubs, we think they were distributed with his knowledge, or even that he was involved in the supply, but we've no evidence to support it. He covered his tracks very well. He was into gaming machines too, one of his sidelines, and might have been running some kind of protection racket among businesses in the north-east. We do know the Inland Revenue and HM Customs are investigating him, too, the latter for VAT fiddles.'

'Has he a record?'

'Yes, years ago. Petty crime mainly, as a youngster. Then he went into bank robberies, he's got form for two armed raids on building societies, and one wages snatch. He served time for those. They were more than fifteen years ago, he asked for all those jobs to be taken into consideration when he was sent down. He was forty-seven when he died and has managed to avoid the courts since his last term inside. We know he's a villain, he's a criminal businessman, we know that, it's just we've never been able to prove anything against him – not for the want of trying, I might add. I think people were too frightened to testify against him.'

'What about indecency? Child abuse? That kind of thing?'

'Oh no, definitely not, nothing like that. He wasn't as warped as that!'

'Enemies then? Had he enemies?' Pemberton asked.

'I'm sure he had, he'd crossed more villains than is good for him, but always managed to keep on top. I'm not sure whether he'd kill to maintain his superiority, but he was ruthless, Mark, a very formidable character. He was the boss, that was never in doubt. Even so, he was always watching his back, he knew he'd made some dangerous enemies. We're checking those right now, his business acquaintances and so on, some are as dodgy as he was and they'll be jockeying for top dog position now. We've got some good leads about deals that have gone sour in the past, deals which gave the loser a reason for getting rid of Abrahams, but we've no-one in the frame yet.'

'Has he lived elsewhere? Lincolnshire? Norfolk?'

'No, he's always lived and worked in the north-east, in the Newcastle area.'

'A white motorhome was seen near the scene of our murder, it's got blue stripes on the sides of the roof and a spare wheel bolted to the rear but our witness doesn't know its make or number. It could be a Renault, we think, with false plates, and we've a dark-haired man, probably in his forties, who was seen with the van. Do either of those ring any bells with you?'

'No, Abrahams didn't have a vehicle like that and we've none reported so far, and we've no dark-haired suspects right now. Our problem is we've got no witnesses – it was a lonely spot, miles from anywhere, in darkness in the early hours. Nobody saw or heard a thing, Mark. And the local villains aren't too co-operative!'

'Have your Task Force searched the scene, Jack? Ours didn't find any empty cartridge shells, we think the killer took them away.'

'The mark of a professional assassin, eh? It was the same here, Mark. The scene is as clean as a whistle.'

'We found some orange pips, Jack,' and Pemberton explained the significance of those.

'We've some road-side rubbish to examine, the sort

motorists throw out of cars. To be honest, I don't know whether there're any orange pips among it'.

'Check it out, Jack. Look for orange pips, keep them for comparison with ours. We've checked ours for DNA – if we get a suspect and all else fails, that might nail him.'

'Thanks for the tip. I thought all we had to go on is Abraham's very shady background. That's our starting point, we're turning over the local underworld for this one, but from what you say, we might have to look further afield?'

'If our man is involved, I think it might extend beyond any local struggle but don't neglect your own underworld characters. We're looking at locals too, especially any old soldier, former soldier I should say, who might keep a Kalashnikov under the bed.'

'From what we've gathered so far, which is not much, it seems the local criminals are as baffled as us, but they want it cleared up, they want us off their backs!'

'You'll get help from them, perhaps?'

'I'm sure we will, especially if we keep up the pressure. They don't want us prying into their dealings but we've nothing else to go on. And there's always a chance they might know somebody with a Kalashnikov and a grudge of some kind.'

'I'm not publicising details of the weapon, Jack,' and Pemberton explained his reasons, adding that he was continuing with his efforts to publicise the motorhome. 'I think chummy has been setting up a false trail so I'm letting him think we've fallen for that. It might be sensible not to publicly link our two crimes, or refer to the make of weapon. We need to keep him in the dark about some aspects of our enquiry.'

'Right, that makes sense. Let's keep the two jobs quite separate in the minds of the press and public. After all, I suppose your man could have disposed of the gun after he'd used it. Some other villain could have got hold of it. That's always possible, firearms can be obtained for a few pounds in Newcastle, no questions asked, courtesy of the underworld. With ammunition, of course.'

'That's something we'll have to establish, whether or not the same man used the gun on both occasions. The orange pips might just do that!'

'You think he eats oranges when he's under stress, or something?'

'He did buy a lot when he was in Roberthorpe,' was all Pemberton could say with confidence. 'And we did find bits of orange peel at places we think he visited – when he tidied up the scene, he overlooked the pips.'

'Right, well, that might help us decide whether the same man was at the scene of both jobs, but proving that won't be easy unless we find the weapon and finger-print it. So, apart from the fact the same gun was used for both crimes, Mark, how is our victim connected with yours?'

'There might not be a connection if their killers were not the same person. That could be the proverbial red herring.'

'Point taken! But if it *is* the same killer, could there be a link?'

'More than likely, Jack. And if we knew what that link was, we'd be half-way to cracking these jobs,' Pember-ton said. 'Abrahams' name hasn't cropped up during my enquiries, nor have any links with Tyneside, so I've only the weapon to link him with Kenneth Flint. There has to be another connection, Jack.'

'Not if a different person used that gun,' he grunted.

'All right, point taken. But if the same man has used the same gun for both crimes we need to establish why. There must be some kind of link between the victims, neither of us can ignore that. Why suddenly start bump-ing off people with a Kalashnikov? The victims are two men with differing backgrounds in different parts of the country, even if they are both villains of some kind. Nasty pieces of work, both of them.'

Radcliffe paused, then said, 'I reckon we need a liaison officer, Mark. Someone to work on both investigations, to spot the link, to identify similarities, to make links with evidence like those orange pips you mentioned. Have you anyone who might cope with that? A dedicated liaison officer perhaps?'

Pemberton's mind worked rapidly. His first consideration was Lorraine, she had the brains, instinct and experience to deal with that kind of responsibility but he wanted her to concentrate on Flint – she was too valuable to lose to another investigation. Paul Larkin was another but he was needed in the Incident Room, and then Pemberton remembered a detective called Ben Silver.

'I've a good officer who's at a loose end just now,' he said. 'Ben Silver, a detective sergeant. He's been on house-to-house but he needs something meatier, besides, his team-mate's gone down with flu. He'd do a good job for us.'

'If you recommend him, that's good enough for me,' Radcliffe said.

'I'll have a few words with him and get him to contact your Incident Room,' promised Pemberton and replaced the receiver. Pemberton acquainted Larkin with Radcliffe's comments, then mentioned the idea of Ben Silver being the liaison officer. Larkin agreed and said he would do all he could to help Silver.

'So, this is a turn-up for the books!' commented Paul Larkin. 'Have we a serial killer at large?'

'Unless the gun has been discarded and used by someone else, it looks ominously like that,' Pemberton admitted. 'The Abrahams job sounds as professional as ours, although the only link does seem to be the rifle. This is the second killing with that weapon, so does it herald more? If so, why? Why suddenly embark on this killing spree? Anyway, I must notify our own teams about this development, I'll do that at this afternoon's conference – but we've decided not to tell the press or the public about these links, not at this stage anyway.'

'Fair enough, but we haven't given details of Flint's past to the press yet,' Larkin reminded Pemberton. 'Maybe it's time we did so? It would generate a little more press interest.'

'You're saying we should tell the world his real name and what he was charged with in the past?' Pemberton asked.

'Why not, sir? It would stir things up and give our enquiry a much-needed lift, and I do know the civil liberties bunch will come up with the hoary old argument that he's not here to defend himself.'

Pemberton nodded, 'I think we've reached the stage when the public has helped as much as it can. Maybe his real name will generate more response? And his past, those misdeeds under his own name, might be the very thing we now need to concentrate on.'

'It'll get publicity, I agree with that, and it will upset the villagers when they realise they've had a killer living among them. He's had them fooled all along.'

'He has, but it was his decision to change his name, he did it to cover up his activities and now his cover has been blown, as they say; now it's the day of reckoning.'

'Murder will out, as they say.'

'They do indeed. I think we should be careful not to say he was guilty of those murders, we'll stress that he was tried for one and suspected of another, which is the truth. So, yes, let's bite this particular bullet at this evening's news conference.'

'And we can release his name, the vicar's completed the formal identification for us, so this will all feature in tomorrow's newspapers.'

As the teams of detectives returned to the Incident room after their daily stint, Pemberton spotted Lorraine and Andy Williams. He called them over and explained the development, saying, 'You're still busy with Flint's background? Can you bear in mind the Northumberland crime as you go along, you might come across the name of Abrahams or some link with the north-east.'

'Sir,' smiled Lorraine. 'The victim, Abrahams, was a known criminal so you've told us. Do we know the extent of his criminal life?'

'You'll get details from the Northumberland Incident Room, and I'm appointing Ben Silver to be liaison officer for the two investigations,' he said. 'All Detective Superintendent Radcliffe told me was that he had previous convictions and lived a criminal life-style, possibly with involvement in drug dealing, protection rackets and so on. They're looking into his past to try and find a motive. It won't be easy, those sort of people don't talk to the police.'

'I was wondering if he'd ever been tried for murder?'

'That wasn't mentioned.'

'It wouldn't be in his records,' she smiled. 'Like it's not in Flint's criminal record, but Flint was tried but found not guilty of one, and suspected but never tried for another. We were lucky to be told about that. Andy and I were chatting this afternoon, either of those cases could provide a motive for Flint's death, not his lesser paedophilia. We've not established that, have we? Whether the motive for his death might be something else?'

'We did consider that in the early stages of this enquiry and came up with nothing, we found no vengeful family members lying in wait . . . I think we decided that neither his acquittal nor the non-trial were likely to provide a revenge motive for his death.'

Williams nodded, 'I realise that, sir, at the time we thought it might be his more recent actions that had prompted the gunman, that the motive could rest with someone whose little girl he'd been abusing. That was our thinking then. That's not produced anything, we're coming up against dead ends all the time.'

Lorraine took up the conversation, 'In spite of extensive enquiries into his recent life, we've not found anyone with a motive, sir. We've come up against a brick wall. It's not that people are withholding information, I don't think they are. I've the feeling there is nothing to know, that our killer is not someone from Flint's recent past. For that reason, I thought we should go back to those earlier crimes, back to the acquittal and the non-starter. We've gone a long way into Flint's past, but I do think the clue might lie in that acquittal – and my view is reinforced by what you've just told us about Abrahams.'

'So what are you suggesting, Lorraine?' There was a frown on Pemberton's face as he tried to understand the direction of her questions.

'I wondered if Abrahams had ever been found not guilty of a murder, or whether he'd been suspected of one which had not proceeded to court for some reason. Both victims were villains, we know that, very different kinds of villains, but villains nonetheless. We know the same gun was used for both murders and it does look as if both were some kind of professional execution. No evidence left behind, the most recent being a man waiting for his victim to come home in the early hours. There were no witnesses.'

'You mean a vigilante of some kind?'

'It's a thought,' she smiled at him. 'We know he's good with a gun, he might be a soldier or ex-soldier, he's clever enough to create false trails. Does that suggest SAS training, for example? Or some kind of undercover military background? The killer might be on some kind of personal mission, sir.'

'What made you come up with that idea?' he asked.

'As I said, Andy and I were discussing the crime today, musing over it and I wondered if the death was

116

due to those past crimes, the ones for which he'd not paid a price . . . and now you tell me about another villain who's died by the same gun. So I wonder if Abrahams has ever stood trial for murder, or some other serious crime. And more important, was he found not guilty which means, in some eyes, that he has not paid the penalty?'

Pemberton now understood the sheer horror of her suggestion.

Without wasting a moment, he picked up the phone and dialled the Northumberland Incident Room.

'Pemberton here', he announced. 'North Yorkshire. Is DS Radcliffe there? It is urgent.'

He waited and soon his call was answered.

'Jack,' he began. 'Can you answer this. Has Abrahams ever been prosecuted for murder, or some serious crime, and been acquitted? Or perhaps been charged with a major crime which did not proceed to court for any reason?'

There was a pause, then Radcliffe said, 'Yes, twelve years ago. He was charged with murdering a prostitute, the Crown Court jury found him not guilty. He had a witness who said he was sure he'd seen Abrahams in Sunderland at the material time; the prostitute was killed some miles away in Newcastle. We were sure the witness was lying, but it was enough to sway the jury. And it created enough doubt for the judge to think a guilty verdict was dangerous. Abrahams was found not guilty – but we knew he was as guilty as hell. Blood from her clothing matched blood on his trousers, he had scratches and she had skin under her finger nails, there was other circumstantial evidence too . . . he was as guilty as hell, Mark but for reasons we may never know, the jury rejected our evidence. How I wish we'd had DNA in those days!'

'DNA could still wrap the case up for you, to close the files, if you've samples left.'

117

'It could. I think we kept all the evidence, but when it was all over, all we could say was that we were not seeking anyone else for the crime. But all that was twelve years ago! We are looking at the file, to see if any of her relatives could have decided to take a late revenge, but I doubt it. Do you honestly think it's relevant to this murder?'

'Our victim was found not guilty of one child murder and he was suspected of a second, both of them several years ago, although the second never went to court. A lack of evidence, so it was claimed,' Pemberton said.

'So you're saying that's a second link between our crimes, Mark.'

'It could be.'

'If it is, it changes everything,' Radcliffe went on. 'It looks as if we have a serial killer on the loose, someone at the start of his campaign, some nutter armed with a bloody Kalashnikov! Someone not local to my area, or yours. So where do we start looking? And who's he going to kill next?'

'We need to look beyond our two murders,' Pemberton spoke quietly now. 'If this man has begun a sniping campaign against people who've been found not guilty, or whose cases have never reached court, it means there are hundreds of potential victims out there! They're spread throughout the country. They've got to be warned.'

'And how do you propose to do that, Mark? Without causing one almighty panic among the public? Besides, we don't know it is the same killer yet, do we? Same gun, yes. Similar clean scenes. Two villains have bitten the dust – but that's all we have. There's no pattern, we've no conclusive evidence that he's actually set about wiping out a section of the public.'

'But if he is . . .'

'If he is, we've got to catch him before he kills again.

And I suggest we keep this to ourselves for the time being. After all, it is just speculation.'

'Speculation or not, if the press gets hold of the idea, they'll blow it out of all proportion. I can imagine the headlines in the tabloids – and there'll be widespread panic among hundreds of people who've been found not guilty of all sorts of crimes, big and little. It's not just them who'll feel at risk – everyone will feel vulnerable, everyone who's done the slightest bit of wrong!'

'The last thing we want is hundreds of people demanding police protection . . . we've got to keep the lid on this one, Mark. And you can see who's going to get the blame for whatever goes wrong – the British police service! Good job we've got broad shoulders. Right, so I'll pressurise the Tyneside underworld for information and I'll tell the press that's what I'm doing, while you continue your bucolic investigation, but behind all that, we'll be quietly seeking – jointly seeking – a man with a murderous mission and a mighty effective gun.'

'My intentions entirely,' Pemberton said.

'One thing worries me, Mark,' Radcliffe spoke in hushed terms. 'If this character is snuffing out selected victims for this reason, where does he get his information?'

'You're thinking he might be a member of the force?'

'Or an ex-member,' said Radcliffe. 'With firearms training and a good knowledge of CID work. We're talking of old cases here, my victim's murder trial was twelve years ago, yours was what?'

'Fifteen or thereabouts.'

'That could be another factor, Mark.'

'Right. Or he might just be reading the newspapers and watching television. Some of those police dramas are very accurate so far as CID work is concerned. He could pick up some skills just by watching them, or learn from the Internet.'

'Skills, yes, but not the names of his victims. How's he making his selection, Mark? We need to get that sorted. Look, we've had a useful and very productive chat and I appreciate what you've told me. We must liaise very carefully, daily or even more than daily, give your man Silver a full briefing. So what are your plans now?'

'I'm making a splash of trying to trace the motorhome and the dark-haired suspect, but in reality we're digging deeper into Flint's past.'

'Good. Keep in touch.'

'And you.'

Pemberton relayed the key points of his conversation to Paul Larkin, Andy Williams and Lorraine, and as Lorraine and Williams left his office, he sank into his chair and said to Larkin, 'I don't like this one, Paul.'

'We'll catch him, sir, he's bound to slip up sooner or later.'

'But at what cost, Paul? How many innocent lives is he going to take?'

'Innocent lives, sir?' and Larkin's eyebrows rose as he queried that word.

'Innocent until proven guilty, Paul? Isn't that the keystone of English justice? Anyway, this whole scenario bothers me. I think we're up against a sophisticated operator. But we can't sit here brooding. News conference time!'

At that evening's news conference, Pemberton confirmed the identity of Kenneth Flint but at the last minute, due to the import of the Northumberland case, decided against adding that the deceased had changed his name from Kenneth Bourne or that he had lived in Norfolk and Lincolnshire under that name. Thus he made no reference to any criminal record of Flint's under the name of Bourne but added that he was still anxious to trace any motorhome which matched the description already circulated, and to eliminate its dark-haired driver from his enquiries. He was pleased that none of the journalists made any reference to the Tyne-side killing – clearly they had not associated it with Flint's death. Not yet.

After the conference, Larkin said, 'I thought you were going to reveal Flint's past, sir?'

'I was, but I changed my mind last minute,' Pember-ton smiled. 'It dawned on me that if a clever individual is behind these killings, he'll want to boast about it sooner or later. He'll want to give us a reason for what has doing, so I thought I'd play the dumb cop again, pretend to him that we know nothing about Flint. So far as anyone knows, Flint is nothing more than a seedy church worker with a penchant for little girls, but with-out any convictions – if the press hunt for muck under the name of Flint, they'll find nothing.'

'I understand your reasoning, sir, and you'll ask Tyne-side to keep their man's reputed murder quiet?'

'It's a thought, but when you're dealing with gang-land killings, the odd murder or two in the background isn't all that unusual!' he grinned. 'Gangland killings don't have the same awful aura as killings of innocent children.'

Realising that he must think even more like his adver-sary, Pemberton took yet another look at the Norfolk file. Then he realised that Norfolk was a very long way from Newcastle-on-Tyne – the investigation of those crimes was not his responsibility but they had firmly thrust his own case into the national arena instead of allowing it to remain rather parochial. If the sniper struck again, it could be anywhere in the British Isles – and Pemberton realised he was dealing with a roving assassin who was not operating within the limitations of any boundaries.

*   *   *

The sniper had studied all the newspapers covering both the Roberthorpe death and the more recent one on Tyneside. The nationals had not given very much space to either, each being considered of limited interest beyond their immediate localities, but in the early days of both there had been very extensive local cover. The search for the motorhome and its dark-haired driver had occupied some space in the nationals, but that had been very brief and there had been no follow-up stories, and nothing to say the motorhome had been traced. Furthermore, there was no reference to the weapon, save to say that the deaths, in both cases, had been from 'gunshot wounds'.

The history of neither victim had been mentioned, the death of the former being thought the outcome of some unknown motive while the latter was attributed to some kind of retribution from an underworld rival. The sniper smiled at this – such assumptions were typical of unsophisticated police officers; their enquiries were heading entirely in the wrong direction, which was exactly what he wanted. They'd never catch him and he congratulated himself upon his ability to deflect the investigators in this way.

Now for Number Three.

Chapter Eight

The following day, a Wednesday, it was coffee time in a small but specialist motorhome and caravan hire company in Lichfield, Staffordshire. The receptionist-cum-secretary, Alison Porter, was enjoying her morning break. Business was quiet but as there was no canteen in such a small establishment, she was eating her chocolate biscuit and drinking coffee at her desk. She reached for one of the daily newspapers which she had earlier placed on the counter for the convenience of waiting customers and began to scan it as she sipped from her mug. She found herself reading a short item about the murder in Roberthorpe, that Yorkshire village where the churchworker had been found murdered, and where the police had been looking for a motorhome. She was surprised to find it was mentioned again; this was today's paper and they were still looking for the white motorhome with the blue stripes and the spare wheel fixed to the rear. It had been several days since she'd first read about it and because nothing more had been said, she'd assumed they must have found the one they sought. But no. Here they were, still looking for it!

The snag was that Mr Denton, the manager, was away all this week. She recalled he'd not been too pleased at her suggestion they tell the police about their motor-home, although he had reacted when she'd said the man had paid cash. Later, he'd agreed it was rather unusual to pay cash for such things, most people used cheques or credit cards these days, but he'd said there was nothing criminal in using cash. It didn't prove the hiring was in any way dodgy. He'd also been worried the police might remove the van for examination.

If they did that, it would be out of circulation for a while – and that meant it wouldn't be earning money. However, she'd got the file out that first day, just in case the police traced their van, and now she retrieved it from the pending tray on her desk. She checked on the current situation with that van; it was in the secure compound, available for hire at short notice. She found her heart was pounding at the thought of ringing the police in North Yorkshire, and then she recalled what Mr Denton had said before he left on Friday for his holiday in Spain. He'd given her instructions for the week, and had then added, 'You're in charge now, Alison. I've complete faith in you. Don't be frightened to make decisions, I'll back you if there's problems, you know that . . .'

And so she picked up her telephone, rang Directory Enquiries to get the number of North Yorkshire Police and found herself speaking to someone in the Control Room. The girl said the Incident Room at Roberthorpe had a separate number which she provided, and so Alison rang that number to ask for Detective Super-intendent Pemberton, the man whose name had appeared in the newspaper.

'Can I ask what it is in connection with?' the girl sounded very pleasant.

'It's about the motorhome seen near where that Mr Flint was murdered,' said Alison, knowing from her *Crimewatch* viewing that callers were expected to be precise and factual. Even so, her shaky voice betrayed some slight nerves. 'I work for a caravan hire company, we have a motorhome just like the one you're looking for.'

'Right, and your name?'

'Porter, Alison Porter. Miss,' she added to clarify things.

'Hold on, Miss Porter, I'll put you through to Mr Pemberton,' and in a few moments, a pleasant voice said, 'Hello. Pemberton here.'

'Oh, I'm ringing about that motorhome, Mr Pemberton, we have one here, for hire, and it sounds just like the one you're looking for.'

He began to quiz her about the motorhome, asking for a detailed description and he followed with a request for details of the man who had hired it during the week Kenneth Flint had died. From the open file in front of her, she provided the name of the hirer – David Rushforth – and his address; she recalled his description too, a fair-haired man, thinning on top, who'd said he was going to Cornwall with the van. He was nothing like the dark-haired man seen in Yorkshire. She did explain it was not a new vehicle; its registration number did not include the letters CUB and it was a 1991 model because one of their specialities was the hire of older vehicles which might have some kind of romantic association for the hirer.

'If you'd ridden in a Mark II 1968 Jaguar on your wedding day, for example,' she told him. 'We could rent you one for your silver wedding, you'd be surprised how many people like to do that sort of thing.'

Pemberton listened carefully as she talked and it became increasingly evident that this could be the vehicle he sought. Certainly, it sounded close enough in appearance for Mrs Piper and the dog-walker to be shown a picture.

'I'd like to have a look at the vehicle,' he told her. 'Now, as you're a long way from North Yorkshire, I'll have words with Staffordshire Police. I'll ask them to come and make a preliminary examination for us and they'll check the name and address of the hirer. As you say, Miss Porter, it might be a genuine hire but we must check it out. Will you be there all day?'

'I will,' she said.

'Good, and thanks for calling. I really do appreciate it. You said it is not on hire at the moment and has not been out since Mr Rushforth returned it, but can I ask you to make sure the vehicle is not touched until our officers have examined it?'

'It has been valeted,' she told him. 'When they are returned from hire, they're all valeted and checked.'

'We'll cope with that,' he said, wondering how much evidence might have been lost due to that innocent action. 'And thanks. I'll be in touch later,' and she gave him the telephone number of the office.

She relaxed now, exuding a huge sigh of relief and thinking, 'I've done it . . . I've helped in a murder enquiry like they do on *Crimewatch* . . .' and she made herself another cup of coffee to celebrate.

Pemberton smiled at Paul Larkin. 'This could be our breakthrough, Paul!' he sounded happy as he explained the call. 'It's an old motorhome, no wonder Mrs Piper couldn't pick one out of those catalogues. And it was used by Rushforth – that name's cropped up already. Anyway, Paul, I'll ring Staffordshire now. This is not for the press, by the way, this might not be the actual one. So far as they are concerned, we're still hunting the motorhome – and that's what I want chummy to think.'

Pemberton rang Detective Inspector Blackwall at Lichfield Divisional Headquarters.

'Alan? How's things? It's Pemberton here,' and after reminiscing about their happy days at the Detective Training School in Wakefield, Pemberton recounted details of his current investigation and explained his request, stressing that the press should not be told about this development. Blackwall said he would attend to the matter without delay. The van would be removed to a site on police premises, and in spite of it being valeted, it would be subjected to an intense forensic examination, even down to a search for the orange pips Pemberton had mentioned. And he would check the name and address of David Rushforth.

'You've got digital cameras there, have you?' Pemberton asked.

'Sure, we'll take pictures of it, from all angles, and email them to you.'

'Great, we have a good witness or two, I'd like them to see the pictures. And we have a fraction of a tyre imprint which might have come from it, we can compare that too.'

'I'll get moving right away,' Blackwall assured him.

Wondering whether Northumberland Police had established any links with the Roberthorpe murder, Pemberton rang the Incident Room and spoke to Detective Sergeant Ian MacIntyre. He had been appointed the liaison officer at that end of the joint enquiry. He confirmed their Task Force officers were at the scene now. They were making a second fingertip search of the surrounding area – chiefly grassland but with a few pine trees nearby – and they had been specifically asked to seek orange pips or skins.

It was also felt the killer must have used a motor vehicle to reach and depart from the scene, and evidence of a vehicle was also being sought, not necessarily very close to the place Abrahams had died. Night patrolling officers were being asked to check their operational logs for recorded sightings of vehicles in the early hours of that Sunday morning, and house-to-house enquiries were being conducted across a large area surrounding the murder scene in the hope someone noticed the suspect and/or his mode of transport moving at night. Pemberton was told there was very little more to add, save to say that there was intense police activity among the criminal fraternity by CID teams from Northumberland.

Pemberton passed on the news about the motorhome even though it seemed of little direct consequence to the Northumberland enquiry. If it had been hired by the killer and returned on the Saturday Kenneth Flint had died, it could not have been used in the Northumberland killing – although it might have been used earlier for some kind of reconnaissance visit.

At the morning conference of detectives in Roberthorpe, details of the Northumbrian case were provided by Pemberton, along with an opinion that the same killer might be responsible, He did tell his officers the good news about the motorhome, adding that an email photograph was expected during the day. Copies could then be distributed among the teams and it might prompt further reports of sightings around the village. But the conference did not produce any other dramatic developments; rather, it was a consolidating operation which sought to finalise any local enquiries and to ensure every possible area of enquiry had been considered.

Likewise, the news conference was low key, with no new developments about which the press should be informed, and once again none of the newsmen linked the Northumbrian crime with this one – after all, they were separated by some ninety miles. Pemberton made sure he did not make any reference to it.

Meanwhile in Lichfield, due to the importance of Pemberton's enquiry, Detective Inspector Blackwall had decided to undertake it himself, albeit with Detective Sergeant Tony Clarke as his aide. His interview with Alison Porter had been very useful – she had provided a history of the vehicle along with the names of its previous owner and former hirers and all would be interviewed. Similarly, she'd given a very good description of the fair-haired, balding man called David Rushforth, a fit-looking man in his early forties, and she could recall her conversation about his stated intention of visiting Cornwall. She showed Blackwall his signature on the booking form which contained his name and address; Blackwall said he must seize as evidence the entire file relating to the vehicle, and to that particular booking. He would issue a receipt and the papers would be returned in due course. He asked her to make a photocopy for her own records in the meantime. He did stress that she should not inform the press about this, not at this early stage. She had to treat it as highly confidential and if there was an opportunity for her company to use the incident for later publicity, then he was sure it could be agreed in the fullness of time. And so, in the space of a few hours, Alison had seen the motorhome being carried away on a police low-loader for an indefinite period and, worse still, a part of her office filing system removed. At the police station, the vehicle would be photographed and copies sent to North Yorkshire. Maybe its picture would appear in the papers? If it did, she hoped Mr Denton would not be too angry!

For Alan Blackwall, the visit produced a good lead – the name and address of David Rushforth. It was a street in Stafford and so he decided to drive there without delay. He and Clarke located the address, a semi-detached house near the outskirts of Stafford with the M6 traffic roaring in the distance, but when they knocked, they were told by a neighbour that Mr Rushforth would be at work. Furthermore, his wife was visiting her mother in Eccleshall. Work, they were told, was a solicitor's office in Stone. The address was given by the helpful neighbour and immediately Blackwall drove there. There was a brass plate on the outer wall announcing Rushforth, Taylor and Co., Solicitors, and when he arrived at reception on the first floor, he was told Mr Rushforth could see him. He had no clients at the moment. Rushforth was a stout man in his middle fifties, far from a fit-looking man in his early forties; he had a rounded face, rounded spectacles and a balding head with a few strands of black hair clinging to his pale crown.

'Detective Inspector, Sergeant, what can I do for you?' he rose and greeted Blackwall and Clarke with a show of warmth. Blackwall could guess the answers to his questions even before asking them, but he had to go through the motions.

'Mr Rushforth, did you hire a motorhome recently? From a company in Lichfield?'

'A motorhome? Good Lord, no! What would I do with one of those? Give me a nice hotel for my holidays, not one of those dreadful caravan-things.'

'A Renault motorhome was hired from Lichfield and driven to Yorkshire. The hirer gave your name and address, and this was checked against your driving licence.'

'Good Lord! I did have my wallet stolen a few weeks ago, driving licence, credit cards, the lot . . .'

'Did you report it?'

'Yes, immediately, to the local police. It was when I was on the sports field here at Stone, I played in a charity cricket match one Sunday. I hung my jacket in the pavilion while I was on the field and, sometime during the match, a sneak thief relieved me of my wallet and contents. Cash and credit cards, driving licence, club membership cards and so on. And he took some other wallets and cash. No-one saw a thing, Mr Blackwall, we've never had trouble before with people sneaking into the pavilion, but I've not heard anything about the matter until now.'

'Was there much cash in your wallet?'

'Well, the event was to raise money for charity and I was prepared to spend a good deal. I think I had about £150 or so. My friends, who lost their money, had similar amounts, we think he netted over £850 that afternoon. I expected he would throw the wallets away once he'd abstracted the cash.'

'That's the general pattern, Mr Rushforth but it seems he's made additional use of yours! Now, I must ask this, but can you prove your whereabouts over the past three weeks?'

'Well, yes, I've been here, at work during the week, my secretary can vouch for that, and I've been at home over the weekends. My wife could back me on that, we've had guests for the past couple of weekends too, they'll support me on this. Look, Inspector, am I permitted to know what all this is about?'

Blackwall explained and Rushforth listened intently, adding, 'This is dreadful, Inspector! A murderer, I mean a suspected murderer, using my name . . . I wonder if he's used the other licences he took that day? Or do you think he was merely after the cash?'

'We don't know. I'll check with the Stone police next, for a list of names. Did anyone see a stranger around at the time of the thefts?'

'Well, the ground was busy with lots of strangers, Inspector. It was a charity match, for a range of local charities, and so we got a lot of support from all quarters. It's a bit of fun really, I'm no cricketer but I don't mind making a fool of myself if it raises cash for the disadvantaged. But as far as the thief is concerned, I can honestly say no-one stands out in my memory . . . there must have been three hundred spectators there that day.'

Blackwall quizzed the solicitor at length, at the end of which he concluded Rushforth was not a suspect; his alibi would be checked, of course, but in the meantime he was thanked for his co-operation, and then Blackwall headed for Stone police station. The theft of Mr Rush-forth's wallet and contents three months earlier was recorded along with others taken at the same time.

There was a total of five wallets among which were three driving licences in the names of David Rushforth, Jeremy John Hazel and Gareth Reade. All lived in this area of Staffordshire. Blackwall noted the names; they would be passed to Pemberton in case his killer made further use of them and these facts were logged in the Police National Computer for future reference. Black-wall noted that the total amount of stolen cash came to £924. Not bad for an afternoon's work!

From enquiries at Stone police station, however, Blackwall discovered that no description of a suspect had been forthcoming and all enquiries at the time had produced nothing. It seemed as if a search for the thief was pointless, unless he made a mistake and was caught in possession of some of the stolen property.

It was towards lunchtime when, from Lichfield, email photographs of the motorhome arrived at the Incident Room. Pemberton studied them – they were very clear and Blackwall's officers had done a good job in taking the pictures from various angles. The blue adornments and the spare wheel on the rear were clearly visible and the transmission was accompanied by a note saying that Blackwall would contact Pemberton by phone in due course. It added that the van was currently being exam-ined by forensic officers, a task which was expected to take some time, and tyre impressions would be taken for comparison with that found by Pemberton's Task Force. In addition, of course, efforts would be made to trace Rushforth.

Pemberton decided he would personally speak to Mrs Piper about the van and so he told Larkin about his plans and left for Elm Tree Cottage.

Mrs Piper was busy in her kitchen but said she could spare a few minutes and so Pemberton settled at the table where he spread his selection of photographs.

'Oh, yes, Mr Pemberton,' she nodded vigorously after studying them for a few moments. 'Yes, that's the van all right, see it's got the skylight and those blue lines and that wheel on the back.'

'So it is like that van you saw, or do you think it is the actual van?'

'Well, I suppose there must be a lot of them about, but if you ask me I'd say it was the same one. It's got that sticker on the side, you see? A squirrel . . . somebody's put a squirrel on the side, painted it on mebbe, see?'

She'd not made any reference to this until now, but when he peered closely, he could see the silhouetted outline of a squirrel on the offside of the upper roof space, towards the rear of the vehicle. It was a dark grey, standing some eight inches high and it was the sort of stick-on souvenir some people might gather when they visited stately homes, nature reserves or theme parks, except this was the only such embellishment that was visible. He'd have to ask Blackwall to talk to Miss Porter about this – was it a feature of all such vans, or had someone personalised this one? Nonetheless, he did feel a tremor of excitement – he sensed this was a tremendous breakthrough.

After thanking Mrs Piper, he decided to visit the village shop, recalling that the shopkeeper had made reference to seeing a motorhome outside her store when the suspect had bought his oranges; her name was Peggy Page.

She recognised him instantly and when he showed her the pictures, she nodded and smiled. 'Yes, it was just like that one, Mr Pemberton. I remember those blue lines now. A nice smart vehicle, I remember thinking.'

As she had seen only the side of the vehicle as it had parked outside, she was not able to provide any further details, but her testimony was sufficient for Pemberton to believe that this was indeed the vehicle they sought, not merely a matching model. Buoyed by this development, he thanked her and returned to the Incident Room.

'Paul,' he took Larkin into his office. 'Both Mrs Piper and Peggy at the shop believe this is the actual vehicle they saw in the village. Even if it isn't, the similarities are good enough for us to make use of these pictures. There's a few actions here for the teams, get them to revisit everyone who saw a motorhome like this. See if we can get any more sightings and timings of it, people using it and so on. And if it was hereabouts for a week or so, the driver must have bought food somewhere and he must have topped up with petrol. Check local cafes, pubs, garages and so on, will you? He might even have used a credit card for some of his purchases, if he did, we can nail him!'

Meanwhile, in Lichfield, the forensic teams were making a thorough search of the motorhome. Even though it had been valeted, there would be evidence of human usage within the vehicle – there would be lots of fingerprints, various DNA deposits from all sorts of people and tiny particles of things like chocolate bars, biscuits and other food which would be hidden in small crevices into which the vacuum cleaners would not penetrate. Pemberton had specially requested a search for orange pips or particles of skin or pith – a DNA match between the pips left in Green Lane and any found in this vehicle would prove the presence of the same man. Or woman. A task of this kind could not be hurried. Pemberton and Blackwall were prepared to wait.

In Northumberland, the task force had produced a

134

result. In searching an extensive area around the scene of Abrahams' death, they had covered a small, unfenced forest of conifers which grew beside a minor road. Comprising mainly spruce and larch, the floor of the woodland was smothered with a thick layer of needles through which little else grew, apart from the occasional fern or briar, but detectives found traces of a wheeled vehicle having entered the forest. Access was simple – anyone could drive over the grass verge from the unclassified road leading into East Creston, and then drive deep into the forest along wide firepaths. The surface was sound enough to tolerate the weight of even a fully laden timber wagon but the needle-covered surface of the ground would not reveal the detail of tyremarks. The fact that a vehicle had driven along that firepath was evident enough, but it was impossible to discern the pattern of the tyres.

The faint track could be followed into the trees, and then into a small space off the firepath where the vehicle had parked, turned around and then been driven out the same way.

Had anyone seen a vehicle parked deep in the forest at night, they would probably have assumed it had been a courting couple although, at this depth among the densely planted trees, it would not be visible from the road. Having traced the tracks to the turning point, the detectives, working from a detailed map, realised it was less than a mile from Abrahams' mansion; furthermore, the forest covered the ground to within fifty yards of his main gate. Thus a killer could have driven into the secrecy of the forest, left his vehicle and walked through the darkness while staying concealed among the trees until within fifty yards of the gate.

He might even have been able to remain concealed when the trigger was pulled. In those dark and early hours, it would be easy to walk back to the vehicle,

135

emerge from the forest when no-one was around and head off in the opposite direction. Unseen.

The officer in charge of the Northumbrian Task Force, Inspector John Craven, had been fully briefed about the Roberthorpe murder and so he ordered his men to inspect every inch of the forest floor from where the car had clearly come to rest, to where chummy must have emerged from the wood, or stood on its edge, to fire his fatal shot. And if an orange pip had been dropped anywhere along that route, his men would find it. And so they did. They found three near the turning point – as if the man had been seated in his car, and spitting pips from the open window as he awaited the time to make his move. They found two more at the edge of the wood.

Standing at that point, the mansion gates were clearly visible in daylight and the road leading to them from the south, from Newcastle and Morpeth, could be seen rising and falling over the hills in a long, straight line. A former Roman road. And there was plenty of cover for a waiting sniper. All the evidence they had gathered was recorded and labelled, and John Craven felt his officers had performed a very useful task. But they found nothing else which might be linked to their local murder, or the death of Kenneth Flint. However, Craven knew that these insignificant fruit pips were critical – if they had come from the mouth of the killer, they would provide sufficient DNA evidence to place him at this scene. But Craven and his team did not find a single expended cartridge shell. The killer had been very careful. But not careful enough.

Detectives searching the motorhome in Lichfield also found an orange pip. It had clearly been dropped by someone sitting in the driving seat and it had rolled or been kicked under the seat to become wedged between the base of the seat and the carpet; there was a small gap between the edge of the carpet and the metalwork, and the pip had lodged there, perhaps being thrust deeper by the driver's foot or even by the vacuum cleaner's brush before the suction had had a chance to swallow it. But the detectives found it. It was the only one, but it was cared for as if it was one of the crown jewels. Pemberton would be pleased. ❡

The Sniper, in early stages of planning his campaign, had decided that the element of surprise was beneficial and it was now time to swiftly repeat his Northumberland success. He had realised that too long a gap between his adjudications could result in a lack of understanding or appreciation by the general public and that appeared to be the case already. Not one newspaper had identified a link between the Yorkshire case and the one in Northumberland – in the minds of the readers, there was absolutely nothing to link one with the other and he felt sure that was due to police incompetence. It was clear that they had not collaborated on their enquiries, they had not established any kind of link between the deaths. The fact that these deaths, these necessary deaths, were the actions of one man dispensing justice on behalf of his fellow citizens had so far escaped the country's attention.

How, then, could anyone appreciate his actions? If the great British public had no idea these missions were being undertaken, let alone not knowing *why* they were occurring, what was the point of his dedication and positive action?

The whole point of a campaign was to arouse interest among the public and to influence them, or even to persuade them to adopt similar tactics. But so far, his actions had not produced that effect – although, if he was honest with himself, that was what he had anticipated in the early stages. The fact that the punishments had been imposed at such great distances from each other, geographically speaking, meant the police had not even considered any association between them. That merely showed how incompetent they were but, in any case, he had come to realise it might take time for the impact of his actions to be fully understood.

He had considered a series of anonymous telephone calls to the police or the press, or even sending anonymous letters to highlight the fact that one man was responsible for this ongoing administration of justice but he knew that such actions could, if he was not very careful indeed, lead to his identification and capture. Even calls from mobile telephones could be traced, and so he had decided not to follow any of those courses of action. He would let his faithful Kalashnikov do the talking. And surely, in the course of time, the police or the press would recognise the work of a dedicated campaigner?

With these thoughts in his mind, and with plans already in place to launch his swift follow-up to the Northumbrian sentence, he eased his rifle from its hiding place, checked it, cleaned it and oiled it, and then pushed it under his bed. It was ready again.

Chapter Nine

Every morning at 7 a.m., Leroy Campbell, a Brixton resident in his late thirties, set off to take his daily exercise in Low Wood Park. This welcome patch of urban greenery comprised almost sixty surprisingly charming acres of grassland, paths, shrubs and trees, and it lay just off the A23 as it passed through Lambeth in south London. Leroy, six feet tall with broad shoulders, ran around the park for an hour, usually with a small knot of friends to accompany him. He followed the same circular route each morning, running up the sloping paths and down them again, in and out of the trees, around the scattered benches and shelters, to jog a total of some seven or eight miles during his stint. Some very observant people might have detected a definite swagger in his running motion, a visual display of arrogance and confidence. Afterwards, feeling exhilarated due to the exercise, he returned to his basement flat for a shower before setting off for his work as a gentlemen's hairdresser. The salon he rented was in Brixton and it specialised in a range of ethnic styling, being well patronised by the Brixton community; for Leroy, it was a very successful business. Among his peers, Leroy was regarded as a powerful and fit man and very skilled at his profession; indeed, some considered him famous, an example to others, a person to respect, and certainly he did attract a considerable following of acolytes. Others, however, felt he exuded an aura of fear – beyond doubt,

Leroy was a redoubtable leader of his section of the local community. No-one argued with Leroy, that understanding affected a considerable area of this part of London; there were whispers that he always carried a knife, and that he was not afraid to use it.

On Thursday morning, as a nearby church clock was striking seven, Leroy, with six of his companions, trotted through the tall green west gates into the park to begin his morning routine around its network of paths. As Leroy ran, two of his friends were ahead of him, side by side, another two ran at his side, one on his left and the other on his right, and the remaining two followed immediately behind in what might be described as an effective, protective formation. In some respects, it resembled the jogging routine of an American president with his human shield of security officers. And so this small phalanx of runners moved at a steady and smooth pace along the path. After a hundred yards or so, past the first bench, the path began to rise and their pace slowed just a fraction to cope with the gradient. At the top was a copse of young copper beech trees which effectively concealed a toilet block and the runners were heading in that direction, intending to continue beyond the trees, down the other side of the hill and return via a different, rising path before executing a second circuit. Traffic was busy on the A23. The sound of it filled the air as people were already on the move, some commuting to central London and others to Brighton, Croydon and elsewhere. The park itself was virtually deserted, save for a couple of dog-walkers and a girl jogger in the distance, but later in the day it would grow busy with retired people, mums with children in pushchairs, lovers meeting surreptitiously and office workers wanting some fresh air or just popping out for a smoke. Now though, it was quiet; it was always quiet at this time of morning.

It was seven minutes past seven.

Whether or not anyone heard the very brief rattle of shots is questionable, but Leroy suddenly produced a strange, gasping scream-like cry and fell to the ground as spurts of deep red blood burst from his chest and saturated the front of his tee-shirt. For the briefest of moments, not immediately seeing the blood, his companions thought he had tripped and fallen, or that he was having a coughing spasm, but it took only another instant for them to realise the truth. Even as one of them was dragging out his mobile phone to call the ambulance, it was clear he was already dead.

His friends looked around in horror and panic, wondering if they were going to be gunned down and not knowing what to do in those first awful seconds; they crouched for safety but no more shots followed. The park was deserted. That was imprinted on their minds, they would never forget those dreadful moments when everything seemed to move in slow-motion. But right now, there was no-one to help, there was not one person within their view, not here, not on the level stretch near the gates, not among the trees on top of the hill. They crowded around the body, kneeling on the path, calling his name, glancing around nervously, terrified of what might still happen. But it was too late for Leroy.

'Don't move him, call the police,' said Justin Jones, the one who had been running on his right.

'He needs an ambulance, man, mouth-to-mouth . . .'

'No, it's too late for anything like that, look at that chest wound, no-one could survive that, he's dead,' said Justin. 'Shot down like a rat! We shouldn't touch him . . . it's important we don't . . .'

'I'm getting an ambulance anyway . . .'

'No point! The police will bring a doctor!' said Justin.

'We don't need no police. . . they won't do nothing . . . let's just get him out of here, home, we'll see to him.'

'No,' Justin was now in charge, someone had to take

141

the lead and he was very capable of doing so. 'We call the police like I said, now. And we wait here, we see who's in the park, who might have done this to Leroy and we watch out for ourselves . . .'

'There's no place to hide, no place at all . . . not here in the open . . .'

'They got Leroy, man, they got him . . . he said they would, in the end . . .' Damien Brown was crying and shaking with anger and fear.

'We don't know who got him!'

'I know who got him, man, we all know who got him, he knew they'd get him, they never give up . . .'

'Give me that phone!' snapped Justin, grabbing it from Damien's fist. He took it, dialled 999 and waited a few moments. Then he said, 'Low Wood Park, Brixton, a murder. A man shot in the park, he's dead. I'm sure, yes. Up near the copper beeches . . . yes, I know him, he's a friend. Yes, I'll wait. My name? Justin Jones,' and he provided his address.

'They said to stay here, not to move anything, they'll be five minutes. They'll bring a doctor anyway, they said.'

And so they waited, some of them weeping over the still form of their leader, others looking nervously around, as if expecting another shot, another death.

But there was no-one in the park. It was all so eerily silent, save for the noise of distant traffic as the people enjoyed what was, for them, a normal working day.

At ten o'clock that same morning, Detective Superintendent 'Ted' Edwards of 'L' Division of the London Metropolitan Police addressed teams of detectives who had already assembled in the Incident Room at Streatham Police Station.

'This is going to be a tricky one,' he told them. 'The dead man is Leroy Campbell, thirty-eight years old, who

142

described himself as the owner of a specialist hairdressing salon. In fact, he did sometimes work there, he did rent the premises and he did employ genuine hairdressers. That was a cover – he was an extremist on the far left, an active trouble-maker who saw racism everywhere and he is known to the police, well-known in fact. He ran a publishing house behind his shop, turning out inflammatory leaflets and a newspaper, most of which had an anti-police bias. A list of his convictions is shown on the noticeboard – they're mainly associated with rioting, arson, public order offences, criminal damage, assault on police and so on. But his chief notoriety was in 1987; there was severe rioting in Brixton, with burning of houses, buses and cars, and a uniformed police sergeant, Sergeant George Coulson, was murdered. Stabbed in the chest. Leroy Campbell was charged with the murder but was found not guilty; there was a very hostile crowd around Coulson at the critical moment, up to a dozen or more rioters.

'No-one could be sure exactly which of them had used the knife so the judge ordered a not-guilty verdict. A year later, Leroy was interviewed, it was the anniversary of the troubles, and he admitted killing the policeman, knowing he could not be charged again with the same crime – he knew about the *autrefois acquit* rule. In the view of his followers, that confession elevated him almost to the status of a god, certainly he was a hero in their eyes, the conqueror of police oppression. You can see how careful we have to tread with this one. Whether or not his friends will co-operate with us remains to be seen, but at least they did call the police to the scene of the crime. We shall do our best to find this killer, ladies and gentlemen; we have to. You'll not find it easy, going into some of those ghetto areas, in fact there will be downright hostility, but we must do our best to show the community in which Leroy lived that we are to be trusted, and that we will do our best to find his killer. Now, about the scene.

'We are confident that the fatal shots – four of the them – were fired from a gents' toilet on the top of the hill up which Leroy and his friends were climbing. A small window in one of the cubicles overlooks the hill and provides an ideal view of the pathway he was using. He was, in fact, facing his killer, we believe, although Leroy would probably not be able to see him; the window is small, about eighteen inches wide by six inches high. It opens outwards on hinges at the top; it is possible to rest the barrel of a rifle on the bottom of the frame and to aim it with the window only a fraction open. It's a very good sniping position, a gunman locked in there can operate unseen by anyone else using the toilets and by anyone outside.

'We have already carried out a superficial examination but we have not found any ejected cartridge shells. The cleaner had not visited the toilets, we've checked that, and they are open all night and all day. But we were on the scene within minutes – it seems the killer had tidied up after himself. We found nothing else of note in that cubicle, although it is being subjected to a detailed forensic examination. Motive? At this point, we have no idea. Leroy did mix with some odd people from all sections of society, and we must endeavour to determine a motive. So, we need house-to-house in the vicinity, we need to find who was using that park at that time of day and earlier, the gunman must have arrived very early to set himself up at his firing position, and, of course, he must have known Leroy's movements. Was it someone known to him? Someone close to him? Has he been involved in some kind of major dispute? The gunman shot him accurately in the chest in spite him being surrounded by his regular guardians. A very cool and skilled marksman, so it appears. A post mortem is being carried out later this morning when we shall recover the

144

bullets from the body; they will be sent to the Met Forensic Lab for analysis. Then we shall have some idea of the type of weapon used. The entire park has been sealed while officers conduct finger-tip searches, and we are already making a search of Leroy's salon – he lived above the premises, by the way. We're going through his personal and domestic stuff to see if it provides any leads.'

Detective Superintendent Edwards had no reason to link this death with another two in the north of England, nor did he know anything about orange pips and the need to trace and retain any found near the scene.

Furthermore, bullets removed from the body of Leroy Campbell would be sent to the firearms department of the Met's own forensic laboratory, not to Nottingham, and so any association with those recovered from the two other deaths would be most unlikely.

But Damien Brown had every intention of making this murder a well publicised matter. Once he had made his statement to the police, he took the tube into London and presented himself at the offices of a news agency.

About the time Damien Brown was talking to the freelance reporter, Pemberton received a telephone call from Detective Inspector Alan Blackwall of Lichfield.

'One or two things for you, Mark. First, that squirrel logo. I've checked with Alison Porter, it's been on the vehicle as long as they've owned it. They obtained it second-hand, a one-owner vehicle with a very low mileage, ideal for their fleet but they didn't attempt to move the sticker in case it damaged the paintwork. So it stayed. There isn't a matching one on the other side, it's a one-off adornment. It's been there so long it looks as though the manufacturers included it, but they didn't.'

'Great news, Alan! That makes it distinctive. It means it is the actual vehicle seen near the scene of our murder

– it was used by the killer, I'm sure about that, and that means we need it here. I'll send a transporter to pick it up. Where is it now?'

'It's sealed in one of our road traffic garages. Our Scenes of Crime team did a preliminary search as you requested . . .'

'And?'

'And they found an orange pip! Wedged between the carpet and the base of the seat.'

'Brilliant! Let's hope it proves chummy was in the van – we'll need all that, the pip and any other rubbish collected from it. We'll give it our own forensic going-over along with DNA tests, but in the meantime, I'll send someone down to collect the samples. I'll ask them to liaise with you.'

'Glad to be of help in this one. Now, the hirer – Rushforth. The real Rushforth is genuine, Mark, he's got an alibi for the material time, we've checked it and it holds up. And he looks nothing like the description of your suspect or the fair-haired, balding man who hired the motorhome. The genuine Rushforth is a large round man in his fifties and he had his wallet nicked, along with his driving licence, other papers and credit cards. He did report it – and several other people had theirs taken at the same time, along with a total of over £900 cash. From clothes hanging in a cricket pavilion during a charity match in Stone. No suspect was seen, no-one's been arrested for the thefts. Now you know how chummy finances his activities – he uses stolen cash.'

Blackwall assured Pemberton his officers would continue their enquiries in the Staffordshire area in the hope they could trace the wallet thief, the motorhome hirer or any other evidence of value to the Roberthorpe investigation. It was always possible that the murderer/thief lived somewhere around the Staffordshire area; Blackwall would not lose sight of that likelihood.

Pemberton thanked him for his efforts and his help.

146

This call was swiftly followed by one from Jack Radcliffe in Northumberland who confirmed that orange pips had been found on the floor of a coniferous plantation very close to the scene of Steven Abrahams' murder. He told Pemberton of his belief that a vehicle had been used by the killer who had apparently concealed himself, and the vehicle, in the cover of the trees until moments before his execution-like killing. No ejected ammunition shells had been traced and Radcliffe could not say what kind of vehicle had been used, except it was four wheeled and quite small, probably a private car or even a light van. Bearing in mind the motorhome's role in the murder, Pemberton did consider the Northumberland vehicle might also have been hired. He suggested that Radcliffe's men visit hire firms to see whether 'David Rushforth', 'Jeremy John Hazel' or 'Gareth Reade' had recently hired a vehicle and Radcliffe agreed to put some of his teams on that action. Meanwhile, he told Mark, there had been no new development – the under-world of Tyneside had not been able to suggest the name of any likely killer and that meant the police continued to dig deeply into their various furtive business dealings.

Having been informed about those two important developments, Pemberton began to feel more optimistic – instead of being faced with no evidence whatsoever, he was now gathering snippets from around the country, tiny, apparently unconnected, pieces of trivia but, when viewed holistically, they began to produce a panorama of important information.

His renewed enthusiasm was transmitted to his teams as he chaired the morning conference of detectives; he told them about these developments, hoping the squirrel logo might prompt others to remember seeing the motorhome, although later his public presentation to the press indicated he was still seeking such a vehicle.

By midday one of Pemberton's teams had found a

rural garage which had twice served petrol to a motor-home fitting the description of the suspect vehicle. It was about five miles from Roberthorpe and each time the buyer had paid cash – £15 on one occasion and £12 on another – and on the second occasion, he'd checked the tyres for air pressure. The girl in the kiosk could only provide a brief description of the driver – a man with dark hair who would be about forty, she thought, with nothing unusual about his build or style of clothing. The only reason she remembered the vehicle was because it had a grey squirrel motif on the side of the roof. The man had not said much to her, commenting only on the weather and the beautiful countryside. But it was another sighting, it could be logged into the time-chart and it might eventually help to provide a map of the van's movements.

Pemberton was pleased. His investigation was progressing, if slowly.

A post mortem had been swiftly conducted upon the body of Leroy Campbell. Beyond doubt, the cause of death was by shooting and prior to his death, he had been a very healthy man. There was no evidence of drug abuse either. Four bullets had been recovered from his chest and heart. The pathologist had studied the bullets and realised they were unusual – they were 7.62mm calibre.

They would have to be examined by a ballistics expert but they were quite distinctive and he felt there would be no difficulty determining the type of weapon from which they had been fired. He rang Detective Superintendent Edwards with that news, saying a full written report would follow.

Edwards was also pleased because one of the community constables patrolling the vicinity of Low Wood Park shortly after six-thirty this morning, had noticed a man walking through the park. Striding was the word he had used. He'd been of average height, white skinned, and had been wearing a colourful woollen hat with a pompom on the top. Although his hair was not visible, the constable had gained the impression it was long and dark because, at a distance, he'd thought a few stray strands were protruding from beneath the hat. His dress had been casual – faded blue jeans, a light blue tee-shirt without any message on the front, and a dark blue blouson-style jacket, worn open. He had white trainer shoes and had been carrying a tan-coloured guitar case slung over his right shoulder while hurrying towards the copse of copper beeches and the toilets. The constable had observed this character while he was patrolling past the south gate; he'd been too far away for the policeman to hail and he'd assumed he was a musician who had recently left a local venue after an all-night session of some kind. Or, of course, he could be en route to an early-morning recording session. Whatever his purpose, the man had disappeared among the trees, ostensibly to make use of the facilities to which he was hurrying, and the constable had continued his foot patrol. There was nothing at all suspicious in the man's behaviour, and the constable had not seen him again.

Edwards decided to release this description to the press, not seeking to trace the man as a suspect but as someone he would like to trace for elimination purposes or as a possible witness; this information would be given to the press at the afternoon news conference. He would have to be careful how he presented this case to the media. It was hoped that publicity might persuade the man to come forward if he was innocent. And, of course, if he was innocent, he might have seen the killer – it was quite feasible he would have been in the park around the same time. Finding this man was important for all sorts of reasons, mused Edwards.

However, his carefully laid plans for the news con-

149

ference were disrupted when he received a telephone call.

'Jim Cowan, Mr Edwards,' said the familiar Scots voice. 'I hear you've got an interesting murder for us?'

'Who told you that?'

'You know I can't reveal my sources. All I need is confirmation.'

'I can confirm we are investigating a suspicious death, Jim, but there'll be a news conference at half-past four this afternoon. I'll expect you there.'

'I can't wait that long. Leroy Campbell, I have it on good authority. The victim.'

'You are ahead of me there, Jim, but we've not had the deceased formally identified. You know I can't confirm his name until then. All I can say is we believe he is a resident of Brixton who's probably in his late thirties.'

'That's good enough for me. A revenge killing, you think?'

'Revenge?' asked Edwards.

'Come on, Mr Edwards, you know Leroy! Cop killer, self-confessed knifeman . . . he got away with it and now you've got him. You think he's got what he deserves, an eye-for-an-eye sort of syndrome. That's what my source alleges.'

'I should be very careful what you accept from your so-called source, Jim.'

'He said Leroy was in permanent fear of his life, fearful the police would get him. He's been told they'd get him one day, according to my source. Leroy had guards whenever he went out running, and at other times. He was a frightened man, Mr Edwards.'

'You know better than to print that kind of rubbish, Jim. Your source sounds like a loony leftie to me, anti-police, and using any excuse to have a go at us. All I can say is we're investigating a suspicious death, it occurred this morning in Low Wood Park, I have already de-

150

scribed the deceased and I can add that an incident room has established at Streatham. We have sixty-five detectives engaged on the enquiry, many on house-to-house enquiries in the vicinity and we are anxious to trace a witness – a man believed to be a musician, carrying a guitar case, medium build, dark hair. He was wearing a coloured woolly hat with hair protruding, and he had blue jeans, a blue blouson, light blue tee-shirt and white trainers.'

'That's all pretty bland stuff, Mr Edwards. All right for your local weekly, but not for me, not for the high-circulation tabloids. My bread and butter! So am I right in thinking you are denying the police were involved in this killing? Might it have been a rogue copper, out for revenge perhaps?'

'I am keeping an open mind,' said Edwards, using the simple, familiar response.

'You're not denying it, then?' returned Cowan.

'We are investigating every possible avenue, Jim.'

'That sounds like an admission to me, it says you haven't ruled out the possibility.'

'Jim, you know I cannot rule out anything, I have to examine every avenue and then I base my action on the evidence we have gathered.'

'You must admit it is a good story, Mr Edwards. The death penalty resurrected, vengeance from the wronged and all that.'

'All I want to do is to find the person responsible for the death of this unfortunate victim and I hope the press will help us to do that. There you are, a quote for you. One you'll never print.'

'Watch the papers tomorrow, Mr Edwards! I'll give you headlines!'

'Bloody journalists!' cursed Edwards as he replaced the telephone.

*   *   *

151

The call came from the eighth floor of New Scotland Yard.

'Superintendent? You'd better withdraw Justin Jones from the Brixton infiltration job. Campbell is dead, we don't want his pals realising who Jones really is. His cover could be blown now. So withdraw him, immediately. Give him a safe posting, out in the sticks maybe.'

'Very good sir,' said the Superintendent.

The sniper had left the park by the north gate, caught a bus, then another and finally a tube to Waterloo. Before nine that morning, less than two hours after completing his task, he'd boarded a train for home. He found a double seat on the Intercity Express, large enough to accommodate him and his precious guitar case, and he made sure he never let it out of his sight. Even when he went to the toilet, the case went with him.

'It's a very valuable instrument,' he smiled apologetically at a middle-aged couple at the other side of the aisle when he declined their offer to look after it during his short absence.

When he emerged from the train, he caught a taxi to a large department store, went into the gents' toilet, changed out of his jeans and blouson and replaced them with a pair of light tan slacks and a brown sweater which had been just two of the items in the guitar case. The colourful hat, the jeans and the blouson were packed into a plastic carrier which he produced from the guitar case, and then he left the premises. Walking quickly along the street, he slipped into a Help The Aged store, handed over the plastic bag and said they were a few belongings from his late brother, nearly new clothes, which they could sell for whatever they would bring.

'Every little helps,' he said to the blue-rinsed lady behind the counter.

'You are very kind,' she smiled. 'We'll make good use of them.'

From a fruit shop, he next bought six small oranges in a large brown paper bag and after eating one of them, pushed the others into his pockets. Then, in another public toilet, he slipped off his wig and pushed it into the brown paper bag.

A hundred yards along the street, he slipped the brown package into a street waste bin. The Sniper then went home. Already, his next mission had been partially planned and this afternoon he would pop into his library to obtain the information he required to complete his work. And tonight, he would clean his Kalashnikov in readiness for its next job.

Chapter Ten

It was a warm and sunny day, so Pemberton announced he was going to disappear on to the moors for a couple of hours, a working lunch-break, he called it. Instead of eating at his desk or joining Lorraine and the others in the pub, he said he'd buy a bread roll at the shop, along with some tomatoes and cheese, and he'd have a picnic washed down with a can of Coke and sweetened with a crisp Cox's orange pippin.

'I need some thinking time, Paul,' he told Larkin. 'I'll be back in a couple of hours or so – and my mobile will be switched off!'

'Sure, boss.'

It was while driving on to Roberthorpe Beacon for his moments of peace that he first heard news of the murder of Leroy Campbell. The item was broadcast on his car radio as part of the one o'clock news and he almost missed it. Tucked among the political news and the sporting latest, it was a very brief announcement to the effect that police were investigating the shooting this morning of a man believed to be Leroy Campbell in a south London park. 'Leroy Campbell was well known in the Brixton area; a fiercely political activist and publisher, he had earlier been acquitted of stabbing a police sergeant to death during a riot.' The newsreader added that Detective Superintendent Edwards, speaking from the Incident Room at Streatham Police Station, had not discounted a revenge attack by police officers. He did say, however, that he had an open mind and consideration would be given to a racist motive, or indeed any other. And there the news item ended.

The impact of this snippet of news so affected Pemberton that he pulled on to the wide moorland verge and sat there for a few minutes with the radio burbling meaninglessly as he wrestled with the notion that this might be yet another in the Kalashnikov series. But was it? There'd been no mention of a Kalashnikov, no mention of a suspect and no hint of a skilled execution, but a significant factor was that the killing involved the shooting of a man who'd been acquitted of murder. Pemberton did not lose sight of the fact that this crime had occurred in a south London park, many many miles from Roberthorpe and even further from Northumberland. Nonetheless, the likelihood of a link could not be ignored. He picked up his mobile phone, switched it on and rang Paul Larkin.

'Pemberton speaking, Paul,' he announced.

'I thought that thing was supposed to be switched off!' laughed Larkin.

'It was,' he chuckled. 'But listen. I've just heard the news, a political activist has been shot dead in south London, this morning, in a park. The victim had been earlier acquitted of a police murder. It's a slim chance, Paul but there might be a connection with our job. Can you check it out? Ring the Met, Streatham Police Station, ask for Detective Superintendent Edwards. Tell him about our case and Northumbria's.'

'Right away, sir,' said Larkin. 'Now you can enjoy your thinking time!'

Pemberton drove higher on to the moors and left the car for a short walk as he clutched his brown paper bag of food and drink; he knew a high point nearby. There was a large flat rock upon which he could sit and gaze almost into infinity as the panorama of Yorkshire countryside spread before him, with rolling moors and deep valleys rich with trees and glistening with silvery ribbons of fresh water which flowed from the hills as rivers and streams. Perhaps he looked rather incongruous, a tall, elegant and very smart, dark-suited man sitting on a rock in the middle of the wilderness, but it was a world in which he could lose himself for a while as he struggled to make sense out of two – or maybe three – crimes which, to date, had linked factors. In two cases, the same weapon had been used and there was the fact the victims had been suspected of murders for which they'd been acquitted or not prosecuted. Flint's victims had been two small girls, Abrahams' victim had been a prostitute and now there was Campbell, who had killed a police officer. Was there any link between those victims – the little girls, the prostitute and the policeman – other than the fact their killers had allegedly evaded justice? He thought not, but it was something which would have to be checked. He pulled out his notebook and jotted down a reminder to get Larkin to arrange for enquiries to be made.

As he tried to understand the mind of the killer – assuming one person was responsible – he did conclude he wanted the police to pursue something which might not be there, to follow a line of enquiry which came to an inconclusive end, such as the motorhome with its false plates. But he'd used a different tactic in Northumberland so this man was not following the usual modus operandi of a criminal – most criminals followed the same, or a very similar, pattern as they went about their nefarious business.

And no suspect had been mentioned for the London murder.

The killer was not following any discernible pattern – apart from using the same Kalashnikov. That was a crucial linking factor. If the weapon used in London was also a Kalashnikov, or the *same* Kalashnikov which had been used in Roberthorpe and East Creston, then it provided indisputable proof that the crimes were linked. But why? If they were linked, there must be a common motive – and the fact all the victims had been acquitted of murder, or not prosecuted due to a lack of evidence, did seem to provide that motive. It presented a powerful reason to impose justice on those who had apparently avoided it but was this the real motive? Or was there some other purpose behind the killer's actions? None of the families or friends appeared to have wanted to kill the person who had destroyed their loved one, and all had sound alibis anyway – not counting the Campbell killing, of course. That enquiry was scarcely under way at this early stage but did the London killing fit the pattern? At the moment, he had no idea. But the fact that these crimes, in different parts of the country and against victims with such varied backgrounds, were almost surely the act of one man – or woman – was highly significant. It was a man who used disguise, who used a different tactic for each murder but who knew enough about his victims to carry out his crime in a highly effective way. What sort of person was the killer? Cold, skilful, chillingly ruthless and well organised, knowledgeable, able to move freely around the country, so he probably had his own transport; he was one who knew how and where to find the information he required . . . and how to put his knowledge into positive action.

Oddly enough, he seemed nervous to a degree. He did seem to eat oranges shortly before committing his crime. Was that for pure refreshment or were they some kind of calming agent? People in the spotlight, or about to undergo some kind of stressful activity, often did resort to a range of personal treatments in order to calm their nerves. Some chewed gum or even pencils, other preferred mints or boiled sweets . . . it seemed this man had chosen oranges.

It did enter his mind that the villain might be a rogue

police officer with firearms training or skills – some of the witnesses had said the dark-haired man in Rober-thorpe had the appearance and demeanour of a police-man. But would – could – a police officer have access to a Kalashnikov? True, he could obtain one illegally if he was so minded – anyone could, so long as they had the cash and the right contacts. Or had any been surren-dered to the police during the recent amnesty? And then stolen by a rogue police officer? He had to acknowledge that that was not impossible.

And then Pemberton's mind turned to soldiers. More than one person, himself included, had referred to the military precision of the killings, the coolness in com-pleting the act, the fact that the man actually sat down to have his breakfast minutes before killing Kenneth Flint . . . and an ex-soldier, with the right training, might be capable of doing that. He'd work to a routine, to a plan and he would consider there was nothing personal in what he did – shooting the enemy on active service was part of his job.

Could he, or would he, if the circumstances were right, be capable of doing likewise in his civilian capac-ity? Or was this man a serving soldier? Pemberton thought not – it would be difficult getting time off to travel as the killer had done, unless he was on leave. Sick leave perhaps?

Then there was the question of the Kalashnikov. He had been told that it was not unknown for soldiers, coming home from a campaign, to smuggle captured Kalashnikovs into Britain in their kitbags. In some cir-cumstances, captured weapons could be regarded as trophies of war, but a fully-operational Kalashnikov? However, this was an old weapon because it was using pre-1974 ammunition according to the ballistics wizard; that did not mean the user was necessarily a former soldier. It meant the killer had access to such a weapon, one which had first appeared for service in 1947 as a means of protecting Russia against future German invasion. Old weapons of this kind were still in use around the world; more than 70 million had been manufactured and such was the popularity of the Kalashnikov that it had become almost legendary; many said the weapon was indestructable, that it would even function when it was rusty and dirty. Such a huge number meant that not every one of them could be accounted for. How did one find the right one out of so many millions?

Pemberton then realised his teams had not examined that issue on a wider scale. Certainly, they had targeted either serving or former soldiers with local connections, but this was no longer a local crime. It was nationwide. And bearing in mind the probable reason for the killings, how far back did Pemberton need to research? On a national basis, how many soldiers had been recruited or discharged since, say, 1970? Was there any way of tracing them, or even a selection of them?

Was there a central record of soldiers who had been recruited, those who had left the service for any reason, and those who had retired? Or did every regiment maintain its own records? If so, how many regiments were there, and how did he gain access to their files? He remembered the description of the man with the motorhome – in his forties, so Mrs Piper had thought, with a good head of dark hair, although a dark wig could knock a few years off a man's apparent age. Alison Porter, the motorhome hire girl, had described him as a fair-haired man, balding slightly but also in his forties. But was that also a disguise? It was easy for an older man to dye his hair or even to wear a wig. And the fact he had the bearing of a policeman could also mean he had the bearing of a serviceman.

As he sat alone on that lofty rock with a skylark singing somewhere in the heavens, Pemberton's belief that the killer had some link with the army began to grow stronger. The mode of killing and the behaviour of the suspected killer suggested that and it was supported by his use of the Kalashnikov. Any villain might acquire such a weapon but few could use it with the skill of a trained operator. And this man was skilful. He'd used military skill *and* a military rifle.

But if the killer was a serving or former soldier, why would he suddenly embark on such a catastrophic catalogue of murder? Was it someone with a mental illness? Did he think he was justified in killing those who had avoided justice? Was this some kind of war for him? Was he somehow connected with any of his victims' victims? Was there an ex-soldier somewhere in the country who was nursing a huge grievance because someone had killed a relative and got away with it? Was this his way of getting revenge?

As these thoughts turned and tumbled through his mind, Pemberton realised it was a near impossible task to track down such a man – the combination of factors was such that a methodical search of every record, a mammoth, time-consuming task, would not necessarily produce the result he wanted. He began to see that he would have to tempt the killer to come forward, to reveal himself in some way, but he was not in charge of the other enquiries – he had no jurisdiction over them or the way they were investigated. It began to seem that some kind of co-ordinated effort was required but the danger – a continuing and increasing danger – was that the only way the killer could show his power, his determination or even his contempt for the police, was to kill another person. In view of what had happened so far, and in view of the number of people who'd escaped conviction for murder or other crimes, the risk was very high indeed. Pemberton realised the country was rich with potential Kalashnikov victims. So how many would lose their lives before the killer was trapped?

First, though, Pemberton knew he must seek the help of someone with army experience. He required that kind of expertise to further his investigation and his immediate thought was an old friend and ally, Colonel Ian McKay of the Royal Corps of Military Police at the Provost Company Detachment Offices in York. The two men had regularly worked together on a variety of cases and were always willing to assist one another. So Pemberton returned to his car, checked his pocket contact book for the right number, picked up his mobile phone and rang McKay.

'Pemberton speaking, Ian,' and for a few moments they exchanged mutual pleasantries.

Pemberton then explained about the series of murders, stressing he knew little about the Brixton killing at this point, but adding that he suspected the killer may be a soldier or former soldier who had possession, illegally or otherwise, of an old Kalashnikov.

McKay listened intently, then asked, 'So what do you want from me, Mark? How can I help?'

'I know it's a tall order, but I'm told that lots of soldiers, returning from wars like the Falklands, the Gulf and so on, smuggled guns back home, in their kitbags.'

'Right, they did. Trophies of war. If they actually get the guns into the country undetected, they can be allowed to retain them, with the necessary documentation and safeguards. But we used to carry out spot checks as they returned to base, we confiscated a lot but we never found them all. If you're asking me if we can trace those guns, the answer is that we confiscated every one we found and disposed of them, melted them down.'

'We do that too, with confiscated weapons.'

'Right. From our point of view, no serving soldier is allowed to keep them. If a squaddy did manage to get one through the system and then went into civvy street with the gun in his possession, he would have to apply for a firearms certificate from the civil police, claiming it

161

was a legitimate war trophy. That did happen sometimes, the guns were usually rendered incapable of
being fired, that was a condition of the firearms certificate, but we haven't those kind of records. Your own
records will show who's authorised to possess a war
trophy.'

'Right, we've checked those records – the local ones
that is – with a nil result. At the moment, Ian, it's the
personnel I want to trace rather than the weapon, I'm
anxious to find soldiers whose terms have expired.
They'll be in civvy street now, so are there records of
them?'

'You'd have to contact individual regiments for those,
Mark, you're talking of huge numbers, with men leaving for all kinds of reasons after long- or short-term
engagements. We wouldn't keep that kind of record, not
in Provost files. Look, can I make a suggestion?'

'Sure!'

'If you look for a killer, what's the first thing you
do?'

'We check our records to see if there's anyone who fits
the profile, we check our intelligence files and criminal
records. If it's a sex-related crime, we check for convictions for sexual crimes, for example. In this case, we've
run checks of several kinds, owners of firearms
included, but we've drawn a blank in every case.'

'Right. So if this character is a serviceman, or an ex-
serviceman, are we talking about one with a criminal
record?'

'It doesn't necessarily follow, but it would make
sense,' Pemberton agreed. 'I think, to commit this crime,
we're talking about a man of violence, or one who's not
averse to violence, some hard case who can turn to this
kind of cold-blooded killing. Gentle old ladies go for
poisoning while manly villains go for shootings or stab-
bings, so I'm told, and this doesn't look like a sudden

urge to kill, like a lost temper. It's a well-thought-out act of deliberate murder. An assassination, I'm convinced.'

'From what you've told me, I tend to agree. Now, if the squaddy was convicted of a serious criminal offence, in a non-military court, he'd be drummed out of the service. And we would keep a record of that – our Central Criminal Record and Intelligence Office does liaise with your central Criminal Records Office at Scotland Yard for such cases and our SIB keep tabs on anyone with a service history who might be a security risk. So yes, we have our own criminal and security records.'

'On computers?'

'Yes, we're right up to date. We maintain very detailed records in case squaddy tries to rejoin – and we won't have him back, not if he's collected any kind of major criminal record in civvy street. As for the minor stuff, well, we might accept him – things like driving offences or even petty theft. Every minor case is dealt with on its merits. But armed robbery – no! Or rape, murder and so on, definitely not.'

'And what about a man who's left the army? And who goes wrong, gets himself a criminal record after he's returned to civilian life? Would you know about that?'

'Probably, but not necessarily. It's the sort of thing our security branch would be interested in, especially if he was a former soldier convicted of, say, rape, after he'd returned to civilian life – or murder, espionage, rioting, racialism, that sort of thing. We want to know about it, just in case he does make application to rejoin, or, of course, we need to know for a variety of security reasons. SIB records are quite substantial and we do maintain our own database of servicemen or known ex-servicemen with criminal records who might be security sensitive.'

'Well, our man is a killer, Ian, he's trained in that

special skill, I'm sure of that. He's demonstrated he knows how to use a rifle. I'm guessing he killed in his army career, and now he's using his skills for a private civilian campaign.'

'We do maintain records of soldiers who are convicted of murder in the civilian courts. They're not retained as servicemen unless there's an appeal and the conviction is overturned. There's a fine line between shooting the enemy and shooting a civilian you think is the enemy. That used to worry us in Northern Ireland.'

'Right. So if a soldier was drummed out because he had killed someone while on duty, through being charged with a murder which he thought was a legitimate killing, he might want to take revenge, mightn't he?' Pemberton was thinking aloud now.

'He might, I suppose, it could prompt a man with some kind of mental problem to set about killing those who he thought had got away with murder. Some kind of perverted revenge. Do you want me to search our records for any such characters?'

'It would be useful, Ian, yes. Is it much of a chore?'

'Not with computers. I can soon arrange a print-out for you. I can produce a list of ex-soldiers, of all ranks, who've been convicted, while serving, of murder, rape, robbery, violence, sexual crimes and other serious offences, and who've been drummed out of the service over the past forty years. I can also produce a list of former soldiers, male and female, who've been convicted of murder, or some other serious crime, since leaving the service, including those regarded as a security risk.'

'Brilliant!' said Pemberton. 'At least it provides us with a whole new focus of enquiry.'

'Call me tomorrow, we'll see how we get on by then. You can come in to collect the data? It should be ready for collection by mid-morning. I prefer to deal personally with this, I don't want to commit it to the post or a courier.'

'Yes, no problem. And in the meantime I should find out more about the Brixton crime. I'll update you on that one.'

'Keep in touch, Mark, glad to be of assistance,' and McKay replaced his phone. Pemberton, feeling elated now that something positive had flowed, decided to return to his office to find out more about the Brixton murder.

Upon his return, Paul Larkin briefed Pemberton on the Brixton case, confirming he'd spoken to Detective Superintendent Edwards in person and had acquainted him with the orange pip clues, the role of the motor-home, the suspect with dark hair and the links with the death of Steve Abrahams in Northumberland.

At the time of speaking, however, Edwards had not received any information from the Met Forensic Laboratory about the bullets, although, thanks to the pathologist, he did know they were 7.62mm calibre. That did suggest they'd been fired from an old Kalashnikov AK47. The moment confirmation was received, he would contact the Roberthorpe Incident Room. In Edwards' opinion, having heard about the two other cases, it did seem that the murder of Leroy Campbell was third in the series – but whether or not the musician with the guitar case was relevant was not yet known. That man had not been traced, he confirmed, and he added that, contrary to press reports, he had no reason to think this was an instance of police revenge, although it was true that Campbell had been acquitted of murdering Sergeant George Coulson but had later admitted the crime. Larkin did say he had explained Pemberton's reservations about exactly what should be released to the press and Edwards said he would welcome a chat with Pemberton about policy and tactics as soon as it was convenient. Pemberton said he would ring him.

'So how was the thinking spell?' smiled Larkin.

'Useful. Two things emerged, thanks,' returned Pemberton. 'One – I think we must encourage the killer to reveal himself, or to reveal his motive – and we can do that by *not* linking these cases publicly. If he is on some personal campaign or vendetta, it's my guess he'll want to tell the world about it. The minute he starts doing that, he's likely to betray himself. Second point – we need to think much more deeply about the likely military connection, Paul, and it has to be done nationwide.'

'That'll take some organising!' breathed Larkin.

'It has to be done, we need a wider net,' Pemberton explained his discussion with Colonel McKay. 'He'll give us a list of a few of the most likely lads, we can set about checking those and they might lead us to others. We're moving again, Paul, but we've a lot of work to do.'

It was while they were having this discussion that Edwards rang from Streatham. Pemberton took the call.

'Good afternoon, Mr Pemberton,' the well-spoken voice sounded strong and lively with just a hint of a southern accent. 'Nice to make your acquaintance, and thanks for putting me in touch with events in your part of the world. Seems we have a sniper at work here, eh? A man with a mission of some sort.'

'Those are my feelings,' Pemberton agreed. 'I'm pleased you rang because I was going to suggest we co-ordinate enquiries, there's a lot we shouldn't reveal to the press – in fact, I don't think we should reveal the links between these murders.'

'Really? And why not?'

Pemberton explained his reasoning, adding that he felt the killer was someone with military experience.

166

'I couldn't agree more, Mr Pemberton. So yes, why don't you set up a meeting between us all, so we can exchange information and ideas. I'll be happy to come along. Just give me the date and time and I'll make myself available.'

'I have to go to York, probably tomorrow,' Pemberton said. 'To collect some data from the Assistant Provost Marshall's department which might be relevant, so maybe a meeting in the Royal York Hotel? It's next to York railway station.'

'That sounds fine to me. Give me confirmation when you can. Now, my reason for ringing. Those bullets, they are from a Kalashnikov. Our firearms experts have just confirmed it.'

'Just as we thought. Now we'll need all the bullets to be seen by the same experts,' Pemberton reminded him. 'To determine if they all came from the same weapon.'

'Who's your contact in the Nottingham Lab?'

'Lightfoot, Chris Lightfoot in the Firearms Section.'

'I'll call him, I'll arrange for him to examine our bullets. I'm betting they are from the same Kalashnikov, Mr Pemberton. Now, you said you're getting some relevant data from the military police?'

'I am,' and Pemberton explained the relevance of Colonel McKay's assistance.

'Why not invite Colonel McKay to meet us all?' suggested Edwards. 'What he's got to say might be important, even if I am looking for a guitar-playing suspect and Radcliffe hasn't anyone in the frame.'

'I'll invite him to join us, thanks for the suggestion. Now, are you publicising your musician?' Pemberton asked.

'I am, I'm using the line that he's a valuable witness, not a suspect. We've had some coverage down here, thanks to Damien Brown, but no-one's come forward. Having learned about your case, I tend to think it was the killer, using disguise as he did in your part of the world.'

'All the more reason for letting him think we've fallen for his ploy,' said Pemberton.

'OK, and we'll not refer to any links with your cases, not in the press. I just hope the press themselves don't link them! Confirm our meeting soon, Mr Pemberton. I'll pencil tomorrow in my diary.'

Pemberton immediately rang Jack Radcliffe in Northumberland, first with the news about the Brixton bullet, second about McKay's role and third to invite him to the meeting. Radcliffe was very enthusiastic, saying there'd been little development in his own investigation, with no sighting of a suspect and no names in the frame, so he would welcome the opportunity for this kind of dialogue. Pemberton rang the hotel, fixed a small private room and settled on a lunch-time meeting, with a meal – all very civilised! To the outside world, it would seem just like any other meeting between four businessmen – and Colonel Ian McKay said he would be delighted to join them; he'd fetch the data for Pemberton, with sufficient copies for his colleagues.

Almost immediately, his phone rang again; it was Kirsty Brewer, one of the assistants in the Force Control Room.

'I've got the driver of the RTD low-loader on the radio,' she said. 'He's got a motorhome on board, from Lichfield, and wants to know where you want it delivered, Mr Pemberton.'

'Where is he now?' he asked.

'On the A1(M), south of Dishforth.'

'Right, it needs to go to Rainesbury DHQ, Kirsty, to be sealed in a garage so that our own SOCO can examine it and compare tyre marks. But first, I'd like him to come here, we've a news conference at four o'clock and photos of that van will make a good feature for tomorrow. So get him to come here first, to the Incident Room, it's in the parish room at Roberthorpe. It's only a short diversion on his route to Rainesbury. I reckon he can make it before four.'

'I'll tell him,' she said.

'And I'll alert the press office to this photo opportunity,' he said.

After hearing the news and reading the early editions of the evening papers, the Sniper felt a small glow of satisfaction. His efforts in Brixton had produced a considerable response, and he looked forward to tomorrow's daily papers; if the stories already published were any guide, then he could expect banner headlines tomorrow. It was true that his personal campaign had not been mentioned, however, with some papers hinting the killer might be a disgruntled copper but at least the publicity did highlight the fact that Campbell had got away with murder – well, he had until now. Now he had received his just punishment.

Even so, there had been no reference to similarities between the Brixton death and those in the north of England. Clearly, even now, the police had not established any links and although the Sniper had no wish to smother himself in glory and no wish to have his campaign halted by being arrested, he was of the opinion that it was in the public interest for the public to become aware of the reason for those killings.

They were not random, they were not done without cause, and they did involve a lot of thought, research and planning.

But, he reasoned, it does take time for such patterns to become evident in the mind of officialdom; with the due passage of time, someone must realise that all these killers were themselves being executed, that all were receiving the same treatment, that all had been shot by the same dedicated campaigner . . .

His present dilemma was whether to follow the Brixton case with another swift repeat, or to allow a week or more to elapse before embarking upon his next mission. Three successes in fairly rapid succession was a considerable achievement but he did want to build on that success. After all, there were plenty of candidates – eighteen on his list – and so he had plenty of choice. But he decided to have a break, he might even take a short weekend holiday in the Lake District so that he could plan his next operation without distractions.

His gun would be quite safe, of course. Not that he would leave it at his grandmother's house; it would tucked away in another attic in its guitar case. Not even granny knew where his other home was – when he was not with her, he told her he was travelling, looking for work or going to gigs. Even so, her attic contained one of his guitar cases, and she always welcomed him back when he had been on one of his musical tours. An accompanying guitar case, complete with guitar, did make things look real. After all, he was her favourite grandson, the only one on this side of the family, and because he had moved around a lot in his army days, with no home to call his own, she had continued to accommodate him.

'There's always a bed here for you,' she'd told him time and time again. 'And a good hot meal!'

He had a lot of things in her loft, but because she was old and infirm, she never managed to cope with the ladder. There was no need, all the stuff in her loft belonged to him and it was quite innocuous, but she'd always said the bungalow would be his one day. She'd often said it was so nice to have a musician in the family, even if she had never been to one of his concerts.

Having decided to take a break, therefore, he began to pack a few belongings into a rucksack, find his hiking

170

boots and socks for an enjoyable weekend in the mountains and lakes. He'd book into a nice country pub somewhere, for bed and breakfast. He would tell granny he was going off looking for work, probably in Wales.

And while he was away, he'd fine tune the plans for the next stage of his campaign.

Chapter Eleven

Before Pemberton went home that night, he received a second call from Detective Superintendent Edwards in Streatham. He announced that his Task Force, after a second search, had found three orange pips in the long grass outside one of the windows of the gents' toilet in Low Wood Park. It seemed, according to Edwards, that chummy had been standing with his face close to the small aperture formed by the open window. Probably he'd been awaiting his target and at the time he'd been chewing an orange. He'd apparently spit the pips out of the window but as no sign of orange peel was found, it seemed he had removed that. None had been found during either search. Edwards said he would log the pips as exhibits for his own case, but he would have them examined for traces of DNA which could then be compared with the DNA taken from pips already in police possession. It was another good result which hopefully would produce evidence – or even irrefutable proof – of chummy's presence in Low Wood Park. Edwards felt that expert evidence on the trajectory of the fatal shot would show that it had been fired from, or very close to, that ideal sniping position.

Pemberton went home feeling happier than for some time. It did seem he was moving closer to his quarry even if, at this point, he had no idea who it was or where he was. With a new sense of optimism, he made a tasty beef curry for himself and Lorraine, then they had settled down to eat it informally on trays in their favourite chairs with classical music playing in the background. It was a comfortable, domestic evening.

Next morning's tabloids shouted to the world that Leroy Campbell, once wrongly accused of murdering a police officer, had been savagely gunned down in a London park in front of his friends. One paper even used the headline 'Cops' Revenge in the Park?' – the question mark was deliberate. There were blatant but unsubstantiated suggestions that his assailant might have been an aggrieved cop or ex-cop and the piece concluded with a veiled suggestion that the police were incompetent because they had no idea where to start hunting the killer. One paper even hinted they might not be interested in finding him while another suggested that a killer-cop, using his inside knowledge, could prevent his own arrest and remove any suspicion of him by his former colleagues.

Only one paper referred to Leroy's admission of guilt – the others maintained he was a person who had been wrongfully accused of murdering a police sergeant but had been fortunate to be found not guilty. Thus, in the eyes of the law, he was an innocent person – but that lone paper suggested his 'confession' was little more than a publicity stunt for his left-wing views and known hatred of the police. One report suggested that Leroy's 'confession' had been done to take the pressure off the real killer, with Leroy safe in the knowledge he could not be prosecuted again for the crime. In reading the reports, Pemberton was pleased to note there was no link with the northern crimes, although several of the items did feature the police request for the guitar-carrying musician to make himself known. As a potential witness, he might have seen something or somebody in the park, suggested the reports.

Following Pemberton's news conference yesterday afternoon, the local morning papers and, indeed, some of the nationals, did carry colour photographs of the motorhome. It was not stated anywhere that this was the actual vehicle seen near the scene of the murder; as Pemberton had been careful to point out to the journalists, this was a vehicle which appeared to be identical to the type still being sought. Pemberton was pleased at this presentation – if the killer did read these items, he would know the police had been following his false trail. Meanwhile, the van was being subjected to a detailed forensic examination, including tyre checks.

At the conference of detectives, Pemberton informed his teams of the current developments and asked them to look at and carry pictures of the motorhome for examination by potential witnesses. He wanted to trace its movements while it had been in the vicinity and he also urged his teams to have another look at the array of pornographic pictures removed from Flint's bedroom. They were now presented in an album in the hope that at least some of the children might be identified even if they were now adults; he wanted another check on firearms certificate holders to see if any held trophies of war, a further check on the movements of former military personnel living in the area and an appraisal of local persons with convictions for violence – any kind of violence whether against the person or against property. He asked for another determined attempt to trace any other person who might have used Green Lane on the morning of the murder and for the villagers to be given yet another opportunity to suggest a possible motive or name for Flint's killer.

If none could be found locally, then it added strength to his decision to expand the enquiry across the nation. A further reason for this concentration of enquiries was that it might jog the memories of those who'd earlier been reluctant to come forward.

At the news conference which followed, there was little to add; that is what he wanted. He wanted a period

174

of low-key publicity which concentrated on finding the motorhome and tracing the black-haired suspect – false messages firmly directed towards the killer. There was little else to highlight and, quite deliberately, Pemberton created a lack of exciting developments so the press were not tempted to expand their own enquiries – even now, the murder of an unknown church-worker from a quiet moorland village had not attracted much media attention. No longer was it the lead story, not even in the local papers.

Meanwhile, in Northumberland, a similar situation prevailed – Jack Radcliffe had succeeded in making everyone believe the killer was from the local criminal fraternity as he publicised the fact that no suspect had been seen and to date he had no prime suspect. He stressed his own team's continuing enquiries in the criminal underworld and, as a result, the villains of Tyneside were having a rough time. They began their own concerted effort to identify the killer, if only to prevent the police poking noses into their sensitive operations. Similarly in Brixton, Detective Super-intendent Edwards was publicising his efforts to trace the guitar-playing suspect while allowing, without any contradictory comment from him, the anti-police theme to persist in news reports.

What none of those senior detectives could know, however, was that their mutual strategy was beginning to have its impact on the Sniper. They had hoped for such a development and now, in his Lake District bed-and-breakfast accommodation, the Sniper scanned the nationals. He now realised that, although the ruse of his false trail in Yorkshire had succeeded, the simple-minded police had still not linked his three crimes. Should he tell someone? Or dispose of another killer who was living free from prosecution? After all, there were plenty of candidates from whom he could pick and choose . . . he'd think about that as he tackled Helvellyn this morning.

He was not to know, however, that the three police officers whom he had supposedly deceived, were now en route to a very important meeting in York.

Upon arrival at the Royal York Hotel, the senior detectives had been advised in advance by Pemberton to report to reception and ask for the venue of Mr Pemberton's lunch party. They had been accommodated in a small dining room overlooking the gardens with the city walls and Minster in the background, and Pemberton had arranged for a pre-lunch aperitif. The table had been placed before the window – to which none objected for security reasons – and it was laid ready, while at the other side of the room was a coffee table with four easy chairs, along with cups and a full percolator. Also available was a choice of sherry in carafes, along with glasses.

As the detectives arrived, Pemberton made the introductions and offered drinks – there was Jack Radcliffe, a tall thin individual in his early fifties with rather gaunt features and the meagre remains of auburn hair on his scalp; Ian McKay, also in his early fifties, with a rather stocky frame and a mop of fair, wavy hair, plus a distinct military bearing in spite of wearing civilian clothes, and Ted Edwards from the London Metropolitan Police in Streatham, a man with a Mediterranean appearance – his dark eyes, black hair and faintly olive coloured skin came from his Spanish mother – and he spoke with a faint south of England accent. He was younger than the others, in his mid-forties, estimated Pemberton. Like businessmen at a vital meeting, all were smartly dressed in suits and carried briefcases. It was twelve-fifteen – lunch had been ordered for one o'clock and so they

176

welcomed the coffee and biscuits after their journeys, then settled down with their sherries.

After the pleasantries, it was time for business. Pemberton, being the instigator of this meeting, acted as chairman. He began with an outline of his own case and had asked the others to follow with an up-dated résumé of both the Northumberland and Brixton murders, highlighting any relevant details.

Sipping his sherry, he summed up by saying, 'The common facts are these. Each victim has either been cleared of murder or not prosecuted for murder. Now, as if in retribution, each has been shot in the heart, three or four times. The gunman is an expert. He does not leave evidence in the form of spent bullets, he clears up the scene afterwards. He does not leave any kind of message as one might expect if he is on a personal mission and he has not contacted the press to publicise his efforts. However, he does leave orange pips at or near the scene – we think he does not realise this – but he leaves no peel. He leaves a very clean and tidy crime scene, gentlemen, which, I think, tells us a lot. He's behaving like a professional assassin. He uses a Kalashnikov AK47, an old weapon because it fires 7.62mm ammunition which went out of date in 1974, and we know there are lots in this country, held illegally, often by former servicemen or villains who had managed to acquire them.'

'About the Kalashnikov,' chipped in Edwards. 'I forgot to mention earlier. I got a phone call on the train. After our chat, I rushed one of our samples up to Nottingham, I wanted an answer for this morning's meeting. I got it. We are talking about the same gun in all our cases. I can confirm the bullets came from the same Kalashnikov and that must point to the same killer throughout.'

'Good, that helps us go forward very positively,' smiled Pemberton. 'Now, we need to produce some kind of strategy, to agree on tactics particularly as far as the press is concerned – and by press, I include radio and television. To date, they have not noticed any link in these crimes. I think that is only a matter of time, especially if we release the fact the victims were all shot with Kalashnikovs.'

'And that they're all unconvicted killers,' added Radcliffe.

'Right, except it might not be wise to be so categoric in print! Now, I believe in my case, the killer deliberately set up a false trail,' and Pemberton explained his reasons for that belief, then asked, 'Ted, what about your guitar player? Could that be a false trail?'

'It could, I can't deny it,' he smiled. 'We're publicising him, you know that? We had just the one sighting of him, happily by our community constable who chanced to be nearby at the time, in uniform, I might add. Other than that, we've heard nothing more about guitar players or any other sighting of a suspect.'

'He's trustworthy, your constable, is he?' asked McKay.

'We've tested his story, it holds up,' nodded Edwards. 'I don't suspect that policeman. But yes, the guitarist might have been the killer making himself prominent when in fact he looks nothing like a musician. It could have been done to mislead us.'

'Jack? Nothing yet in your case?'

'Not a sighting, we've combed the area, on house-to-house, and checked all drivers known to use that road in the early hours, but it's a remote spot and a very quiet stretch of road. No-one saw our suspect, so I can't help – but the fact he has not been seen has made us concentrate on the local villains – and that could be the red herring he's presented in our case. We've been busy turning them over when in fact none's guilty, it's a time consuming business and employs lots of manpower.

After talking to you, I'm convinced it will lead nowhere.'

'That is one area of strategy I'd like us to agree on,' Pemberton said. 'That we publicise our efforts to trace and interview those fictitious suspect characters, that we make our man think we are chasing them, or turning over the villains of Tyneside when in fact we're concentrating on other matters. If he thinks we are not on his tail, he might grow careless – or even bolder. It gives us a chance to surprise him as a result of our genuine enquiries. We do to him exactly what he's trying to do to us; we might even lead him to reveal something of himself.'

'Fine, yes, I agree with that,' nodded Edwards.

'And me,' said Radcliffe.

'So far as my motorhome is concerned, I have found the actual vehicle in Lichfield, but I'm not letting chummy know that. It did have an orange pip under the driving seat, the tyres match a mark left at our scene, and a witness has agreed it is the one she saw. But I shall continue to pretend I am seeking one just like it.'

'Fair enough,' said Edwards. 'I've no vehicle in my frame.'

'Me neither,' said Radcliffe. 'Well, not one I can describe, he did use one to drive into the forest prior to shooting Abrahams, but at this stage we have no idea what it was. The consensus is that it was a small vehicle, a car or van perhaps.'

'And we are agreed we will not refer to the type of weapon in public or through the media?'

'One half of me says that if I publicise the fact an old Kalashnikov was used, it might lead to someone suggesting where we might find it. But this is an odd case, so no, not at this stage. In view of the circumstances, though, let's keep that knowledge to ourselves, at least for the time being,' said Edwards.

179

'Along with the fact the victims are all unconvicted killers?'

'Yes, we needn't publicise that,' Edwards continued. 'Don't forget, though, that Leroy Campbell was known as a police killer, that's no secret.'

'Abrahams was well known too, and he was a killer who got away with it, but in my case his murder looks like an underworld job. There's no other link, nothing the press will latch on to, I'm sure.'

'And Flint was not known, by the public, to be a child killer. So we'll keep that to ourselves. If the press do raise the issue, we can say we have no reason to suspect any connection between the murders – after all, the press do not know about the weapon, the cluster of bullets all in the hearts or the orange pips.'

'If they do raise the question, we can dismiss it as speculation, unfounded speculation,' said Radcliffe. 'We could even suggest one of them was a copy-cat killing, done by someone emulating an earlier killer. That kind of thing does happen.'

'We'll cope, we'll all do our best to follow that line,' said Edwards, adding, 'I'll discuss it with my press office. But Mark, you do appreciate we might have to change our minds, depending on how each case pro-gresses – or if he shoots anyone else. I don't want any decisions taken here to be cast in iron; after all, some are contrary to our established procedures and against our policy of openness with the media.'

'I realise that and I know operational requirements must take precedence but for the time being I believe the end will justify the means. I am prepared to risk official complaints about my actions in this case but, in my view, we are involved in a very unusual series of, events. That's my justification. Shall we liaise with each other prior to making any decision to opt out of this agreement?' Pemberton put to them. 'I do think that is necessary, in fairness to our joint enquiries.'

'Of course. You know I'll do my best,' was all Edwards would say. 'And if he does kill again, in another police area, you've got all this routine to impress upon that CID chief whoever he is.'

Radcliffe also signified his general agreement.

'I'll cope with that when and if it happens,' said Pemberton. 'Now, it's time to hear what Ian has to say. He's here because my own gut feeling, supported by my teams, is that chummy has some military experience. Ian?'

'Thanks,' McKay smiled. 'Hearing your accounts of the killer's behaviour reminds me of training undertaken by the SAS and our undercover units, but not exclusively. Anyone with common sense, or the ability to search the internet for websites which provide advice on military tactics, undercover or otherwise, could do the same.'

'Point taken – except for the coolness he's displayed. Eating a meal before despatching someone! I think that is exceptional. Ted, what about you? What do you think? Any indications your killer had military experience?'

'Yes, I was drawn to the same conclusion. I was impressed with the accuracy of the shots, especially as they were fired from a distance, and the fact he despatched his victim while he was surrounded by henchmen – another example of coolness. There's also the fact he managed to get away afterwards without being seen – yes, I'd say there's more than a hint of covert military expertise here.'

'One man against the world, eh?' said Pemberton.

Edwards said, 'I ought to add, under strict secrecy, that one of the guards accompanying Leroy when he was shot was an undercover police officer . . . he's been withdrawn now, for his own safety, and given a safe address. He called the police but said he saw no sign of the assailant. He thinks he ran away down the far side of the hill, under cover of the panic he'd created.'

'In my view, it's definitely the work of a sniper,' Radcliffe made his contribution. 'In my case he used thick conifers and darkness to conceal himself, he chose a site where he'd not leave footprints or car marks, and he left a clean and tidy scene. And he was amazingly accurate. Yes, I'd go along with the fact he could be a soldier or ex-soldier, or from some other branch of the services – Marine commandos or something. With bags of nerves, the sort who'd be iron-cold in executing his duties. A good front-line soldier in other words.'

'Those are our views, Ian,' Pemberton said. 'We might be totally wrong, but it's over to you!'

'Thanks, Mark. Well, gentlemen,' he spoke in a crisp and clear Scots accent. 'I do think you have a rogue soldier, or ex-soldier on the loose. The pointers are all there but I doubt if a serving member would undertake this kind of long-term freelance project – he'd be missed by his colleagues for one thing, they'd notice his absence and they'd recognise his handiwork. Men like this know each other's traits, they'd put two-and-two together, they'd soon realise he was the villain but they wouldn't let him continue, not with those kind of murders. He'd be reined in pretty smartly. Serving soldiers will cheerfully allow their mates to kill the enemy in a proper theatre of war, and they'll give their full support to each other, but they call a line at murder in civvy street. But yes, I'd go for an ex-soldier with a grievance, or perhaps one suffering from mental problems or a disease. Even the so-called Gulf War Syndrome which can cause soldiers to go wrong in spectacular ways.'

'Well,' smiled Edwards. 'If we are looking for a former serviceman, this narrows the field down somewhat – at least it's not one man out of millions in the public sector but it's still a lot of soldiers. So how can we find him?'

'Mark rang me yesterday,' and Ian McKay told them of his conversation with Pemberton. 'As a result, I arranged a computer sift of all likely former soldiers, bearing in mind their sickness records, their criminal records and of course their service records plus their status as a security risk. I'd better say here that our records are far more comprehensive than you might think. On service matters, especially those with national security implications, we do work closely with the civilian security services and with New Scotland Yard. I must stress, of course, that not every ex-soldier is listed here. I had to be selective. These names are a selection upon whom some kind of suspicion must rest, men I would want to check if I was undertaking your enquiry. My list ranges from those with civilian criminal records to those with security risk status of varying degrees and even those known to us who have some degree of mental illness. From your point of view there is a difficulty because they are spread across the whole of the United Kingdom and overseas, they're not all living on or near your own personal patches! I am minded that Mark Pemberton's suspect did hire his motorhome from Lichfield. From a UK point of view, that's a very central location. Significant perhaps? You might care to bear that mind when you read these papers. They're all yours, gentlemen,' and from his briefcase, he gave each detective an identical file of computer print-outs, several of them on different coloured papers, each in a category of its own. He retained a copy for his own reference.

It was evident, right from the start, that there were hundreds of names, all of whom would have to be traced, interviewed and alibied. For a few moments, each detective scanned the lists in silence, each with their own thoughts and wondering how such a mammoth task could best be approached. Even now, it was clear it would involve most of the police forces in

183

England and Wales, as well as some in Scotland and overseas – and all that would take time, time none could really afford.

McKay noticed their discomfort, 'I hope you don't mind, but I did a little analysis of my own, bearing in mind military requirements and my own brief knowledge of the Roberthorpe case. Thanks to our own data bases, I came up with a short list of seven. I've got two suffering from Gulf War Syndrome, one with a conviction of manslaughter after a fight in a pub, two with convictions for smuggling firearms into Northern Ireland, one convicted of assault with intent to cause GBH, and one with a conviction for murder. In addition to those factors, however, they're all in our top list of a select group that we, the military authorities, need to keep under covert observation for a variety of reasons.'

'That seems a good starting point, so we can take our pick!' smiled Pemberton. 'Or did you look at their records in depth?'

'I did. All these men are atrained in the use of firearms, some have served overseas on active campaigns – the Falklands for example, or on secret engagements in places like Oman. Some have also served in Northern Ireland. They are all men who could have fired your shots, gentlemen, they've all got the kind of skills your man has displayed, even down to ice-cold behaviour. In my opinion, you will need to have all seven interviewed and eliminated – and if all these *are* eliminated then you'll have to look at another bunch! I can furnish a second team for your consideration, but these are my first seven.'

'And who would you place at No. 1 in your frame?' Pemberton asked.

'The one convicted of murder, followed by the two Gulf War Syndrome sufferers. They're my three top candidates. I think it is very significant that No. 1 denied committing the crime for which he was imprisoned. He maintained he'd been wrongly convicted but later, after eighteen years in prison, and quite inexplicably, he changed his mind. Quite suddenly, he admitted the crime which meant he was eligible for parole. He couldn't get parole unless he admitted his guilt and showed genuine contrition. Earlier, he'd refused to do that on the grounds he was innocent, but a long-drawn out campaign, with at least one appeal to the High Court, failed to establish his innocence. He did eighteen years inside and he's out now, back in the community, on parole. He's not in the army, I might add, and he's not working at the moment but has worked as a driver in the past.'

'A man wrongfully convicted, eh? He sounds like someone with a grudge,' commented Pemberton. 'Eighteen years inside for a crime he did not commit? So who is he, Ian?'

'His name is Michael James Steele,' Ian McKay told them. 'He's halfway down the green sheet in your hands. He's forty-two now. He joined up at the age of eighteen and served five years. He was just short of his twenty-third birthday when he left, he had a chequered career with us. He was in the SAS, a brave and very daring young man, not afraid of taking risks, very skilled in everything he did – especially with firearms. He did some undercover work for us, in Oman and Northern Ireland. A very capable man. But he had a weak spot – whenever he was on leave, not just a week-end leave, I mean, an extended period like a month, he missed the excitement of his army life – and took to crime. He burgled several houses, he got into fights outside clubs, he was convicted of GBH on two occasions and so we got rid of him. It was a pity – if he'd kept his nose clean, he'd have made a superb soldier, a real man of action. He is bright and intelligent, cool under pressure . . . an ideal man for specialised work in

185

the army. Then, not long after he finished with the SAS, two elderly people were murdered during a burglary. Steele was caught and denied the murders, but admitted the burglary. There was substantial evidence against him and the jury would not accept he was responsible for the burglary but not guilty of the murder. He maintained the old couple were asleep in bed throughout his burglary, he got away with their savings, over seven hundred pounds in cash. They were bludgeoned to death, there was no blood on his clothes and nothing to link him with the murders, except he'd been in the house, illegally, around the material time. Anyway, the jury found him guilty in spite of his protests of innocence and he got two life sentences.'

'And his personal life?' asked Pemberton.

'Sad, really. His father killed his mother, then committed suicide. Michael was six at the time and went to live with his grandmother. He's an only child, we've no details of his behaviour at that age, but he did moderately well at school, he attended a comprehensive in Wolverhampton where his granny lived – and still lives. He got a few dead end jobs on leaving school, stacking shelves, spells of lorry and van driving, work on building sites, and then he joined the army. He's never been married, by the way, and his current home address is his grandmother's house. It's shown in your files. She's still alive and in her late eighties. He's there most of the time, but tends to go away a lot, looking for work he says. She thinks he's a musician, going off to gigs and concerts. He has a car, a second-hand Vauxhall Astra. A white one. We do visit him from time to time, undercover, to keep tabs on him but his granny is a very wary old thing. And now you'll be wondering why I selected him out of the hundreds on my list?'

'Go on, surprise us!' laughed Radcliffe.

'His music?' laughed Edwards.

'No, he's got a passion for oranges,' said McKay.

'I remember Mark telling me about the pips you'd recovered.'

'That makes him very interesting!' Pemberton felt a tingle of anticipation as he discovered this piece of news. 'You've a very comprehensive file on him!'

'It's in our interest. As I said, we supervise those we feel are a security risk and we feel he is. Even after all this time out of the service, he's classified as a risk to national security and to the army in general, due to his training, his knowledge of covert techniques and his unstable character. Men like him have been used to burgle Government offices and the homes of ministers suspected of espionage or treasonable behaviour; you can understand why we want to keep tabs on him. There is a photo in each of your files, by the way, covertly taken three years ago. Sadly, it's not a very good likeness. His hair's thinner now, for one thing.'

Pemberton and the others searched for the photograph. They saw a fresh-faced man with handsome square features, fair hair with just a hint of curls round the neck, blue eyes, clean shaven with good white teeth and small, neat ears.

'He looks like a model!' laughed Edwards. 'Or he would, if he had more hair.'

'I don't think he was ever short of an admiring crowd of girls,' said McKay. 'Perhaps that explains why he never married.'

'So if he's not married, where is he right this minute?' asked Edwards.

'As I said, his official address is his grandmother's house in Wolverhampton. He's using that while under supervision by the Parole Board and probation service; as you know, it's a condition of release on licence that he notifies the authorities of any change of address, but we understand one of his main interests is the exploration of remote upland regions like the Lake District, and he says he needs to travel in search of work. He has worked as a driver, HGVs or buses, taxis even. The Parole Board is happy for him to travel around if he lets them know where he's going.'

'Like his trip to Cornwall when in fact it seems he came to Yorkshire?'

'Could be!' smiled McKay.

'So we've a base for him,' smiled Edwards. 'That's good, we can always mount a surveillance exercise to greet him when he returns from one of his trips. Right, gentleman, he's got to be interviewed, we need to establish his whereabouts at the time of all our murders, but the question is: which of us gets to interview him?'

'I think we'd better alert Wolverhampton police to our interest,' Pemberton felt that caution was needed. 'We can't just breeze into their territory and lift him. We might interrupt some exercise or supervision role of theirs which involves him!'

'Anyone with contacts in the West Midlands?' asked Radcliffe. 'I haven't!'

'I have,' Pemberton said. 'I did my Police College Junior Command Course with Jim Deakin, he's the Detective Super at "G" Division of the West Midland Police, that's Wolverhampton.'

'I think a word with him is the first thing we must do,' suggested Edwards. 'First, his troops will know Steele, he'll be in their records, they'll know he's out on licence and they'll be keeping tabs on him. They'll know if he's at his granny's or touring or looking for work or whatever excuse he's got for not being there.'

'We've got to be careful, we don't want his men blundering in and ruining anything we might establish,' Radcliffe knew the dangers of having too many police forces involved in the hunt for one killer. 'There's no suggestion he's killed in the Midlands, is there?'

'Not at this stage, but I'm sure Deakin will co-operate,' Pemberton said.

'Fair enough, but we don't want him to scare away

our quarry, not if we're on the point of getting close to him,' said Edwards. 'It seems to me that one of us, with backup, should go and find Steele first. We've got to establish whether he is a genuine suspect, and we can't do that from a piece of paper in a file. We've got to visit him.'

'All of us?' asked Radcliffe.

'There's safety in numbers!' laughed McKay.

'I still think we should involve Wolverhampton,' said Pemberton. 'Not just as a matter of courtesy, there might other crimes for which he's under investigation locally, Wolverhampton will know what they are. We can't just breeze in there and take over.'

'The ideal scenario would be for Wolverhampton to nick him on our behalf and take him into custody straight away, before he can get rid of any evidence, or hide his gun or whatever. That can be done legally. Once he's inside, we can turn his house over, contact his mates or whatever to see what he's been up to, and each of us can interview him in the comfort of our own custody suite once we've got enough evidence to nail him – and all within the provisions of the Police and Criminal Evidence Act.' Edwards was right. This seemed the only way.

'OK, you can have first crack at him, Mark,' said Radcliffe. 'Yours was the first murder.'

'I'll ring Wolverhampton now,' and Pemberton hauled his mobile from his pocket.

The Sniper's plans to despatch another of his targets were well advanced. It was a man who had got away with murder because the body of his wife had never been found. The Sniper had made a decision to act speedily because neither the police nor any of the news outlets had recognised the reason for any of his killings. There had been not a single column inch, not a mention on TV or on radio and so the great British public was unaware of what he was doing on their behalf.

It was time to make them aware of his dedication but for that, he would have to return home for his Kalashnikov.

Chapter Twelve

'It's Pemberton speaking, Jim, from North Yorkshire.' The two detectives swopped gossip for a few moments with Pemberton giving him the number of his mobile before continuing. 'I'm at a meeting in York,' he went on to explain the purpose of both the meeting and his call before saying, 'We're interested in talking to a man who lives on your patch, name of Michael James Steele, he's just been released on licence after doing a stretch for murder.'

'We know him,' Deakin had no trouble recalling the man or his deeds. 'He accused the police of fixing the evidence but he was found guilty. There've been appeals, they've all been turned down. I was a young DC then, I was on the case, I know he killed those pensioners, Mark, sure as eggs are eggs, no matter how much he denies it. He admitted it eventually, you know that? Then he got parole.'

Pemberton explained his knowledge of events, then acquainted Deakin with the suspicions currently exercising the minds of himself and his colleagues.

'We need to have Steele interviewed and a sample DNA taken if you can arrange that, Jim; we need to know his whereabouts at the material times of our killings, so how about lifting him on suspicion straight away?'

'We can do that. Do you want us to search his house as well?'

'He keeps his Kalashnikov somewhere, so yes. See if he keeps it under the bed, or hidden in a guitar case. And the ammo. Make sure he doesn't see you first though, I don't want him using your lads for target practice.'

'I'll send a team around immediately, Mark, and the minute we've got him inside I'll call you.'

Pemberton, unsure whether or not his meeting would conclude prior to Steele's arrest, provided the number of the Roberthorpe Incident Room where a message could be left if his mobile was out of range. For Pemberton and his colleagues, however, it was time for lunch. By the time they reached the coffee stage, they hoped Michael James Steele would be in custody – and that would provide a cause for celebration.

In Wolverhampton, Detective Superintendent Deakin wasted no time. He summoned two senior detective sergeants to his office, men qualified to carry arms, and he explained the order.

'We need to lift Steele,' he said quietly. 'He's wanted for questioning, by three other forces, for a series of murders with a Kalashnikov. So draw yourselves weapons and get round there; be very careful but make sure you arrest him and arrange for his house – well, his granny's house – to be searched for the weapon and ammunition. It's evidence so be careful with it – and make sure he doesn't take you out as well! Clearly, the man's dangerous and, from what I've been told, he knows how to use a rifle.'

In separate plain cars, the two teams of detectives drove along Ring Road St George's to the roundabout, turned off to drive along Bilston Road and then along Steelhouse Lane and past the end of Gordon Street.

After some eight hundred metres, they turned into a cul-de-sac called Tower End and sought out No. 18. It was the last house on the right, a small end-of-terrace property with a dark green door and lace curtains at the front windows. There was a patch of lawn not much bigger than a pair of doormats placed-end-to-end, and a straggly shrub of some kind hanging over the brick wall which bordered the street. The first car, call sign Sierra One, contained Detective Sergeant Patrick Temple and Detective Constable John Skinner, and it eased to a halt at the end of the street, well away from the house and beyond the sight of anyone inside. The second car, call sign Sierra Two containing Detective Sergeant Dudley Russell and Detective Constable Stephen Mander, drove along the rear of the street until it was out of sight of the first car.

Temple contacted Russell on the dedicated radio-link.

'Confirm when you're in position,' he said as the second car slid to a halt outside the back door of No. 18. Seconds later, the acknowledgement came. 'Sierra Two, in position.'

'We're going in,' said Temple. 'We'll knock and await an answer, no fire brigade entries this time . . . gently does it . . .'

Sierra One moved forward and came to a smooth halt outside the front of No. 18 and the two detectives emerged from their car, touched their concealed shoulder holsters for reassurance, and walked the few feet to the front door with more than a hint of nervousness. There was an old-fashioned brass knocker in the shape of a lion's face and Temple used it to rap loudly.

It produced no response; he waited and then rapped again, but this time the door opened and an elderly woman grumbled, 'All right, all right, I can hear you!'

She had iron grey hair fastened back with a dark blue ribbon, and a characterful face rich with lines and sporting a deep ruddy colour. A small woman, she looked aggressive and not to be trifled with. No con man pretending to be a waterboard official would get past her, Temple decided. 'Is your Michael in?' he asked.

'Who wants to know?' She was accustomed to such visitors and instinctively knew these were police officers.

'We do. Police,' said Temple, showing his warrant card to emphasise the point.

'He's out,' she said.

'Mind if we look?' was Temple's next logical request, knowing the back door was under surveillance. If he tried to do a runner that way, he'd be caught.

'I do mind, you've no right to harass him, he's done his time and he wasn't even guilty, not of the murder. You're always on to him, never leaving him be. Why can't you let him alone?'

'We'd like a look inside,' persisted Temple. 'We can do it the easy way, like you inviting us in, right now, or we can stay here until my colleagues get a warrant.'

'What is it this time?' she snapped.

'We just want to talk to Michael,' said Temple. 'And if he's not here, we'd like to have a look at his room before he gets back. So where is he?'

'He went off looking for work, that's what he said, to Wales. A driving job of some sort. He might do a gig or two as well, he could be away a week.'

'Whereabouts in Wales?'

'How should I know, he never tells me. Just Wales.'

'In his car?'

'He took his car, yes.'

'Right, so how about letting us check the house, just to make sure he's not hiding in a cupboard or lurking under the bed?'

'Please yourselves, you will anyway,' and she stepped back to let the two detectives into her neat, and tidy home. With arms drawn, they conducted a swift but very thorough search, checking cupboards, under the beds, in the bathroom and every other likely and unlikely place; they even went into the loft but apart from the guitar case lying against the rear wall, and some tea-chests full of crockery and glass, there was nothing. Temple looked inside the guitar case – it was of blue canvas and contained a guitar. Certainly, there was no-one hiding there and no sign of a firearm of any type, nor any accoutrements such as cleaning materials and oil. They returned downstairs, checked all the ground floor rooms, then went into the backyard, into the out-door toilet, the coal shed and the wood shed. In every place they checked for loose floorboards and other places likely to conceal a rifle as large as a Kalashnikov, but found nothing. They made their exit into the lane where Sierra Two was waiting.

'Nothing?' asked Temple.

'He's not come out,' confirmed Russell.

'He's away in Wales, according to his granny,' Temple told him. 'For a week, she thinks.'

'Seems she's telling the truth. His car's not in the street either, he usually parks it out here at the back. A white Vauxhall. I'll contact the boss,' and Russell activated his radio then explained in detail what they had done, including the lack of indication of any presence of a gun.

Deakin listened and said, 'All right, leave the guitar case where it is, the Met might want to see it but if we do move it and he finds out, he'll smell a rat. Besides, it's the wrong colour. Bring something likely to carry his DNA, a toothbrush or mug or something. Then return to base and we'll try again later. When you get back, circulate a description of him and his car, some alert copper might pick him up before he gets home. And contact all the Welsh forces, just in case he is in the valleys.'

'Understood, sir,' acknowledged Russell.

'If the gun's not there, he must have got it with him. That means he might be intent on another job. I think we'd better issue a warning to Wales and our own mobiles. Has he gone to kill a Welsh person? Or is he going to bump off a local by any chance? Who do we know in Wolverhampton who's recently been cleared of murder?'

'No idea, sir, not off the top of my head,' returned Russell. 'So shall we keep obbo here or return?'

'We haven't enough spare men to hang around there just on the off-chance he comes back today or tomorrow, next week or whenever. Return to base, we'll issue a memo to all foot patrols and mobiles to get them to pay regular attention to the house and report his return if and when it happens. That's all we can do – it's not our case anyway, but I hope somebody picks him up before he comes home. I'll call Pemberton.'

Pemberton and his companions were still in York when Deakin's call came through. Pemberton listened, then said, 'Well, Jim, if he's the man I think he is, and if he's said he's gone to Wales for a week, then my guess is that's the last place we'll find him. You say he's got a car?'

'Yes, we've details of it, we do have a comprehensive file on Steele. I can circulate a description for his car to be hunted. If he is touring in it, you'd think some bright-eyed young motor patrol officer would spot it.'

'I think it would be best if the circulation was just to observe and report its position, not to arrest or question Steele. We don't want him alerted to our interest. We don't want him concealing his movements either, or hiding that gun. Or using it against the police.'

'The gun wasn't in his granny's house,' said Deakin. 'Although our team did report a guitar case in the loft – with a guitar in it. We left it.'

'So he could be armed now, wherever he is? You did

right to leave the guitar, the Met might want it. They're looking for a guitar-man.'

'I don't think his granny will touch it – besides, I don't think it's the one the Met is looking for.'

'Good point,' agreed Pemberton. 'Hang on, I'll ask Ted Edwards, he's right beside me.'

Edwards agreed with that course of action. 'Right, we don't want him alerted to our real interest, leave the guitar case there, especially if it's got a guitar in it. Ours was tan coloured, those Midlands lads are on the ball. I reckon the one our witness saw was the one which concealed the gun and we can seize the Wolverhampton one later if we think we should let Forensics have a look at it. But in my view, it's not vital evidence. I agree with the plan to "observe and report". Granny will say the police have been but he might not realise why, and we don't want him to know our real reason. So yes, keep tabs on the house until he comes home, watch for his car and issue a warning that he could be armed. We can ask all forces to look out for him on those terms, with strict instructions not to approach him.'

Radcliffe nodded his agreement.

Pemberton returned to his conversation with Deakin. 'Right, Jim, we're all agreed about this. Search and report but under no circumstances interrogate or stop Steele. All we want is a report on his whereabouts and current movements, then we'll decide when, where and how to arrest him for questioning. And thanks for your co-operation.'

'Sorry I can't spare men for round-the-clock observations on the house', said Deakin.

'I understand,' and Pemberton hoped they would trace Steele before he returned home. But if he was out somewhere in his car, without the gun being found at home, was he already stalking his next victim? Or was he innocent anyway? After all, there were other men in the frame – Ian McKay had produced a very satisfactory

197

list of other possible suspects and so Pemberton returned his attention to his colleagues. He said, 'Well, gentlemen, that's Steele taken care of. What about the others on Ian's list?'

In the Incident Room at Roberthorpe, there had been a good response to the additional publicity about the motorhome. Sightings of similar, or even the same vehicle, had been reported from several locations throughout the country and those reports were all logged and entered into the time chart. In Larkin's opinion, however, it merely suggested the vehicle had been very popular and that such popularity might explain its presence in all kinds of odd places through-out the nation. Sadly, all those reports were long before it was known the suspect had hired his motorhome and a check with Alison Porter revealed the hirers' names and addresses. All would be visited and interviewed for elimination, even though Larkin felt none could be regarded as genuine suspects. It was just possible, how-ever, that one or more might be witnesses. The unfortu-nate fact was that no further sightings had been reported in and around Roberthorpe during the material time – for most of the residents, one caravan or camper was just like another, and few villagers paid any atten-tion to them, other than to complain about them as they passed continuously through the village.

The second sweep among the holders of firearms certificates did not reveal anyone else who held, or who had held, authority to possess an automatic or semi-automatic pistol or rifle which was registered as a trophy of war, nor did the search produce any more former soldiers living locally who might have served in recent combats. Furthermore, no new witnesses were found. It seemed that the teams had exhausted all local enquiries, but when Pemberton phoned Larkin after his conference in York, to provide him with the name of the suspect, the enquiry was jolted back into action. Pemberton, after discussion with his colleagues at the York meeting and with Deakin in particular, was charged with the task of circulating a description of Steele and his car.

If, as his grandmother had said, he was away from home for a week, with his car, then he could have gone overseas although a check with his parole supervisor should clarify that; even so, all ports would be contacted and all customs officials alerted. If he had gone overseas, his destination and his date of return would be known. More importantly, every police force in the United Kingdom would now be circulated with a High Priority Message and photograph; the text would be as follows:

'HIGH PRIORITY. HIGHLY CONFIDENTIAL. NOT FOR RELEASE TO THE PRESS. The below-named is urgently sought in connection with a series of murders in North Yorkshire, Northumberland and the Metropolitan Police District. Michael James Steele, born Wolverhampton 20.6.1959, former soldier, driver, casual labourer. Single. 5'11" (158cm), proportionate build, good physique, fair hair thinning on top, blue eyes, clean shaven, pale complexion, favours casual dress – jeans, tee-shirts, trainers. Home address: 18 Tower End, off Steelhouse Lane, Wolverhampton. Thought to be in possession of a white Vauxhall Astra, Reg. No. M676 HXT, which may be used with false registration plates, and may be touring the country. Is known to favour mountainous districts and remote areas for relaxation. Was recently released on licence following a sentence of life imprisonment upon conviction for murder in 1983. MAY BE ARMED AND DANGEROUS. IF SEEN, DO NOT STOP OR INTERROGATE BUT RECORD DATE, TIME AND PLACE SEEN.'

The message terminated with a note to immediately inform Detective Superintendent Pemberton in the Roberthorpe Incident Room, or anyone who had attended the York meeting. Their personal contact numbers were provided. Once this action had been determined, Pemberton and his colleagues dispersed and each went their separate ways, all thanking Ian McKay for his valuable help. The remaining six top-priority suspects would be visited as soon as possible by officers of the police forces in whose areas they lived; they had to be eliminated from the enquiry and that action had already been instigated.

It was with some elation, therefore, that Detective Superintendent Mark Pemberton drove out of York and made for Roberthorpe. The meeting had been valuable because it had thrown up the name of a suspect, a man who, in his view, seemed eminently capable of committing such crimes. Now, though, the hunt was on.

If Steele was touring the country, the officers of the British police service would trace him. But even as Mark Pemberton was quietly congratulating himself on this unexpected development, he did experience a tremor of uncertainty – knowing of the killer's apparent motive, how many more people would die before he was caught? Would it require another death to trap him? And suppose Steele was not the sniper? He could not lose sight of the possibility that the killer was some other person, someone as yet unsuspected and free to continue. There was always a possibility that too much effort and too many resources were being concentrated upon a single suspect. That was something he must consider when he returned to the office – and he would make sure the other six on Ian McKay's first list were traced and interviewed.

For the Sniper, alias Michael James Steele, the speedy

drive down the M6 from the Lake District was exhilarating, even if he did keep a wary eye open for signs of a police presence. Not that they would have found anything illegal with him or his vehicle – if he had been stopped it was a hire car anyway, a small white Astra very similar to his own – and he was not breaching his parole conditions. He'd been away for a weekend, that's all, looking for work. Who could refute that? It was true that granny thought he'd gone to Wales but his parole supervisor had not imposed such rigid conditions – a weekend away, seeking work, was always praiseworthy.

During this short break, however, he'd had time to finalise the preparations for his next mission.

Out of his eighteen candidates – one for every year he'd been wrongfully gaoled – he had dispensed with only three so far. There were fifteen left. Out of those, John Whittington seemed a very worthy candidate – he'd been charged with murdering his wife and although his past life, along with his mistresses, bad business dealings, allegations of fraud and insurance dishonesty, had been taken into account at his trial to counter his claims of being an honest man, the judge said there was no evidence he had killed her. He did accept she was dead, however, but His Lordship had quoted several other 'no body' murder trials, and had stressed the importance of *proving* the accused had killed his wife. According to the judge, that had not been done to the satisfaction of the court and he directed the jury to return a verdict of not guilty. And so John Whittington had got away with murder – and collected a fortune from his deceased wife's investments and property. It was time for Whittington to face justice, considered the Sniper.

As he approached Junction 11 for its link with the A460, he experienced a certain jubilation. With this particular demonstration of true justice, he would bring to the public's attention the work he had undertaken in the past. It would be done anonymously of course, and with great care, for he had no intention of allowing his quest to be halted prematurely. So it was now Whittington's turn, although the final preparations had yet to be made.

Placing a panama on his head, he drove to the car hire company, returned his vehicle and allowed it to be inspected for damage.

The assistant said, 'I hope we can be of service to you again, Mr Crowther?'

'Of course,' he smiled as he assumed a very realistic Scots accent. That was because the driving licence he had produced, in a certain Alec Crowther's name, had shown a Perth address. 'I'm sure my work will bring me back again. Good day to you.'

With his belongings in a haversack, he took a bus into the city centre, to a lock-up garage he had rented for a few days. Leaving the panama and a pale blue blazer in the garage, he donned a navy-blue fleece and he retrieved his own Vauxhall Astra. Moments later, he was driving through the town centre towards his grandmother's house. He arrived within a couple of hours of the visit by Detective Sergeant Temple and his men, rattled the doorknocker, opened the door and shouted, 'Hi, gran, it's me. Mike. I'm back early!'

She shouted a response from the kitchen and he went through to her, gave her a massive hug, said he'd missed her and sighed that it was so lovely to be back.

'Any luck?' she asked.

'Not a thing. I thought I was in with a chance, a really good job driving continental touring buses, but no, it went to somebody the boss knows well. Mind, I don't think my record helped! I was honest about it . . . still, it was a nice outing . . .'

'Well, better luck next time, Mike. Now come and sit

down, the kettle is on, it's always on, and I've made some scones.'

She led him into the tiny lounge. 'Sit down, I'll get your scone and tea. Now, before I forget, some men came to see you, only a couple of hours ago.'

'Men?' he obeyed as his face showed his deep concern. 'Who were they?'

'Policemen, detectives,' she said. 'Two of them, in a car. And two more went round the back, I saw them.'

'Looking for me? Are you sure?'

'One of them showed me his warrant card,' she said. 'They were policemen, Mike, I'd know them anywhere, it was a real card.'

'What did they want?'

'They didn't say. They just said they wanted a chat with you, and were you in. I said no, you'd gone to Wales and so they looked around the house, in your room and in the loft.'

'Searched the house? And the loft? What for?'

'They thought you might be hiding there . . .'

'Hiding? Why would I want to hide? I've done nothing, gran . . .'

'I said you hadn't but then they said would I ring them, at Wolverhampton office, when you got back.'

'And you said no?'

'I said no, I saw no reason why I should when you'd done nothing and you were doing your best to make a new life with your music, looking for work and that.'

'Then what did they do?

'Well, they left, they said they'd be back when you got home, just for a friendly chat.'

'Did they take anything?'

'Not that I know of.'

'I've got to move the car!' he snapped, jumping to his feet. 'Sorry, gran, the tea will have to wait. Love you,' and he kissed her on the forehead then made for the front door. Even before he emerged, he looked left and right, checked directly across at the other houses, then hurried out to his car. Moments later he was driving along the street, making for another lock-up garage; the car would be hidden there, out of sight and he'd paid a year's rent in advance, in cash . . .

Ten minutes later, after checking that he was not shadowed, he was in the security of his garage. Still inside, he lowered the door and then, from a locked toolbox on a high shelf, took out a dark brown wig. He placed it over his thin fair hair, checked for correctness in the wing mirror of his car, put on a pair of spectacles with plain lenses, and then walked out. He caught a bus at the end of the road and this took him to the other side of Wolverhampton, to a large house overlooking West Park. This had been turned into a block of flats and he rented one. No-one knew about this, not even his granny; the parole board did not know, and, he was sure, neither did the police.

But this was his very own, his real home. This was where he came sometimes when his granny thought he was looking for work or going to gigs. A secret place, a haven for him. Minutes later he was inside; sparsely furnished, it was comfortable and his first job was to visit the loft – with great relief, he saw the Kalashnikov was still there, under the floor boards. He'd dispensed with the guitar case, it had gone into a skip at the edge of a building site. Had it been a mistake to use it in Brixton?

You'd never expect the police to trace him all that way? No, of course not, he'd used a different case anyway, one of several he had hidden away . . . and a different disguise . . . Even so, it did seem things had changed. Why had they come to granny's house? No wonder the police had been quiet . . . they'd been checking on him. But how did they know about his work? Had they been checking all murderers who'd been released recently? But whatever they knew, they would never catch him. As he came to realise they must know something of his movements and activities, he felt the beginning of a new challenge, rather like coming face to face with the enemy, seeing the whites of their eyes. But they could never look ahead, they could never forecast what he had in mind. Who he had in mind.

But that knowledge meant he could take steps to avoid them as he went about his mission to deal with Mr Whittington. It was easy enough, keeping out of their way. And he could always shoot a policeman or two if it meant the difference between capture and freedom! Tomorrow, with his dark wig in place, he would go to the library and then he would clean and oil his rifle.

A policewoman in the Control Room at Wolverhampton attracted the attention of her boss, Inspector Garrard.

'Sir,' she pointed to a frame she had frozen on one of the town's security cameras. 'That white Vauxhall, on the nearside at those traffic lights. It's got the same number as Steele's, the man we're all looking for.'

'Brilliant, Gillian, good work. So he's back in town, eh? I'll ring CID.'

Chapter Thirteen

The instant Detective Superintendent Deakin learned of Steele's return, he alerted Temple and Russell. The two teams raced to Granny Steele's house but they were too late.

'He's gone,' she told them with more than a hint of pride. 'I said you just wanted a chat but he said nothing and drove off. He never said where he was going or when he'd be back. I've no idea where he's gone so don't ask.'

They quizzed her as best they could but apart from giving the approximate time of his return, she was unable or unwilling to provide any further help. The visit did establish, however, that the sighting of Steele's car at the traffic lights had occurred shortly before his return to his grandmother's. It was evident he'd been on his way to her house at that point – and now he'd vanished among the traffic and populace of Wolverhampton.

Using his mobile, Temple rang Deakin. Deakin told him to leave one crew outside Granny Steele's house just in case he returned; Deakin would order the Control Room to alert every patrolling officer in and around Wolverhampton – reminding them to report sightings only, and not to stop or speak to Steele under any circumstances. In addition, they had to search every car park and every street for his white Vauxhall, the registration number of which was supplied. If Steele was in town, he would be found; of that, Deakin was confident.

Deakin also established that there were no other reported sightings of Steele in other parts of the country and so, at the moment, there was no indication where he'd been.

The direction from which he had returned to town did not provide any hint – he could have reached those traffic lights from any one of several incoming routes. Deakin then rang Pemberton and his tone was apologetic.

'Sorry, Mark, we've lost him!' and he explained the circumstances.

'You think he's still in town, though?' Pemberton did not wish to engage in a long conversation or reprisals while driving, so he pulled into a convenient lay-by to continue the discussion. Deakin went on, 'I've got our staff monitoring all traffic cameras and all security cameras on the routes out of Wolverhampton, his number's been logged so if his car goes through one of them the computers will signify so and we'll know.'

'He knows we're especially interested in him?' was Pemberton's reaction as he switched off the engine. 'He knew it wasn't a routine visit?'

'So it would seem,' agreed Deakin with the apology clear in his voice. 'He's sharp enough to recognise the signs.'

'And the fact he's disappeared rather than face the police is an indication of his guilt, you think?'

'I'm sure of it,' Deakin agreed. 'He's either gone to ground, Mark, or he's on the run.'

'Or he's gone to execute another victim! You've not found the Kalashnikov?'

'No, it wasn't there when we searched, but we'll cover the place twenty-four hours a day from now onwards. If the gun is there, he won't get his hands on it without us knowing – and if he does come back for it, we'll be waiting.'

'But if the gun's not there?' asked Pemberton. 'If he's already got it with him?'

'He could have hidden it somewhere else, and that means he's capable of retrieving it and using it,' said Deakin.

'Where can you hide a thing like that, Jim? I reckon he has it with him right now, right this minute, wherever he is, and he intends to use it. The fact he thinks we're on to him makes him even more dangerous, he'll take more steps to conceal himself. He'll have hidden his car too, we can't waste time looking for that. He'll realise it's known to your officers. You say it's his own? You've details of it?'

'Right, he owns it, and we have details on file.'

'Even if it's concealed, your teams might come across it? A search of every likely place in town is not a bad idea. You know what to do if you find it – secure it for our forensic wizards. My view, Jim, is that we're looking for him, rather than his car. He'll have abandoned his car. So any ideas for tracking him to his lair?' asked Pemberton.

'Sadly, no. He might have found another bolt-hole, or had one planned. He does spend time away from his gran's, as you know, so he might have some hiding place we don't know about. We'll sweep the town but so far as our records are concerned, his only address is his granny's house. I'll get our teams to put pressure on the local villains, someone might know what he's up to. We'll scour the car parks and streets for the car, but since his release, he's not established any kind of routine or close relationships, no regular pubs or clubs, no girl friends or male pals. He's been a loner, very much so.'

'A deliberate ploy, perhaps?'

'If he's been planning all this while he was inside, yes it could be quite deliberate. And since coming out, he's behaved himself, according to our books, no heavy drinking, no petty theft, no trouble of any kind, and that means we've not had any close interest in him, apart from the fact he is on licence – until you rang, that is.'

'I know you've a manpower shortage like the rest of us, so what can you do for us, Jim? By the way of searching for him in town?'

'We've more than a quarter of a million residents as well as a large transitional population who come into the city every day for work. Finding Steele among that lot will be like looking for the proverbial needle in a haystack.'

'But you'll try?'

'We'll try,' confirmed Deakin. 'Didn't you say he's likely to disguise himself?'

'It seems likely, especially if he's on the run. I'll keep broadcasting our appeal for sightings nationwide,' Pemberton said. 'If he has slipped through our first net, we might still find him. He can't vanish into thin air.'

'Rest assured that if our officers do come across him, Mark, we'll lift him and he'll be given lodgings in our cells but if he has given us the slip, he might be anywhere, he could be miles away from Wolverhampton in fact. There's hire cars, trains, buses . . .'

'Let's hope our colleagues on the roads and in the towns are alert,' Pemberton said. 'Now, I need advice. Should I warn all his potential victims?'

'How can you do that? You don't know for sure he's going to kill anyone else, do you?' said Deakin. 'He's never said so. And if that is his intention, you don't know who that person might be. I can't see you can do much by way of issuing warnings, not without alarming the whole country. And we don't want nationwide panic, we can't guard every potential victim.'

'He's never said he *won't* kill anyone else either!' retorted Pemberton. 'At the moment, he seems to be taking out killers who've escaped justice, but there's no other pattern, no discernible routine, no chronological order, no sequence of names. To some extent, it looks as if they've been picked at random but he must have some source of information. How does he pick his victims?'

'There've been only three killings!' said Deakin who qualified that remark by adding, 'Well, three to our knowledge. So how many others are we talking about? How many people are living free in this country after escaping justice having killing someone? It's not the sort of statistic you'll easily find in any official record.'

'That's the problem I'm faced with, Jim. I'd like to warn all those people that there seems to be a killer at large who's intent on despatching those he considers to have evaded justice. I'd like to ask them to be very careful in what they do and where they go, and to tell us if they think they're being stalked, but how do I do that without creating panic among the entire public?'

'If the press published the link between these crimes, Mark, that would do the job for you. There's no better way of alerting the public than a big splash in the newspapers and on television. Anyone who's got away with murder will then start to look over his or her shoulder. But the way the press would treat it would create a panic – they'd whip up hysteria in no time, and we don't want that!'

'I've been resisting that kind of publicity for that very reason. I've just come from a meeting where we've decided not to associate the three deaths with each other, not in the public eye, not to mention the kind of weapon and not to reveal that all the deceased are killers who've avoided justice. Apart from the panic angle, another reason is we want to catch the sniper without revealing how much we know about him. We don't want him destroying evidence, like throwing his Kalashnikov into the sea.'

'He might not be planning any more crimes, Mark, that's an important consideration. He might have finished his campaign so you mustn't start a panic when it's unnecessary. If he thinks we're getting close to him, it might persuade him to stop.'

'Or it might make him more determined to beat us, or kill more, but point taken, Jim. Thanks. I'll leave things as they are until there's more evidence that he is on some kind of major quest.'

'I'll agree with that. In the meantime, we'll turn over every stone and every villain in Wolverhampton in our efforts to find him.'

'Thanks, if you need help with extra men, let me know.'

'I'm sure we can manage. I'm sure we'll make good use of our underworld connections; if they're hiding him we'll flush him out, and if they're not hiding him, we'll make them want to find him for us.'

'And his granny's place will be subjected to surveillance?'

'If we can't spare the troops, we'll use electronic methods. It's a condition of his licence that he has to live at his granny's place; if he moves to another permanent home, he's got to inform the authorities – and that means us. Even if he's bolted from town, by train or whatever, he's got to surface sometime, Mark. I'm sure any absence will be a temporary one. If he's innocent of your crimes, he will return, won't he? He won't want to breach the conditions of his licence because that will put him right back inside. And, thanks to cameras and computers, his car can't move in this town without us knowing. I know we can't guarantee to find him, especially if he's trying to avoid us, but we'll do our best, I promise you that. I'll keep in touch.'

'Thanks, Jim.'

'Sorry we lost him.'

'It happens,' and Pemberton switched off his mobile. He continued his drive, expecting to be back in the Incident Room within the hour. During the journey, he found his mind turning to ways in which the Sniper might find information about those who had apparently escaped justice. In the absence of any official record, the simplest way would be by reading newspapers, either live or on the Internet. It was easy for a fanatic to buy daily papers and retain cuttings of subjects they found interesting; it was a simple matter to assemble a file on almost any topic. The fact that some of the Sniper's victims had made their court appearances more than twelve years ago was hardly likely to have been published recently.

It would, however, have been published at the time of the trial and Pemberton began to feel that the Sniper had access to lots of back copies of national newspapers. Back copies can be found in many reference libraries, all stored in chronological order and, in some cases, with key subjects indexed for easy access. He stopped his car at the first available place and rang Wolverhampton again, asking for Deakin.

'Jim, Pemberton again, sorry to nag you, I've had a thought. Libraries. I think chummy might be getting his information from public libraries. Scanning the papers either by reading them or using key words on the Internet, or even using files the library staff have compiled for reference. I wondered if your men might visit your library, to ask if Steele, in disguise or not, has been using their sources? It's something they might know, if he's been a regular user.'

'Great idea, yes, I'll get Temple to send a team around there. Thanks for that – it's a good starting point, better than trudging around the streets and flesh-pots! Leave it with me, Mark.'

Pemberton returned to Roberthorpe and Paul Larkin told him nothing significant had happened during his absence whereas he was delighted to inform Paul about the identity of the No. 1 suspect, the new information of his whereabouts and his idea concerning libraries.

Then he asked, 'Paul, can you get a team to visit the

local library to see if Flint's name has cropped up for any reason? And an alert library assistant might know if a stranger has been in, checking old newspaper files.'

'With modern computer systems, it's very easy to access information, sir, but yes, we'll give it a thorough check.'

The late afternoon news conference was low key, with Pemberton saying nothing positive had emerged. There was nothing with which the reports could fill their pages. Pemberton found this very desirable; with nothing being reported, the killer might react . . . .

Steele, with his long dark-haired wig, had examined the early edition of the evening paper and had listened to the news on local and national radio, but there was no reference to his activities. After the snippet about Leroy Campbell, there had been nothing in the local editions of the national dailies and had it not been for the visit of those police officers to his grandmother's home, he would have ensured the media knew about his work. He'd have told them . . . but now, things had changed. It was evident the police did know about his endeavours, they were not publicising their knowledge, they were being astute and devious and he knew what it meant when they said they wanted a chat! A chat! It would be an interrogation, subtle at first and increasingly more intense. He wanted none of that, he couldn't risk arrest because he had work to complete. And why did they think he was in hiding?

His time in the library had been beneficial and he was now back at home – his real home, not granny's – with the information necessary to find John Whittington. That was a task he'd begin tomorrow. Tonight, he must pack some clothes, make sure his rifle was in perfect condition.

Then he would ring his granny to say he was going to

213

Manchester to look for a driving job after doing a gig in Chester.

At the same time, Detective Sergeant Patrick Temple and his team colleague, Detective Constable John Skinner, were in Wolverhampton Library speaking to the head librarian. She had suggested they speak to Gillian Askwith who dealt with requests for access to old records, newspapers and those reference books which were not allowed out of the building. Gillian, a pretty dark-haired woman in her early thirties, said she remembered a man coming in to request access to the newspaper records, all of which were now on micro-fiche, and she had shown him how to search for the paper in question and to operate the viewing machine. He was in his forties, she estimated, a well-spoken man with thick black hair and squarish spectacles. He was well dressed in a dark jacket, grey trousers and black shoes and said he wanted to look through a selection of national papers for the latter part of 1993. He did not tell her what he was seeking, but did have a shorthand notebook, or perhaps a reporter's notebook in his hand. She left him to his researches and he departed after about an hour and a half, thanking her. She did not know his name or whether he came from the city; those kind of details were not requested when making this kind of search.

'Can we look through the same papers?' Temple then asked.

'Yes, of course. Is there a particular subject?' she smiled.

'Trials for murder,' he said. 'Especially those with not guilty verdicts.'

'Oh, well, we do keep a separate file on those, they're sometimes requested by people doing degrees or doc-torates in criminology and associated subjects. We had a

214

man in about a fortnight ago, he went through the files, the same 1993 ones, he said he was compiling a book of cases where the police had made false accusations and he needed that kind of information. And he's been back a few times, this afternoon in fact, to check on something.'

'Really? What was he like? Can you remember anything about him?'

'Not a lot, but he was about forty, medium height I suppose, with short dark hair. That's about all I can remember. He's been here before, he was here a long time, checking lots of newspaper files.'

'Is he a regular visitor?' was Temple's next question.

'We've had several people in lately,' she smiled. 'Men, doing research. On and off for the past few weeks.'

'Really? How many?' he asked.

'Oh, I don't know. Five or six, thereabouts, but not all the same day but I have noticed there's been a lot of interest in not guilty findings recently.'

'Now that is important, but tell me, could some of those visitors have been one man, dressed differently, with a different hair-style or appearance?'

She looked puzzled at this suggestion and shook her head. 'Oh, I don't know about that. I mean, I never took a great lot of notice but why would a man bother to dress up or disguise himself when he was just coming to look up some information?'

'That's a very good question,' smiled Temple. 'But what about their height and build? Voice perhaps?'

'Well, yes, now you come to mention it, it might have been the same man . . . they were all about the same age and height, same build, similar voice . . . oh dear, have I been tricked into something silly?'

'We can't be sure, but would you think the man who came in today might have been one of those who came recently?'

215

She reflected for a few moments, then nodded, 'Yes, I think so . . . oh dear, I wonder what he was doing.'

'He might have been doing what we are going to do. You said he'd asked for 1993 newspapers?'

'Yes, they all asked for that year, well, most of them did.'

'We're going to check through those same papers for a murder where the suspect was acquitted in court . . .'

And so they settled down at two machines, each scanning the text which was reproduced on their screens, prepared to work into the evening if necessary – the library closed at eight they noted – and then, after an hour's search, Temple found something.

'John,' he called to his colleague. 'Come and look at this.'

It was a report about a murder trial at York Crown Court where a man called John Whittington had been acquitted of murdering his wife; although the prosecution evidence seemed very conclusive, her body had never been found.

The judge did say that he accepted the fact that Mrs Whittington was dead, but the prosecution had not proved, to the satisfaction of the court, that she had been murdered. As a consequence, John Whittington was acquitted and there was a public outcry from his wife's friends, family and neighbours.

'The case was sent up there from Derbyshire,' Temple said. 'Whittington lived in the county, not far from Buxton.'

'You reckon he could be the next victim of this man?' asked Skinner.

'It's a fair possibility, we'd better check to see if there were any more similar acquittals that year. Make photocopies of these articles, John, and if nothing else turns up, we'll give that Yorkshire detective a ring. Pemberton, wasn't it?'

'Right, Sarge.'

And so, for Pemberton and his teams, the day was drawing to a close with no overt sign of increased activity in Roberthorpe, but in Wolverhampton the oncoming shifts of detectives and plain-clothes officers were being briefed about the search for Michael James Steele. Then the phone rang and the caller asked for Pemberton.

'It's Detective Sergeant Temple in Wolverhampton, sir, I think we've found the name of the Sniper's next victim.'

He explained his reasoning and Pemberton listened, then said, 'Great work, Sergeant! Brilliant in fact. Derbyshire, eh? Right, then we've got to find Whittington before the Sniper does.'

The Sniper had already found John Whittington.

Chapter Fourteen

Without wasting a second, Pemberton rang Derbyshire Police Headquarters and asked for Detective Superintendent MacLaren, but was told he'd left the office at six. If the matter was urgent, another officer currently on duty could deal with it; if it wasn't then perhaps Mr Pemberton would call tomorrow? When Pemberton asked for MacLaren's home number, the duty officer refused, saying the private numbers of police officers could not be given over the telephone and if the matter was very urgent, the duty officer would cope. Mr MacLaren was off duty, he was informed. Pemberton then ordered the detective to give his name to MacLaren with the necessary compliments, to do so immediately, and to ask Detective Superintendent MacLaren to ring Pemberton at the Roberthorpe Incident Room as a matter of extreme urgency.

'This is a murder case we're involved in,' Pemberton snapped. 'And if you don't do as I say, you'll have a murder on your patch very soon . . . now get moving, constable! And that's an order! If you frustrate my calls any longer, you'll have to answer to your chief constable.'

The return call came within five minutes.

'Thanks for ringing, Mac,' Pemberton and Hamish MacLaren had known each other for years, and Pemberton explained the reason for his call. MacLaren listened and when Pemberton referred to the case which had involved John Whittington, he recalled the details.

'I remember it well,' he told Pemberton. 'We never found Mrs Whittington's body. Her husband did it, we were sure of that but we could never prove it. He was clever, evil too and even charming but the Crown Court judge said we hadn't proved murder. Whittington was acquitted. What can we do about it? Nothing!'

Pemberton gave the necessary details of the three murders known to be part of the current series and said, 'We're sure Whittington is next,' and then gave his reasons. MacLaren agreed with his logic.

'We've lost touch with him,' MacLaren said. 'After the case he returned to his family home near Buxton, but there was such feeling against him, especially from his neighbours and acquaintances, that he moved house. That would be a year or so after the trial. He was near retiring age during the trial but no-one wanted to work with him after the case, due to his notoriety. Although he is a very unsavoury character with a very dodgy financial background, he wasn't wanted or suspected of any other criminal offence, so we had no reason to keep tabs on him. He'd been a civil engineer, a good one we believe, but after all the fuss he went to live in Derby. I think he had a daughter there, one who believed in his innocence. We thought he'd buried his wife under a new road or bridge somewhere, we did a few checks to see what he'd been working on but you can't go digging up miles of motorway or demolishing every bridge in the off-chance of finding a corpse. We'll leave that to the archaeologists of the future. Anyway, he thought he could become anonymous in the city, lose himself in suburbia or something. We lost touch at that point, it was all over so far as we were concerned.'

'And he's kept out of bother since?'

'So far as I know, there's not been a whimper from him. After killing his wife, his own life seemed to come to a full stop. Maybe he had a reason for disposing of her, she might have driven him to it and he did blame her for his bad financial state. We'll never know the full story. Anyway, Mark, he's not come to our notice since that case and to be honest, I'm not sure whether he's alive or dead.'

'Wherever he is, he needs to be found, Mac, and warned of this threat – protected even. We need to set up some kind of surveillance so that if and when the Sniper makes his approach, we can catch him before he gets to Whittington.'

'Right, leave it with me. I'll get our local lads to trace Whittington, it might not take long, we can start with the electoral register, it's all on computer now. Give me time to ring Derby CID, I'm stationed at Headquarters these days, not in town. If he is at risk as you say, we'll set up a system of personal protection. We'll need your advice . . .'

'The Sniper uses a Kalashnikov,' Pemberton interrupted. 'That's what you'll need to be protected from! He's a skilled gunman, Hamish. Remind your teams about that, we don't want any police casualties.'

'Understood! You are talking serious business. Let me start things moving. How long will you be in your Incident Room?'

'I'll stay here until I get your call,' said Pemberton. 'Hopefully, the bonus for me is that if we can find John Whittington, the chances are that Steele won't be far away.'

'Right. I'll do it now,' and so began the urgent task to find both victim and potential killer.

With so very little activity in the incident room, Mark Pemberton felt frustrated as the enquiry seemed to be extending its boundaries into areas over which he had no jurisdiction or control. Now, the focus had moved to Derbyshire and, in addition, he had to await the outcome of the searches in Wolverhampton. There was nothing he could do to intensify those enquiries. If only he could have driven down there to make his own search for Whittington, if only he could have had the time to knock on doors to find out where he was, to warn him . . . to meet him, to decide whether he was in truth a killer or whether his wife had merely run off. He'd like to persuade him to go away or even to act as live bait for a sophisticated police operation designed to trap the killer – but everything now rested in the hands of police forces other than his own, with officers not under his command. He wondered if the press might help now – after all, the situation had suddenly changed with the appearance – and rapid disappearance – of Michael Steele in Wolverhampton so should Pemberton have involved the recently created National Crime Squad? Before he could seriously consider that option, the telephone rang.

Larkin answered it, pressed the secrecy switch, then said, 'It's for you, boss. A man called Hammond, Austin Hammond, he said. A freelance reporter. From London.'

'What's he want?'

'He insists on talking to you, he says it's about the Kenneth Flint case.'

'OK, I'll take it in my office,' and he went through, leaving the door open. 'Pemberton,' he said as he lifted the receiver.

'Ah, good evening, Superintendent,' said a smooth voice with a strong southern accent. 'My name is Hammond, Austin Hammond, I'm a freelance reporter specialising in crime features for the national dailies.'

'You've not been to our news conferences?'

'To be frank with you, the death of a rather insignificant church clock-winder in a tiny Yorkshire village is not, in itself, the sort of material that interests me, or my editors or readers. There needs to be another dimension before I am propelled into action,' returned the voice.

'Besides, Yorkshire is a long way from my office. The truth is, Mr Pemberton, that I seek bigger stories. Stories with more beef, stories with more impact on the public, big stories, stories that make headlines . . .'

'So why are you ringing me?' was Pemberton's obvious question.

'I have contacts all over the country, Mr Pemberton, as any good journalist should have – top class contacts whose information is reliable – and I am given to believe there are links between the murder of Leroy Campbell in south London and your Kenneth Flint, and indeed a man called Abrahams on Tyneside . . .'

'What sort of links?' Pemberton wondered where this man could have obtained his information. From someone in the forensic services, perhaps? Or a detective who might recognise ways of obtaining a backhander for information?

'The weapon, Mr Pemberton. My sources indicate the murder weapon was a Kalashnikov AK47 – quite an effective military rifle if I am not mistaken, Mr Pemberton, and something regularly found in the hands of terrorists. I am led to believe the same weapon was used for each murder even though they were in different parts of the country.'

'Your informant has that kind of knowledge?'

'Indeed, and it does seem to me that we have a serial killer on the loose, Mr Pemberton, a man of rather special skills.'

'You are very well informed.'

'That is my forte, Mr Pemberton. And I do happen to know that Abrahams was a known villain, a man who had killed but who was not found guilty, as was Leroy Campbell. At this stage I am still checking the background of your Mr Flint and my preliminary information suggests the same might apply. All this does suggest that I have a big story on my hands. One which has been kept under wraps, if I may say so. I find that surprising, given the dreadful, cold-blooded nature of the killer's tactics. It is surely something about which the British public should be warned.'

'When's your deadline?' Pemberton put to him.

'Midnight – although I can tell you that my story has already been written. In draft, I might add. I am now seeking confirmation of some facts. I do like my work to reflect my care and attention to detail, Mr Pemberton.'

'I would like to know your sources, Mr Hammond.'

'I am sure you would but you know how it is, we cannot divulge our sources, that is a very old and well-respected tradition. But my sources are good and reliable, Mr Pemberton. I think you realise that.'

'I need to make a few telephone calls. Can you call back?'

'Of course,' came the smooth voice. 'In, say, half an hour?'

'That'll do for starters,' returned Pemberton.

'I do have the information I need, or perhaps I should say I have most of it,' said Hammond. 'Remember it is chiefly confirmation I am seeking.'

'I'll remember,' and Pemberton put down the phone.

Judging from what the man had said, and noting his accent, it did seem as if the information had come from the Metropolitan Police or perhaps a member of staff in the Met's Forensic Service or even in one of the provincial forensic laboratories. Or, of course, it could have emanated from one of the many detectives engaged on this enquiry – trying to make such a widespread enquiry totally secure was virtually impossible. Pemberton realised he had been somewhat fortunate to keep the tale away from journalistic noses but now, bearing in mind the developments in Wolverhampton and Derbyshire, Pemberton felt he could make use of some positive publicity. If the public had to be made aware of the danger from Steele, there was no better way to effect a warning than a splash on TV and in the newspapers, even if it did generate some kind of panic. Anything published by Hammond would not reach the papers until tomorrow morning anyway, and he felt he could turn this situation to his advantage – and to the advantage of his colleagues elsewhere.

He first rang Ted Edwards. Like Pemberton, he was at work in his incident room. After listening to Pemberton's account of recent developments, and his update on the whereabouts of Steele in Wolverhampton, he agreed that publicity could now become a very useful tool – and he knew Austin Hammond.

'If Hammond has information that a Kalashnikov has been used, he'll have more confidential stuff up his sleeve,' said Edwards. 'He does have some remarkable contacts, Mark, he's always getting good inside information. We can't ignore him, he'll print what he's got anyway, but he does like to check with authoritative sources. Tell him to contact our press office, I'll authorise some kind of release in time for his deadline. I suggest we don't mention oranges!'

'Right,' and so Pemberton then rang Jack Radcliffe in Northumberland who was also on duty in his Incident Room. After hearing Pemberton's reasoning, he agreed that publicity could now be a useful aid to tracing Steele, particularly as he had been made aware of the police interest in his activities. It could help flush him out, it could put him under a new type of pressure. The fact he had fled from his granny's house in Wolverhampton was an indication of his guilt and if he wanted to get rid of his guns he would now do so in the knowledge the police were hunting him. Radcliffe felt that the publicity would not now endanger the investigation and it might help to trace Steele or even save the life of John Whittington. And finally, as a courtesy, Pemberton rang Ian McKay to let him know of this development; his part in the enquiry, however, would not be publicised. Pemberton was now confident he could deal with Hammond when he rang.

But Hamish MacLaren from Derby called first. 'Our lads have swept the computerised electoral register, Mark, and John Whittington did live in Derby, in a cul-de-sac off Arthur Street. His name is still there, it's his daughter's house really. She's not married hence the same name, she's a school teacher, a geography mistress, and she lives near the Children's Hospital. We've been to see her. John lived with her until a few months ago when he became increasingly sick, he needed care, she said, and he volunteered to go into a home, temporarily at first, to give her a break. It's now become a permanent residency. He's in a wheelchair and an added problem is that he's been diagnosed as having Alzheimer's disease, in its early stages. There's no cure, of course, and already he needs constant nursing.'

'So he's alive? Where's this home?'

'You're going to enjoy this, Mark. It's in Rainesbury, a seaside home called Sandside. Whittington always liked Rainesbury, he went there on his holidays as a youngster and fell in love with the place. He always said he wanted to die there.'

'That might well happen sooner than he thought!'

'His daughter, Juliet's the name, believes in his innocence, I told you that, and she goes up there every fortnight, takes B and B in the town and spends time with her dad. So he's in Sandside, Mark, on your patch! Over to you with this one!'

'Thanks a bunch!' said Pemberton.

'We did enquire whether anyone has been asking after him in recent weeks and she did receive a phone call asking for her dad. It was only a couple of days ago, she thinks, and it came from a man she didn't know. He said he was a former colleague of John's, trying to track him down for a visit. He said his name was Crompton, George Crompton, but it meant nothing to Juliet

225

Whittington. She told Crompton where her dad was staying and he thanked her, saying he'd get in touch with the nursing home.'

'Right, thanks,' Pemberton sighed. 'It looks as if we've got to get moving fast . . . thanks, Hamish.'

'Don't mention it. I'm just glad it's not my problem.'

Tempted though he was to rush off to Rainesbury, Pemberton did sit and await the return call from Austin Hammond; after all, it was of great importance to the enquiry and he was relieved when it came less than five minutes later.

'You've spoken to your colleagues, Mr Pemberton? Does that indicate that the relevant police forces are cooperating in this enquiry?'

'They are, and I might say their co-operation has been of the highest standard right from the beginning.'

'It makes a change from destructive inter-force politics. So, Mr Pemberton, this is what I have learned about your case. Kenneth Flint was shot dead in the porch of the village church, he was a regular churchgoer and churchworker, a rather quiet and insignificant person by all accounts. A suspect has been seen – a dark haired man in a motorhome of some kind. You did publicise that. Has he been traced, Mr Pemberton? Or the motorhome?'

'Neither of them, not yet; we have traced one which we believe to be identical but we are exploring various other avenues, our enquiries are at a critical stage at this moment, Mr Hammond.'

'Are they? So is an arrest imminent?'

'It is very possible,' smiled Pemberton. 'I don't wish to say more than that.'

'Then you are ahead of me, Mr Pemberton, and I congratulate you. I just hope your arrest, when it occurs, does not prevent publication of my material. Now, back to the late Mr Flint. He died from gunshot wounds and I believe the weapon has been identified as a Kalashnikov AK47?'

'Yes, I can confirm that.'

'And I believe the same weapon has been used for the other killings?'

'You'll have to talk to the respective police forces about that, I cannot comment on their findings.'

'Oh, come on Mr Pemberton, you and I both know the same gun was used, that's the whole point of this enquiry . . .'

'I can't comment on events within other force areas,' he reiterated. 'I'm not being obstructive, it's a fact of life, inter-force politics as you call it. You know the situation! All I can say is that Northumberland and the London Metropolitan Police are directly involved in this enquiry due to certain similarities in the commission of the crimes.'

'Fair enough. I'll check with them. Now, another point has arisen. My own researches tell me that the victims have all faced trial for murder, and been found not guilty for various reasons. Even your Mr Flint, Super-intendent. As I said, I do have some knowledge of him and I need your confirmation. I know his real name is not Flint, it is, or was, Kenneth Bourne. He was a paedo-phile found not guilty of killing one little girl and sus-pected of abducting and killing another, under his real name.'

'I can confirm the latter, we do know that Flint changed his name but you'll have to contact the other forces for information about their victims,' Pemberton said.

'Thanks for that, I'll ring the others. But I must raise the point, Mr Pemberton, which I'm sure you have considered, that here we might have a vigilante-type person, a killer with a Kalashnikov – and there's a nice alliterative headline – someone dispensing his – or her – own brand of justice. Have you considered this? Let's face it, if only one freed killer had been executed, we might have suspected revenge by family or friends, but a galaxy of victims across the countryside with no known connection except their murderous past does suggest someone with a deep and dangerous grudge against the judicial system.'

'Hardly a galaxy of victims, Mr Hammond. Three to be precise.'

'Three that you know about,' was the response.

'You know of others?'

'No, I must admit I do not. But this is a huge national story, Mr Pemberton, and I am sure you will appreciate that once this tale hits the headlines, other newshounds, far worse than I, will take up the story and they will ask why he hasn't been caught, what are the police doing about it . . . you know the sort of stuff. I shall not dwell on that.'

'I do know how the story might be treated, but we police officers have broad shoulders. We're used to criticism, Mr Hammond, from whatever direction it comes, and no matter how high the headline letters. But if you want a quote for this piece, you can say "the police are examining a wide range of options and hope to make an arrest very soon."'

'Not too soon, or I can't publish my articles!' and Hammond laughed. 'But are you serious, you have a suspect in mind?'

'We have, and we are actively searching for him at this moment but cannot release details at this stage. If you want to quote me, say that a person is being actively sought throughout England and Wales for the murder of Kenneth Flint, alias Bourne. When he is arrested, I expect he will be questioned about the murders of Steven Abrahams and Leroy Campbell. How about that? Any good for you?'

'It sounds very positive.'

'It is very positive,' said Pemberton deliberately.

'And is that your only suspect, might I ask?'

'My mind is open at this point,' Pemberton produced the well-tried response but added his own subterfuge. 'I must stress the man is only a suspect, perhaps he's little more than a witness – I believe he is the man seen with the motorhome to which I referred earlier – and we are looking at a range of possible motives. Our pooled information suggests that the enquiry is proceeding in a very positive manner, but we have a lot of evidence to consider and lots more witnesses to interview. We shall not be hurried or pressurised into making any hasty decisions. And if the dark haired man with the motor-home reads this, and if he is innocent, he might like to come forward to have himself cleared.'

'But you would wish to issue a warning to anyone who has been tried for murder and acquitted? Do you think such people should be given police protection?'

'We have no evidence to suggest the killer intends to murder anyone else, but it would be sensible for every-one who considers themselves at risk to take precautions, perhaps even to vary their daily routine a little . . . and if anyone does think he or she is particularly at risk, they can always contact their local police station to ask for advice or protection. Every consideration will be given to such requests, albeit with police staffing requirements in mind.'

'Good advice, Mr Pemberton,' said Hammond. 'Thank you for talking to me so frankly. It is appreciated. Can I say you have not found any motive other than the one I suggested? It could be a form of revenge on killers or reputed killers who have evaded justice?'

'They're your words, not mine,' said Pemberton. 'That is one of our lines of enquiry, but I should say our minds remain open, we can only proceed on the evidence which comes to light.'

'All right, I've got enough now. I hope you catch him before he kills someone else.'

'With your help, we might do that,' said Pemberton. 'Goodnight, Mr Hammond.'

When he had finished, Pemberton explained to Paul Larkin the gist of what he had said to Hammond, emphasising the piece about the dark-haired suspect, then told him about John Whittington.

'He's on our patch, Paul, would you believe! At a nursing home in Rainesbury, Sandside. I'm going there now, I need to talk to the Divisional Commander as well, about setting up some kind of continuing protection, and I need to speak to Whittington himself if he's capable of understanding me. He's got Alzheimer's, in its early stages. He might have to be moved from that home as soon as we can fix an alternative. I'm not sure what state he's in, but we can't leave him there as a sitting duck.'

'Shall I get Superintendent Tyndale for you now?' suggested Larkin.

'Yes, do that and I'll set up a meeting the minute I get there, but I don't want to discuss details on the phone. Too many eavesdroppers about these days . . .'

Larkin rang the Divisional Headquarters at Rainesbury and asked to be put through to Superintendent Tyndale's private number, specifying it was Detective Superintendent Pemberton who wished to speak to him urgently. Tyndale, a strong-minded Tynesider, responded in his distinctive accent and Pemberton took the handset.

'Hi, Dick, Mark Pemberton here, sorry to bother you at this time of night.'

'You wouldn't do so unless it was important, Mark. How can I help?'

'It's in connection with the murder enquiry I'm currently busy with,' Pemberton said. 'I'm leaving for

Rainesbury within the next few minutes, I need an urgent word with you. Say in an hour's time? Can you meet me outside the Lobster and Lettuce? In the car park? It's very important.'

'It all sounds very MI5, but yes. In civvies?'

'Yes, no uniforms, not yet.'

'See you there,' and so the meeting was fixed.

Before leaving, Pemberton acquainted Paul Larkin with what he expected this evening, who might call and said he would have his mobile switched on. Depending upon what transpired with John Whittington, Pemberton would call and inform Larkin – he might go home, he might have to maintain an all-night vigil or he might return to the Incident Room. His plans were as fluid as that. Larkin understood.

'And tell Lorraine what I'm doing,' he said. 'If I need assistance from the troops, I'll contact you before you go home, Paul, or at home!'

'It's going to be one of those nights, is it?' laughed Larkin.

'I hope we're going to catch a killer, Paul, maybe not tonight, but in the near future. I hope our uniformed colleagues at Rainesbury do the honours, Dick Tyndale will have to come up with something. You might like to ring Wolverhampton, ask for Detective Superintendent Deakin in person, and see what the current state of play is down there, see if they've had any smell of Steele. Tell him what I'm doing, tell him about John Whittington being a likely victim and that Steele could be heading this way. He can get me on the mobile if necessary.'

'Do you want armed back-up, sir?'

'Tyndale will see to all that. Well, I'm off.'

And five minutes later, he was driving towards Rainesbury – and he was exceeding the speed limit. He hoped no traffic patrol cars were prowling the highways and byways; even though police officers could legally exceed the speed limit in the execution of their duty, he had no wish to be stopped and quizzed.

The Sniper had decided to bring forward his plans for John Whittington. A call to Whittington's daughter had revealed his current whereabouts, a nursing home on the Yorkshire coast at Rainesbury and so, in the security of his own flat, he was making preparations. He had a pleasing wig of auburn hair, with hair slightly curled, which completely altered his appearance, and he would top that with a baseball cap, with its peak reversed. His rounded granny specs with the plain lenses would sit on his nose like something out of Dickens, and he would wear his old jeans, battered trainers, green tee-shirt and multi-coloured sweater.

He'd carry waterproofs in his huge aluminium-framed backpack which would also contain his tent and camping gear, and a pair of hiking boots would dangle alongside his tin mug and billy can which hung from the bar at the bottom of the pack. His backpack would contain a selection of other clothes and his Kalashnikov, with its stock folded as paratroopers did and its magazine removed for the trip, would be accommodated among that clothing, wrapped in plastic and well disguised among the tent, the tent poles and the other paraphernalia. Just in case he was away from home for a long time, he had all his ammunition too, enough to dispose of all his victims, and he'd brought his gun oil and cleaning materials. And he would carry a waterproof map holder around his neck.

In this guise, he would head for the railway station tomorrow morning to take a train to Yorkshire; for this trip, he was Gareth Cunningham, a computer worker, who was heading to the Yorkshire coast to meet some friends before tackling the Coast-to-Coast walk. He had Gareth's motorcycle licence and a pocket full of cash –

£650 – which he'd stolen from Gareth's panniers as Gareth had visited a friend in hospital. Upon arrival in Rainesbury, he would find the nursing home and then observe the routine of John Whittington before finalising his plans.

He went to bed early after polishing and oiling his Kalashnikov.

Chapter Fifteen

When Pemberton drove into the car park behind the busy, well illuminated and refurbished seafront pub now called the Lobster and Lettuce, Superintendent Tyndale had already arrived. The two men, colleagues of many years, emerged from their vehicles and Pemberton said, 'Let's walk, Dick.'

He led the way to the wide sand-covered pavement which ran alongside the beach, skirting the bay with a wide sweep of railings, and separating the sand from the seafront road and the array of buildings which followed the curve of the bay. There were hotels, amusement arcades, shops, houses, a museum, even a hospital and lots of wooden stalls from which, in the daytime, seafood was sold to the scent of vinegar and brine. There was a children's playground too, with colourful swings, roundabouts and trampolines, now closed for the night.

They walked to their left, a route which would take them towards the pier and the lighthouse and then beyond, if they desired, to the second bay with its more rugged rock-strewn shoreline. The full return journey could take an hour or more if they wished, and with the waves crashing into the shore as the sun began to slip out of sight in the lateness of summer, they knew their conversation would not be overheard.

'Good of you to come at such short notice,' Pemberton and Tyndale were both based in Rainesbury, Pemberton being in charge of the CID throughout the whole division, while Tyndale was commander of the uniformed branch of sub-division, the town's police in simple terms. If Whittington was to receive police protection, it would be Tyndale's responsibility.

As they strolled, Pemberton noticed the colourful lights reflecting from Tyndale's own light brown hair, wavy and well-groomed. He was in his early fifties, a pleasant, jovial character who was popular with his subordinates. As they walked side by side, like two smart-suited friends taking an evening stroll either before or after a couple of pints in a pub, Pemberton explained the background of the murders and Tynedale listened without interrupting. Their strides took them closer to the pier and lighthouse, and so Pemberton said, 'Let's go along the pier, Dick, it's deserted.'

Sometimes the pier was thick with fishermen or, in the daytime, busy with tourists and bus-trippers but now it was deserted and the incoming tide was crashing against the huge concrete base and sending plumes of spray into the air, some of it blowing on to the wooden walkway which stood on iron pillars, rusting in places.

'So,' Pemberton had by this time provided Tyndale with the necessary background, and said, 'We have strong reason to believe that the Sniper's next victim will be John Whittington. He's suffering from Alzheimer's disease, and he's in Sandside, just along the sea front from here.'

At Tyndale's request, he provided his reasons for believing Whittington was now at risk, adding that he had no intimation of the time-scale involved.

'Chummy could arrive tonight, tomorrow, next week or even next month. I just do not know – or he might not come at all, he might select another victim. It's all as uncertain as that, Dick. Wolverhampton police are trying to locate him, so far without success. If they find him, they'll lift him.'

'They won't put a tail on him then?'

'No, he'd spot a police tail a mile off! We want to draw him into a trap.'

'And Whittington has no idea of all this?'

'No, not yet, although Derby police have spoken to his daughter, but they would not give her any reason for their visit; she would probably associate it with some other on-going enquiry with the police checking his whereabouts; after all, he was once a murder suspect.'

'So what do you want me to do, Mark? Put an armed police officer permanently in the home? Put a guard outside the premises? Have an armed guard accompany him whenever he's out of the building? Electronic surveillance? Have Whittington moved to another secure place? I'm not sure we have the power or the right to move him, unless he consents of course. Perhaps he's not in a fit state to make such a decision? And we can hardly have him sent back home, to his daughter, can we? He'd be just as vulnerable there. And don't forget, I have the safety of my own officers to consider. I don't want any of them picked off by the sniper. Contrary to what the public sometimes thinks, police officers are valuable human beings, not disposable pawns in some kind of entertaining crime puzzle.'

'I don't think the Sniper will enter the home to execute Whittington, that's not his style,' Pemberton said. 'In the current cases, he's fired from a distance, out of doors, he's a sniper with a rifle, not a handgun man. If he has an MO, that's it.'

'If he wants to make sure he gets the right target, he'll need to identify which of the residents is Whittington, not easy when they go out of the place,' Tyndale said.

'That's our problem too,' added Pemberton.

'Touché'! And once he's done that, once he's found out which room he occupies, or uses on a regular basis, he could fire from the outside into the building, it's built into the hillside, the rock behind rises higher than the roof, so there's plenty of sniping positions, Mark. And if he operates from the outside, then he can escape very quickly, he can lose himself in the undergrowth or in the town.'

'One part of his MO seems to be to determine the daily routine of his victims, and then to execute them during that routine. He seems to arrive with enough time to undertake that kind of background research, he doesn't rush these jobs.'

'I do know the residents of Sandside take daily exercises, either in their wheelchairs or on foot, Mark. Some are accompanied by a member of staff, others go it alone, chugging along the seafront in their chairs, some go in groups, or ones and twos. They're a regular sight hereabouts, usually mid-morning and again in the afternoon. If the weather's good, that is. Outside meal-times, that's the general pattern. Out for some bracing sea air and then back for a slap-up meal! Not a bad way of passing the time!'

'What about other outings? Apart from runs along the seafront?'

'They're usually organised in groups, bus trips and so on, to the cinema, a seaside variety show or a trip around the moors. With lots of staff in attendance. I doubt if chummy would risk shooting in those circumstances.'

'Don't you count on it! He shot Leroy Campbell as he was surrounded by minders. If his previous patterns are anything to go by, he'll tackle his victim while he's doing his run along the seafront, but the truth is we can't be sure of anything, Dick. I'm sure we're dealing with a very clever and determined killer, and I can't even be sure he's going to turn up. At this stage, I'm just seeking ways of taking precautions along with a bit of advance planning in anticipation!'

'I realise that, so we need to talk to the proprietor of the home, Mark. And Whittington himself. I don't want to put the wind up everyone . . . it seems to me the simplest answer is to have Whittington transferred to some other secure home, well away from Rainesbury, and while that's being arranged, call a halt to any of his outings along the seafront – that's if he does embark on such outings. You did say he's got Alzheimer's. I could have a guard placed on the home and could always park an empty police car, in full livery, outside the premises! You'd be amazed at the effect that would have – that kind of thing is a wonderful device for deterring speeders.'

Pemberton said, 'So our first job is to talk to Whittington and whoever's in charge of Sandside. Now?'

'There's no time like the present as Mrs Manley once said,' quipped Tyndale. 'We can't waste time, Mark, your sniping friend might already be here, or on his way. Does he know you by sight?'

'No, at least I don't think so. Now, can you arrange a guard for tonight?'

'If necessary, yes.'

'Armed?'

'He'll have to be.'

'All right, Dick, come along. Let's visit Sandside. Who's in charge, any idea?'

'I checked before coming to meet you. It's a woman called Maureen Stockton, Mrs Stockton, a widow, she's the proprietor of the place, she owns it lock, stock and barrel. A formidable lady, I know her quite well through our work and she runs a very efficient business. We don't get complaints about standards there.'

'I hope she's not in bed!'

'She won't be, but if by any chance she is, we shall wake her up. Come along, Mark, it's time to exercise your famous charm and charisma!'

'I'm all right with nurses, but used to be terrified of those matrons . . . they're talking of bringing them back to the wards, I'm told, in NHS hospitals.'

'It's just what they need! Well, this lady is like one of those old-fashioned matrons, but she's likeable,' grinned Tyndale. 'Come along, I'll lead the way.'

Sandside was a fifteen-minute walk from the pier and it was tucked into a huge curved area of the over-hanging cliff, albeit with its front door opening on to the seafront. Behind it, the cliff rose sharply until it towered above the roof, while the slopes were covered with trees, shrubs and thick undergrowth. It was a large, handsome house built of stone, once a former mansion, then a hotel and now a nursing home in private ownership.

With sixteen bedrooms and ample downstairs accom-modation for recreation and therapy, it was ideally situ-ated and very popular – there was usually a waiting list for admission. When the two senior detectives arrived at the front door, having checked they were not being observed by their target, it was illuminated with an overhead light. There was a triple doorbell marked with 'Staff', 'Office' and 'Resident'. Tyndale pressed the one marked 'Staff' and waited. After what seemed a lengthy delay, a white-coated male attendant opened the door, peered out and said, 'Yes?'

Tyndale spoke. 'We'd like to talk to Mrs Stockton, please.'

'She's resting,' he said. 'She said she doesn't want to be disturbed.'

'We're police officers,' pressed Tyndale. 'I'm Super-intendent Tyndale from the town, and this is Detective Superintendent Pemberton, also from Rainesbury. Mrs Stockton does know me personally through her work and mine, so if you would please tell her we are here, and perhaps you could add that we would like to talk to her now, on a matter of urgency.'

'Oh, well, I suppose it will be all right,' and he turned away, leaving them on the doorstep, but with the door standing open.

'So much for security,' grimaced Pemberton. The

nurse took a while; he had to climb the stairs and knock on the door of Mrs Stockton's flat, mutter something inaudible to her and then return.

'She says if you would come in and wait in the lounge, she'll be down in a minute. Can I get you a coffee while you are waiting?'

'Yes, fine, I'd like that,' and Pemberton realised he'd not had his evening meal; a coffee would have to do for the time being. Tyndale also accepted one and the nurse produced them from a coffee percolator which was working in the corner of the lounge. They settled down near a coffee table and after five minutes, Maureen Stockton appeared. She looked slightly ruffled, as if she'd dressed in a hurry.

'Sorry to keep you waiting,' she said, as she closed the heavy door behind her. 'I was just about to get into the bath . . . another minute and I'd have been up to my neck in bubbles!'

'Hello Maureen,' Tyndale stood up and smiled. 'This is Mark Pemberton, detective superintendent from Rainesbury.'

Pemberton also stood up and smiled, reaching out his hand and she shook it formally. 'Nice to meet you, Mrs Stockton.'

'Maureen, please. So, Dick, what can I do for you both?' she waved at the chairs, indicating they should sit down while she poured herself a coffee. 'It looks serious, a double-headed police presence!'

Tyndale left his chair and padded across to the closed door, then whipped it open, but there was no-one around. He closed the door. 'I don't want eavesdroppers,' he said by way of explanation then, after returning to his seat, continued in a quiet voice, 'Maureen, this might alarm you but we have to look at it in a logical and sensible manner. The blunt fact is that we have good reason to believe that one of your residents may be at risk from a gunman. We are taking the

240

matter very seriously, and we are here to seek your co-operation. And his.'

'Oh my God! Why would anyone want to harm any of these old dears? They've enough problems without having someone come to injure them.'

'I fear it is more than just an injury, Maureen,' Tyndale continued. 'Mark, you'd better explain.'

'You might have read about the murder at Roberthorpe,' Pemberton began. 'I am in charge of the investigation which, as you may know, is currently on-going.'

She nodded, adding, 'Yes, I did read about it. A church-worker, wasn't it? Shot dead.'

'Yes. The papers will be full of more about that story tomorrow,' he told her. 'But since then there have been two further killings, both by the same person and by the same method, so we believe. A powerful rifle is used; one additional murder was in south London, with another in Northumberland. The killer is not restricting himself to one area of the country, he works alone and he is very mobile.'

She listened carefully as he presented sufficient detail for her to gain a clear picture of events, although at this point he did not refer to the fact the victims were all killers themselves; as he proceeded, though, he could see her bewilderment increase as the full horror of his story unfolded.

'But here?' she cried. 'You mean one of my residents is at risk?'

'We have reason to believe it will be John Whittington,' Pemberton said. 'And at this point, I think we'd better continue this conversation with John present.'

'John? But why? He's such a harmless old fellow, so nice and refined . . . and far from well, he's got Alzheimer's, you know that?'

'Yes, we do know,' said Pemberton. 'It's not very advanced, though?'

241

'No, but it is present and it is affecting him, he's showing many of the signs, forgetfulness, vagueness, not knowing what day of the week it is or even where he is, then he's lucid for a while . . . he tried to clean his teeth with soap last night, and more than once he's tried to wash his hair with toothpaste and he flushed his alarm clock down the toilet . . . and on top of that, he's in a wheelchair, poor old John.'

'What do you know about him?' asked Tyndale.

'Not a lot, I must admit, he's not local, you know that? He's from Derby, but his daughter said he used to come here for his holidays years ago, when he was young, and he wants to be here now that he's ill. He likes the sand and the sea, childhood memories I suppose, and now he's got the money to pay his way. We had a spare room at just the right time and so we admitted him. He's a retired civil engineer, he spent his working life building roads and bridges, so he keeps telling us, and he lost his wife some time ago. His daughter comes to see him very regularly, she gets accommodation in town and comes for the weekend, or longer in holiday times. She's a teacher. He looks forward to that. He does need full-time care, though, he was getting too much for his daughter to cope with, especially as she is still working.'

'Is he lucid? We do have to talk to him now, Maureen,' said Tyndale.

'Oh, he's quite lucid at times and very entertaining, quite a character really. He's in his room, I heard the television. He's in a wheelchair the whole time, one of those mechanised ones, electrically powered . . . we could go up there, it would be easier than getting him down here, I think.'

'Right, good idea,' said Pemberton. 'Can you ask him first, if he'll talk to us? And I'd like you to be present as we chat to him.'

'I just don't understand all this,' but she left the room

and went upstairs. They heard her tapping on a bed-room door, and she was admitted; after a while, she emerged and said, 'Do come up, gentlemen, John will talk to you. There's not a lot of room, one of us will have to sit on the bed . . .'

They were shown into a small and very tidy bedroom with a television glowing in one corner, a washbasin in another, and a table and chair before the window. A wardrobe occupied one wall and there was a small bookshelf containing a few Readers' Digest fiction titles and former library books. Mrs Stockton switched off the TV.

'John, this is Superintendent Tyndale from Raines-bury, and Detective Superintendent Pemberton, they want a word with you.'

The old man smiled and nodded, then said, 'Hello, can you find a seat?'

Pemberton took the chair near the side of the bed, Tyndale sat on the bed and Mrs Stockton took the one which had been tucked under the small table. Before them was a gaunt-faced man with grey wrinkled skin and thin grey hair; his cheeks were hollow and he looked dreadful, even if he did manage a thin smile. He was dressed in blue striped pyjamas but his skeletal frame showed through. Faced with two policemen, unknown to him, he looked nervous and apprehensive, understandably so. Pemberton wondered if he thought they'd come to break the news they'd found his wife's remains . . .

Pemberton began by establishing that this was in-deed John Whittington from Derby, quoting the address, his daughter's name and other identifying facts. Whittington agreed with nods of his head.

'Mr Whittington,' said Pemberton at length. 'We have a strong reason to believe your life is in danger.'

'I know it is, I've got Alzheimer's,' and he chuckled, a dry, hoarse laugh.

'I don't mean that. I mean we have a strong reason to believe you're in danger from a gunman,' said Pemberton, and he then explained about the other killings in the same terms as he had spoken to Mrs Stockton. Whittington listened and then asked, 'But why me, Mr Pemberton? What makes you think he's coming for me?'

'All the other victims had been charged with murder, and cleared by the courts, or their cases had not proceeded to court,' said Pemberton. 'We think it is someone making his own form of retribution.'

'You mean he knows about me? How can he know about me?' and there was fear in his eyes.

'It was in the newspapers at the time,' said Pemberton, now very aware that Mrs Stockton was eyeing both him and Whittington with shock on her face. 'It is easy to trace you, we found you. If we found you very easily, it means he can find you too.'

'You mean . . .' Mrs Stockton started to say something, but Pemberton put up his hand to stem her words.

'I think Mr Whittington should tell us, if he wishes,' he spoke quietly.

'I was charged with murdering my wife, Mrs Stockton,' his voice was quivering now. 'Some years ago, but she was never found. Her body has not been found to this day and I was acquitted. The judge said the prosecution had not proved I had killed her, and so I was set free. Juliet believes in my innocence, if that's any consolation to you.'

'That is the reason we think you are at risk,' said Pemberton. 'We have reason to believe that the killer was recently scrutinising the newspapers which carried the story of your case. And that is why we are here, to warn you and to find some way of preventing you being harmed. We'd like to discuss your transfer from here perhaps, or perhaps we can talk about some other security arrangement.'

244

'I don't believe all this . . . why would anyone come for John . . . he was innocent . . .'

'I wasn't,' he said quite unexpectedly. 'I did kill her, Mrs Stockton, she was rotten, cruel, a bitch, you ask Juliet, my daughter, she deserved everything that happened, there was nothing good in that woman, she ruined me financially, I resorted to fraud, she drove me to distraction, my life was hell . . . I buried her, under a bridge . . . they'll never find her . . . no-one will, so I deserved this, this awful disease, and I deserve to die, I did wrong, I know, I broke the law but I was at my wits' end . . . and I know I can't be tried twice, can I? For the same crime . . .'

'Oh, my God, I had no idea . . . no idea . . . I mean, John, this means we must have another look at your continuing presence here . . . I mean, I can't have a murderer in the house . . . this is dreadful . . .'

Pemberton held up his hand. 'It has never been proved that Mr Whittington murdered his wife, or even that he might have been guilty of manslaughter. We have only his word for that, Mrs Stockton, the word of a very sick man . . . he might be romancing about it. This kind of admission would never be acceptable in a court but we are not here to discuss that. We are here to discuss ways of avoiding John being killed and at the same time, looking at ways of capturing the gunman.'

'Use me as a decoy,' said Whittington.

'We can't do that,' Pemberton said.

'Yes, you can. How does he operate, this killer? You mentioned sniper. Does he take pot shots from a distance? Let me go out in my wheelchair, let me be his target, that's what he's coming for and if he kills me, so much the better. Look at me! What have I got to live for? Nothing, not with this bloody terrible debilitating disease, it's a living death, a slow and agonising one for my family. I may as well be shot, then I'd die quickly . . . so, yes, I deserve to be shot for what I did to my wife, and

I'd do a bit for society by helping to trap another killer. So there you are, Mr Pemberton, you've got a willing victim. I'd rather die quickly with a bullet in my head than cope with the lingering living death that my fellow Alzheimer's sufferers have to tolerate.'

'I can't accept your offer,' smiled Pemberton. 'Sorry, my duty is to protect life, not to arrange its destruction. I am going to suggest we move you to a secure home, on a temporary basis until we catch the killer. There must be somewhere not too far away, where you will be safe from the sniper.'

'I refuse to go!' and he folded his arms across his thin chest in a gesture of defiance. 'Besides, wherever I go, he'll find me, if he's really determined.'

'Mr Whittington,' said Tyndale. 'There is no question about it. We cannot allow you to put yourself – and our officers or the staff of this home . . . at risk. I admire your bravery in volunteering . . .'

'It's not bravery, it's cowardice, fear of what Alzheimer's is going to do to me.'

'Before we discuss this any further, Mr Whittington,' Pemberton spoke quietly now. 'What is your daily routine?'

'I go out before breakfast, in my wheelchair. Half-six or thereabouts. I can manage that, there's a lift to get me downstairs, a ramp at the side entrance and I like to feel the sea breezes. I go every day, whatever the weather, winter or summer. Right along the promenade, round both bays, it takes me the best part of an hour.'

'Alone?' asked Pemberton.

'Always, I like my own company that time of day. Peace and tranquillity, with just the sea and the sea-gulls.'

'And the same route every day?'

'Yes. A creature of habit, that's me. I get back in time for breakfast, with a good appetite and rose-coloured cheeks. It's no effort, not with that chair.'

246

'Does anyone know you? Do you encounter the same people on your trip?'

'Not really, there's a jogger comes past in a yellow tracksuit sometimes but he never says anything, and sometimes I see a milk float chugging along, or a delivery van or two, but they don't know me, not by name . . . well, I lie! My name is on the wheelchair, across the back, like those director's chairs. Whittington, Sandside, it says in big white letters. In case we get lost or forget who we are. And yes, I do sometimes forget who I am and where I am. That's what the disease does to me. So, yes, the folks I meet on a morning can get to know who I am, unless they think it's the chairmaker's name on the back.' And he grinned wickedly.

Pemberton turned to Tyndale. 'Dick, what do you think? Are our lads good enough to shadow Mr Whittington and protect him?'

'It's a risk I wouldn't want to take,' admitted Tyndale. 'You're talking of a long curved stretch of road, with parking spaces for all kinds of vehicles, the killer's included, with open views from the cliffs on one side and the beach on the other. And lots of hiding places, sniping sites maybe, among the vehicles and on the cliff.'

'I'm willing to die, I've told you that!' snapped Whittington.

'We're not going to let you!' retorted Tyndale. 'We can't cover you during the whole of that route, day after day, just in case the sniper turns up . . . can we use a dummy? Set a dummy off in your electric wheelchair, or even a remote controlled chair with your name on it . . .'

'That's not a bad idea, I've known decoys be used in this kind of situation, with success, I might add. Have we time to give it a test run?' asked Pemberton. 'The Sniper could be here tomorrow . . . or even tonight. He

247

might be here right now, in town, doing his preliminary research.'

'I'll make time,' asserted Tyndale.

'Right. So what do you wear on those runs?' Pemberton asked Whittington.

'I've a blue track suit and a white beret, I wear those,' he replied.

'Always?'

'Yes, unless I got soaked one day and my stuff wasn't dry, then I might use ordinary clothes. But track suit mainly that time of morning.'

'Mrs Stockton,' Pemberton now addressed her; she seemed to be in a state of some shock and bewilderment at this turn of events. 'Has anyone been asking after Mr Whittington in recent weeks?'

'Yes, I did get a couple of calls from an old friend, a Mr Crompton who said he's worked with John and might be in town soon, he wanted to look him up.'

'When? Can you remember?'

'Not precisely. In the last two or three days, I think.'

'Juliet, his daughter, knows nothing of a Mr Crompton, he rang her as well,' Pemberton told her.

Mrs Stockton, now white-faced with the shock of this turn of events, said, 'I did mention it to Juliet last time she rang, and she said a George Crompton had been calling her, asking after her father. That would be yesterday or the day before . . .'

'Our villain is adept at disguising himself and using other names,' Pemberton said. 'If he's used the same name twice, it was either to establish some kind of credibility – or there may be a genuine Mr Crompton somewhere in John's background. What did you tell him?'

'Well, I can't remember really, I did say John was here, and that he went out most days in his wheelchair . . . oh dear, and I remember saying he went by himself

248

at half-past six most mornings, along the promenade, and that his chair had his name on it, in case he got lost or wanders into town . . . we do that with every-one . . .'

'I never knew anybody called Crompton!' said Whittington. 'Is he trying to sell me something? It's a bit late to flog me double-glazing.'

'And do you go out more than once a day?' Pember-ton asked.

'We can do, yes. Sometimes. Not always. Early morning, yes, then maybe mid-morning and afternoon, I go alone in the first instance but with others later. Sometimes we're in a group later in the day,' John Whittington said. 'We have a laugh and a bit of a natter, and we look after each other, although there's usually a member of staff on hand.'

'Well,' said Pemberton, 'The first thing is, Mr Whittington, that you will not be going for your early morning trip tomorrow. I think we might use your chair, though, as a decoy, first thing in the morning, with a police officer on board. We'll have a police presence here tonight, in the home if that's all right with you, Mrs Stockton, and throughout the coming days. And Mr Whittington might have to change rooms. You can fix that, Dick?'

'No problem,' he said.

'Now, we believe that our man read the story of Mr Whittington's trial in a newspaper today, in Wolver-hampton library. Assuming he's decided not to use his car – because the police are checking cars and looking for his – if he got the first train out of there tomorrow, he'd not arrive until afternoon, and that's when your people are out in numbers. John would be on his own the morning after tomorrow. I think that gives us time to set up some kind of trap, but if he came by hired car . . .'

'He could be here now?' and Mrs Stockton shuddered.

'He could, we can't ignore the fact but I think it's unlikely. Wolverhampton Police are watching out for him, if he's seen leaving town, we'll be the first to know. They know he's heading for Rainesbury too! So no news is good news. But he does generally arrive in advance to make a reconnaissance of the town and movements of his target. With all that in mind, we'll have a police presence here all night, discreetly placed,' said Tyndale. 'And that means Mr Whittington can remain here tonight, under guard.'

'I don't mind being shot! I've told you!' cried John Whittington. 'I volunteer now, I make that known, in front of witnesses . . .'

'And we reject your offer, finally,' said Pemberton yet again. 'So, Dick, your men will cover the home tonight and first thing tomorrow? They won't let John out in his wheelchair for his early run, either?'

'He'll be kept firmly in here!' smiled Tyndale.

'And tomorrow, we set a trap for our killer,' whispered Pemberton.

The Sniper slept well and at six the following morning, he climbed from his bed, washed but did not shave, and took a bus to the railway station. He paid cash for a single ticket to Rainesbury and boarded the 7.32 a.m. He kept his backpack at his side but bought a newspaper from the station kiosk.

As he settled into his seat, he saw the banner headline, 'Kalashnikov Killer'. He read it quickly, hardly daring to show just how interested he was, but as he studied the words he realised the police had known all the time, they'd known about the gun, the history of the victims

250

. . . so did they now know he was en route to deal with Whittington? How could they know? But it added a new dimension to his challenge.

Somewhat unsettled, he sat upright in a corner of his seat, pulled an orange from his pocket and peeled it, spitting out the seeds as he came across them.

As he was carried away from the town, a railway policeman chanced to pop into the booking office at Wolverhampton. It was one of his regular calls because the booking clerk was very attractive and she made a nice cup of coffee. As they chatted, she happened to mention the ticket issues for that morning – it was a game they played, trying to guess what people did for a living and why they were heading for unknown destinations – and she said one had been issued to Rainesbury. She told her policeman friend it had been bought by a peculiar man wearing what looked like a wig. She'd never heard of the place until this morning and wondered if her friendly visiting constable knew where it was, but he recalled the name because he'd read that lurid article about the Kalashnikov murders.

That had reminded him there had been a circular from the town police, too, pinned on the noticeboard. And wasn't the detective in charge of the enquiry based at Rainesbury? Thinking the coincidence was very great, and wondering, just wondering if the passenger was suspicious in some way, he picked up the telephone and rang Rainesbury Divisional Headquarters. It would do no harm for the police to meet any train which might carry a passenger to Rainesbury. The train he'd caught had been en route for over three hours already but a trip to Rainesbury would take longer than that.

When the call came through, Pemberton was in his office, having been out before six this morning to observe events on the promenade, but he took the call. He listened to what the railway policeman had to say, obtained a description of the man who'd bought the ticket and smiled.

'He's on his way,' he said to his office colleague. 'Check train times will you? See what time the trains get in from Wolverhampton. We'll have a reception party waiting for our sniper.'

Chapter Sixteen

That morning, Pemberton despatched two of his regular town detectives to the railway station to check the times and await the arrival of any train which might have carried the Sniper from Wolverhampton. It was quickly appreciated that, as he would have to change more than once en route, he could arrive on any one of several, morning or afternoon. The cross-country route from Wolverhampton to Rainesbury was convoluted to say the least, with the possibility of travelling via Manchester and the cross-Pennine service, or even down to Birmingham and then across to Derby and up to Sheffield, taking in places like York, Leeds or Doncaster. It was a maze of possible routes, some with slow-moving local trains and others with mainline expresses. Nonetheless, the two detectives, a man and a woman, both carrying small arms, settled down on the arrivals platform for what might be a long vigil. Even as they watched, a train arrived and they scanned the disembarking passengers, ostensibly as family members awaiting the arrival of a loved one, but no-one appeared who matched the description of the man they sought. But they had all day at their disposal; they could wait and the station buffet did serve decent coffee.

Confident that the Sniper had not yet arrived in Rainesbury, Pemberton directed Lorraine to accompany him to Sandside for another chat with John Whittington. As she was engaged on the Flint murder case, it was quite within her brief to undertake this task – besides, it would avoid the need to drive all the way to Rober-thorpe – and so he rang the Incident Room. He would brief Larkin to deal with the press and also to preside over the morning conference of detectives.

He told Inspector Larkin about the anticipated arrival of the Sniper in Rainesbury, stressed that at this point the uniform branch, under the direction of the Divisional Commander, had the whole of Rainesbury, including the railway station, under armed supervision. He added that he and Lorraine were now heading for Sandside, together with Superintendent Tyndale and members of his Firearms team, for further discussions with John Whittington so that a plan to cope with the Sniper could be devised. Larkin did say there had been no overnight developments in the Incident Room, other than the reported departure of the Sniper for Rainesbury – it seemed that Wolverhampton Police had also picked up that story from the Transport Police but, to date, Steele's car had not been traced. They were confident it had not driven out of Wolverhampton – the traffic cameras would have spotted it, although a car with false registration plates or a stolen car could have been used. Those possibilities could not be ignored but his train trip did seem likely.

Tyndale and some of his officers were already at Sandside when Pemberton and Lorraine arrived. They were accommodated in the proprietor's private office, which boasted a mini-conference room large enough to cope with everyone. John Whittington, whose mental state, particularly so far as his memory was concerned, was not entirely reliable, had been invited. Mrs Stockton had organised coffee too and, after a moment's discussion, it was felt she should join the meeting, just in case there were future difficulties with Whittington. If she knew what was expected of him, she might be able to assist. There were two armed guards outside too, not visible to the general public, but in a position to act quickly if necessary.

Tyndale, in his role as divisional commander, led the discussion.

'Have you seen the papers?' was his opening speech.

'No,' Pemberton said. 'What do they say?'

'There's a massive splash about the Kalashnikov killer,' and he held up several morning papers which he'd spotted in the Sandside lounge and he showed them to the gathering, highlighting the banner head-lines. 'They've gone overboard with this one, the tab-loids especially. It's enough to scare the pants off half the population!'

'That's no bad thing,' Pemberton said. 'We need that kind of fear to generate any kind of reaction. The public ignores our advice most of the time. So what's the general gist? Remember, the stories will all be similar, they were initiated by the same reporter.'

'They're mainly covering the fact that unconvicted killers were the victims, and that one man with a Kalashnikov is responsible. They're claiming it's a ven-detta of some kind, although the victims can't be linked for any other reason. The reports do cover all the mur-ders, Mark, I know it's sensationalism, but the basic facts are accurate enough.'

'I wonder if the Sniper had seen the papers?' asked Lorraine, trying to gauge his reaction if he had read the reports.

'It'll put him more on his guard,' Pemberton said. 'If he has seen these papers, he'll guess we're not far behind him. This man is by no means stupid; these reports will make him more alert, more devious – and therefore more difficult to catch. If he's coming here, he'll be trying to outwit us but he will want to commit his crime.'

'It won't deter him, all this publicity?' asked Mrs Stockton.

'It's possible, although I think he's on his way now, but we'll be waiting for him. He has no reason to know we're here, but if he's seen the papers he'll be very alert and that means he'll be more dangerous and cunning.'

'It means we must get this exercise right,' and Tyndale sounded rather apprehensive now, 'I don't want anyone killed on my patch, so let's get this show moving.'

'Do the papers mention me?' asked Whittington, showing a sudden interest in the affair.

'No, not a word,' Tyndale said. 'But it does mention Rainesbury – due to Mr Pemberton's involvement, that's all. No mention of you, Mr Whittington, sorry!'

'So how does he know I'm in Rainesbury?' Whittington demanded, 'I mean, how could he know? Why's he coming here?'

Clearly, he had forgotten about yesterday's discussions, and so Pemberton re-emphasised the fact that both the nursing home and his daughter had received phone calls, ostensibly from a former colleague asking for Mr Whittington's whereabouts and movements. He felt that, this time, Whittington did absorb the information, and that he would co-operate. There was no indication, on this occasion, that he was prepared to be murdered rather than face the prospect of life with Alzheimer's.

Tyndale said, 'The situation is this. My task is two-fold. I must prevent a crime being perpetrated against Mr Whittington, and I must apprehend the suspect, bearing in mind he has already killed three people. To deal with the former is very simple. We keep Mr Whittington out of harm's way. We can do that without any great difficulty. But there is a downside to that strategy. If Mr Whittington is known to be in hiding, the sniper may decide to try and find him, or he might decide not to continue with his plans. He could fade into the background again, we'd lose him and that would leave him free to kill someone else. He has to be caught if we are to prevent more murders. I regard that as our priority. At the moment, we are within an ace of catching him and we need to draw him into a trap – a trap he is surely anticipating . . .'

'I've told you I'll willingly be the bait,' said Whittington, obviously now recalling last night's talk. 'I'm serious. There is no point in living with this disease . . .'

'And we've told you we can't allow that,' Tyndale was adamant. 'If we have to use real bait, we will use a police officer, one who's armed and protected with body armour. That's something we have to decide. No-one's going to get killed while I'm in charge!'

'John,' said Mrs Stockton, 'You do as you are told, we don't want you wandering into town while this is going on, you listen to the police, you stay here! He does forget things and he has a habit of wandering, gentlemen – hence the name on his chair . . .'

'I'll do it,' said Lorraine.

'You won't!' snapped Pemberton. 'I'm not having you risk your life when we've a madman at large, especially one armed with a Kalashnikov! No way!'

'We've got to decide our strategy, and we have to do it quickly,' snapped the normally placid Tyndale, hoping to quench these digressions. 'I have a suggestion.'

'Good, because I'm at something of a loss with this one!' sighed Pemberton. 'There's no way I can risk a human life as bait for this killer.'

'Earlier, we considered a dummy. Well, my brother's son works for a television company in the props department and, about six months ago, he rigged up a remote-controlled wheelchair. It's one of those motorised buggies like John uses, but it's been adapted so it can be controlled externally. You might have seen it in that comedy programme *Age Will Not Wither Me* where three old chaps in electric wheelchairs get into all kinds of scrapes . . . well, some of the stunts were done with a dummy, and the chair was remote controlled. I can get that chair, I've already done the ground work. It could be here within two hours. We could despatch that chair along the promenade tomorrow morning, with Mr Whittington's name emblazoned across the back and a dressed-up dummy in the seat . . . there are plenty of places from which it could be controlled, well out of sight . . .'

'What about the dummies?' asked Pemberton, 'The one's I've seen don't look very lifelike! You've just got to look in a shop window to know that dummies look like dummies.'

'We can get one from the motor museum, one they used to test seat belts and safety-bars in crashing cars . . . they're very lifelike. Male . . . tall . . . very flexible, well-dressed . . .'

'Just like me!' beamed Whittington, 'But it would never work! I'm no dummy . . . I move and wave my hands and whatever, I stop for a chat – no dummy can do that!'

'Yes, but our killer doesn't know that, he's never seen you. Besides, we have to accept some limitations, but at the same time we've got to make it work,' said Pemberton. 'What we need is for that chair-borne dummy to follow your exact route and your timing, Mr Whittington, and we need every inch of its journey to be covered with armed officers, all out of sight.'

'We can do that,' said Tyndale with confidence. 'The controls are simple enough and security's no problem – I've already discussed this with these lads. Tell them, Sergeant.'

Sergeant Wilkins, one of the firearms officers, then outlined how he and his officers had undertaken regular exercises to test their ability to respond to armed incidents along the seafront. It was part of their ongoing training, and for that they had obtained the consent of many occupiers of seafront properties – cafés, hotels, private houses, the coastguard station, the lighthouse, even beach chalets and toilet blocks, 'We can bring any of those locations into use at short notice,' he said. 'With six strategically placed officers, with rifles and in radio contact with each other, we can cover the whole of the promenade.'

'You can bring the whole town to a halt, in other words?' asked Pemberton.

'If necessary, sir, with a few strategically placed vehicles and officers,' confirmed Wilkins. 'We might have to do that if he makes a run for it. Now, so far as the far end of the promenade is concerned, vehicles do gather at daybreak, sea fishermen, for example, overnight campers in caravans or cars, goods vehicle drivers taking a break, very early morning workers, that sort of thing. We can place a few undercover vehicles among them if necessary, with armed officers on board, or merely observation crews. It's amazing what you can do inside a white van!'

'And with all that firepower, do you think you could protect a man who's acting as bait?' asked Lorraine.

'I like to think our teams are good enough for that, I'm sure we could take out the killer before he fired, but you know, and I know, I can't guarantee that. The risk is always there, and we can't afford that kind of risk, however small. For that reason, I favour the dummy, sir, to be honest, for safety reasons.'

'Fair enough. Now, I'm thinking of tomorrow morning, Mr Whittington. Your normal time to leave Sandside would be half-past six?'

'Yes, and I take about an hour, there and back, stopping along the way to gaze out to sea, stopping for a chat to the milkman or a jogger, or maybe to watch a ship passing, or the seabirds, or porpoises in the bay or a fisherman or something. There's always something happening at break of day. It's a time I really enjoy.'

259

'Could you show us your route now? We'd like to see precisely where you go, where you stop, how often you stop and so on.'

'No problem,' and so they all trouped outside. Tyndale checked with his security officer; there was no sign of an intruder or anyone hanging around outside and no reports of the Sniper's arrival.

In his powered wheelchair, therefore, Whittington emerged from the side door, trundled through the gardens and down the slope to the promenade, turned left and for the next fifty yards motored along the left of the carriageway. He came to a pedestrian crossing, halted and drove across it, then mounted the wide footpath. On the seaward side were stout metal railings and he moved close to those; his retinue followed and then he slowed down to drive as close as possible to the railings, to look beyond them, on to the rocks below and out across the crashing waves. There were several gaps where ramps reached down to the beach, but he used none of those, preferring to maintain his run along the smoothness of the broad, paved footpath. In time, he arrived at a point overlooking a deep pool within a circle of huge, seaweed-covered rocks, and he halted. Beyond, on the end of the promenade, was a circular large-windowed restaurant which was open throughout the summer, and on his left, on the inland side, were cliffs topped with hotels and private houses. At their base, there were parking spaces on the roadside upon which he was driving. Several flights of steps mounted the cliffs, and stretching in a long row behind the car-parking areas were two dozen beach huts, one or two ice-cream kiosks and a block of toilets.

'Chummy's used a toilet block before,' said Pemberton to Tyndale.

'So have we,' said Tyndale. 'They make good hides!'

About four hundred yards from the restaurant,

Whittington stopped, gazed across the sea for a time, and then turned around.

'I usually stop here for a while,' he said. 'Sometimes there's people around, I chat to them, like the milkman or the window-cleaners, then I go straight back for breakfast. Home for half-seven. I'm never longer than an hour, and sometimes less. Not a lot less. Quarter of an hour, maybe. That's if I remember to go back. Sometimes I forget, you know, I forget what I'm doing here, then they have to come and find me.'

'OK,' called Tyndale. 'Your memory seems all right just now and thanks for showing us this. Now, home it is. See you back there.'

Back in the little conference room, Pemberton asked, 'Dick, can you cover Mr Whittington's route with your firearms teams and observers? All the whole way there and back.'

'Apart from some thick bushes in the garden, no problem,' he said. 'Sarge?'

Sergeant Wilkins nodded. 'Once he's out of the garden, there's plenty of cover for us and plenty of open space for our subject to manoeuvre but nowhere for him to hide. We do need the dummy, sir, if we can arrange it in time, and we need a test run with our teams out of sight, preferably at six-thirty tomorrow morning.'

'Sure. If we use the dummy tomorrow morning, and if chummy is here to witness it, he'll accept it as the normal thing . . . a moving chair with Mr Whittington's name on the back, doing that journey carrying someone who doesn't speak to anyone . . . after all, the person in the chair is very ill,' Pemberton said, 'From what we know of the Sniper's tactics, he does seem to arrive in good time so that he can make a recce . . . and in this case, we think he's already established that Mr Whittington undertakes that morning routine. We can't ignore the fact he might turn up tomorrow with his gun, in which case it will be the real thing. Your exercise will have more than a touch of reality!'

'We can cope,' said Tyndale with confidence.

'The nursing home will be under 24-hour guard too?' Mrs Stockton sought reassurance.

'It will, we'll have surveillance in town and here, nothing and no-one will get past us. You'll not be aware of my officers, but they'll be there. Some you will see, of course, those indoors, in here.'

'What if he calls here in person, or rings up?' she then asked. 'How shall I know if he's a genuine caller for Mr Whittington, it could be the killer?'

'We'll have a plain clothes police officer here all the time; if you show your visitors into the lounge, to wait, they can be vetted. You'll know your regulars, won't you?'

'Oh, yes.'

'So it's just a case of being wary of strangers, whoever they are asking for. Perhaps it would be wiser to move Mr Whittington out of here?'

'And where would I go?' Whittington demanded, 'How can I get the treatment I need . . . no, gentlemen, I'm not moving. I'm safe here, the place will be guarded. You'll have to make sure I'm safe because I shall not move out. No way. Sorry. Put me in another room if you wish, but don't move me out. Anyway, if I do move out, I shall still be at risk, shan't I? He'll find me if he knows I'm not here, there aren't many places you can hide a man with Alzheimer's . . . so leave me here. As I've said, I don't mind being bumped off . . . it'll be a blessing.'

'Mr Whittington's right,' said Pemberton, 'Here we know where he is, and here we can guard him, we know the people here, and they know him. And to catch our villain, we've got to make things look as normal as can be. Strangers will stand out, as will a change of routine. I think this is ideal, provided it is secure.'

'All right,' agreed Tyndale. 'You stay here, Mr Whittington, we can make the place secure. I'll continue the round-the-clock guard. Now, I'll get that wheelchair as soon as I can, and the dummy too, and tomorrow at dawn, we'll need a dress rehearsal . . .'

The Sniper read the article about the Kalashnikov killer several times but his face betrayed no emotion; he could not let himself be seen to be elated or angry or surprised or even really interested, but the fact that this piece had appeared did mean the police knew more than he had realised – and this had been supported by their visit to his grandmother's house. He could never guess how much they really knew, although he was supremely confident in his own ability to continue with his campaign and to avoid capture. Nonetheless, this development did mean that his strategy would have to be amended, just slightly, because it was distinctly possible that the police would be waiting in Rainesbury. He had not missed the expression on the face of the ticket clerk when he'd asked for a ticket to Rainesbury – he'd had to repeat the name for her. If that clerk had any brains at all, she must surely connect the ticket with the headlines about that Detective Superintendent from the same town, the man whose name was all over the reports, looking for a dark-haired man and a motorhome.

The Sniper knew she'd seen the paper, it was on the counter beside her when she dealt with his ticket. Whatever thoughts had gone through her mind at that moment, the Sniper considered it possible that she would alert the police; she could say that a man was on his way to Rainesbury from Wolverhampton.

That's how his own mind would have worked in such circumstances – but perhaps he was cleverer than a mere ticket clerk? However slender those chances were, it meant the sniper had to be careful because he was not

263

going to be deflected from his cause. Anyone with a true cause could not allow themselves to be deflected . . .

To his advantage, he had time on his side . . . he had no timetable or deadline with which to comply; he thought the word 'deadline' was very apt for his mission. But for his purpose one day was as good as any other and he had discovered, by ringing the nursing home, that Whittington undertook a daily outing at half-past six every morning. It never ceased to amaze him how willing people were to impart information to strangers over the telephone! Whittington went out every morning, not necessarily tomorrow or the day after, but every morning. So the Sniper could wait; he had money in his pocket, time on his side and infinite patience. In fact, he believed he had more patience than the police.

For that reason, therefore, he did not take the first available connection when he changed trains. Alert to the possibility of plain clothes railway police officers looking out for him, he made small changes to his appearance, using the clothes he carried in his backpack and he spent time waiting on the platforms in Manchester Piccadilly as if waiting for a train heading in the opposite direction; he left his train at Leeds and had a meal, he left the station at York for a potter around the town and then, when he returned an hour later to catch his final link, he decided not to disembark at Rainesbury.

Instead, he would leave the train at Wentford, two stations prior to reaching Rainesbury, then catch a bus. Before catching the bus, though, he would put on a red kagoul from his backpack and change his baseball cap to black instead of red. It was amazing what difference a change of clothing could make.

It was not until early evening that the sniper reached Rainesbury. As he left the bus, he looked at the assortment of people who were queuing for the outgoing services and, to avoid looking conspicuous, tagged on to the end of a queue marked 'Scarborough and Whitby'. From there, he could survey the whole bus station as he sought the tell-tale presence of a waiting police officer, but there was no sign. As the queue began to move forward when the coach pulled in, he slid away from it, muttering something about the wrong queue, and hurried past the front of the vehicle to disappear around the end of the wall which divided the bus station from a department store. Now he was in a busy, narrow street packed with visitors and locals alike even at this time of day; he saw a sign saying 'Seafront; Harbour; Beach; Promenade' and hurried that way, seeking bed-and-breakfast signs as he walked. There were many such signs. The town, eager to attract tourists for longer than just a day trip, had encouraged the proliferation of places of accommodation and he could take his pick.

Many were eagerly seeking guests – people came for day trips now, rather than paying for overnight accommodation and so the guest houses were keen to attract business. Eventually, he found a suitable small boarding house called Sea View. It overlooked the seafront and when he examined the available room, he was delighted to see it provided a long view along the Promenade. This was precisely what he wanted; he congratulated himself on selecting this place.

'This is excellent,' he smiled at the plump landlady who must be approaching sixty-five. 'I'll pay in advance if you like . . .'

'I'd appreciate that, but I don't do evening meals,' she warned him.

'No problem, I'll get something in town. Bed and breakfast is what I want, for the whole week?'

'I don't allow smoking or loud music!'

'I don't smoke and I have no radio with me,' he said, dumping his backpack on the floor. 'I'm a very quiet man, I'm here for a bit of peace and quiet, I'm trying to

265

write a song, a pop song I must admit, but it will be a ballad, a romance . . .'

'Oh, well, I'm sure you will be happy here, Mr . . .'

'Cunningham. Gareth, call me Gareth. I'm from Stratford-on-Avon, my dad works for the theatre, you know, backstage, lighting, but he's got contacts, he says, and so if I get this piece written, well, I could be rich and famous! I thought I'd use the sea as my inspiration, the early morning atmosphere, that calmness before the tourists come and clutter the place . . . that's why I'm here, I came on spec, a last minute decision really, but this room is just perfect for me . . . especially that view . . .'

The landlady, Mrs Gwendoline Crabtree, thought how nice it would have been to have had a son so charming and talented – and good looking – and so she offered him the room. She added that it had not been booked for next week either, so if he decided to stay longer, he'd be more than welcome. And breakfast was downstairs in the dining room at eight o'clock sharp, and she expected him to be out of his room daily at ten and not return before six. He could leave things in the room while he was out and if he wanted to stay out later than eleven, she could provide him with a key. He smiled his consent and he handed over enough cash for a seven-day stay. She said she'd give him a receipt later, she'd push it under his door if he was out.

'I know this will be just right for me,' he oozed. 'I would like to go out very early some mornings, to catch the atmosphere, you understand, my inspiration, I call it. I can let myself out can I?'

'So long as you don't wake the others by banging doors and flushing toilets too loudly,' she agreed. 'And I'm up at seven anyway, so the door will be open then, for you to come in. It's a Yale, so there's no problem letting yourself out. Just drop the latch as you leave.'

'This sounds just perfect,' he smiled at her.

266

'You can leave your things in your room tonight,' she said. 'If you want to look around town. There is a key to your wardrobe, so you can lock things away, not that I've ever had dishonest people in the house but you never know . . .'

And so the Sniper found a refuge; tonight, wearing his blue baseball cap, a sweat shirt with a Four-X advert, and pale slacks, he would explore the seafront and promenade, find somewhere for a meal and have an early night. There were combination locks on his back-pack, and it was locked in the wardrobe. Its contents would be safe, Mrs Crabtree would see to that. And tomorrow morning, he would go jogging.

Chapter Seventeen

Pemberton, equipped with a radio and his mobile phone, was in position at 4.45 a.m. the following morning. It was a misty morning, typical of the coastal locality and marked with a heavy drizzle which came off the sea. The far views were shrouded but, to date, there were no problems with near visibility.

The seafront house in which Pemberton was based belonged to an army officer who understood the requirements, and he gave permission for it to be used for the surveillance exercise for as long as necessary. He provided a key too, so the police had uninterrupted access to the vital part of his house. It was large enough for their purpose without interfering with his domestic routine. From the attic, there were sweeping views along most of the Promenade. The only part not visible was the short stretch through Sandside gardens to the seafront, and then for about a hundred yards until the Promenade began to curve around the cliff face. Once the Promenade materialised, there was an open view for almost a mile as it passed below and curved its around two bays towards the circular restaurant. Tyndale had arranged for armed supervision of the route not within Pemberton's view – the entire route to be traversed by Whittington's substitute chair was therefore under armed supervision.

Although the chair's remote control system could be countermanded by anyone riding on board, one minor operational problem had emerged. To manipulate it from a distance with the hand-held control box, the chair itself had always to be within range of the controls, even if it was sometimes out of sight. It would not move through its own momentum, even downhill. Once contact was lost, it stopped.

After various tests and exploratory exercises, it had been discovered that contact could be maintained from the streets, roads and paths on or near the clifftop. There was a surfaced road along the top of the cliffs, footpaths down some parts of the face away from sheer drops, and access to the cliffs was possible even where there were no footpaths. There were plenty of places for the controller to move so that he could stay in contact with the chair while shelter was provided by the dense vegetation on the cliff face and by the inevitable cars parked above.

Tests had shown it was possible to run the remote-controlled chair from Sandside to a point very close to the circular restaurant. Due to worries about the unrealistic appearance of the dummy passenger, the chair had been equipped with a plastic hood, a variation of the kind mothers use to protect infants in prams, and this had helped disguise the figure within. The figure was held upright by a small quick-release seat belt. Although the hood was made from clear plastic, its creases and scratches did partially obscure the passenger, who looked realistic enough not to attract unwelcome attention. With Whittington's name, plus 'Sandside' on the back of the chair, the entire outfit did look most effective. As things had turned out, the typically damp North Sea weather made the hood look completely normal – such all-embracing plastic hoods were a feature of many small invalid carriages and most were large enough to accommodate shopping and other objects on board.

The remote-controlled chair would make a run this morning, leaving Sandside at six-thirty, and emulating almost exactly every facet of Whittington's morning journey. By five, therefore, every armed officer and observer was in position.

Whittington himself, who'd forgotten what this was all about, would be kept by the staff in Sandside, while in strategic positions along the route, concealed police photographers with still cameras and video recorders would capture the entire exercise on film. It was hoped to compare photographs of persons using the Promenade with those of Steele – indeed, every officer would be shown a picture of him, the one taken some time ago, in the hope they might recognise him in Rainesbury. It was emphasised, however, that he was a man who seemed to regularly change his appearance so there was no guarantee he would or could be identified. It had been decided not to interview or halt members of the public who passed by this morning, or indeed any morning. To start quizzing them might alert the Sniper – indeed he might be one of them. They needed to catch him, to draw him into their net, not frighten him away – and Whittington was no longer in danger from him.

As the police waited that first morning, therefore, it was surprising how many people and vehicles passed along the seafront. A window cleaner's van, several fish delivery lorries, cyclists in chef's clothing going to work in hotels and restaurants, a newspaper delivery van, several paper lads on bikes, post office vans, joggers including one in a yellow tracksuit, a milk float full of rattling bottles, and several cars going about private business. There were people walking dogs or riding bikes with dogs running behind, a police car blissfully unaware of the activity nearby – these and more all passed along the Promenade before six-thirty; each vehicle and person was recorded both on paper and on film, along with their times, direction of movement and any identifying features.

At six-fifteen, Pemberton activated his radio, knowing

each of his officers could hear every broadcast, 'Kilo One to Control.'

'Go ahead, Kilo One.'

'Kilo One checking. Kilo Two in position?'

'Roger.'

'Kilo Three?'

'Roger.'

And so he went through the entire list of twenty-five police officers in their pre-arranged concealed locations, until he said, 'Kilo Mobile?'

'Kilo Mobile in position,' came the response of its controller, 'No problems.'

'Received, Kilo Mobile. Go now. All stations alert, Kilo Mobile is beginning its run. Action and observations as planned. Kilo One out.'

There was a long silence.

For what seemed an eternity, nothing happened except that the people on the Promenade continued their normal activities – a group of five fishermen had unexpectedly arrived to cast their lines into the sea, a caravan moved away from an overnight parking area, more joggers moved along at a steady pace – and then the invalid carriage appeared in the distance to Pemberton's right. It was chugging sedately along the wide footpath beside the railings which bordered the beach, and the figure could be seen inside. From this distance, in Whittington's blue track suit and white beret, it did look very realistic, just like an old weakened man. Pemberton focused a pair of binoculars on the trundling vehicle and it looked most impressive – then he realised it was heading towards the group of fishermen who were standing at the rails. However, the operator on the cliffs noticed the obstruction and steered the carriage away, buzzing it around the group, and it continued without any of them taking a scrap of notice.

Pemberton was quite intrigued to see that several people waved at the moving carriage – the driver of the

271

milk float waved cheerily, a couple of joggers running side by side each waved and so did a jogger on his own, an auburn-haired man dressed in a short and gaudy orange plastic rainproof jacket. These were obviously regulars, people who passed this way every morning, and they'd not spotted the deception. None had seen fit to stop the vehicle, not even to see if the occupant was all right. He smiled with relief. The plan was clearly effective.

The invalid carriage reached the point of the Promenade close to the circular restaurant where it had been decided to turn it around for the return trip. The controller, as instructed when there was no-one close to the chair, turned it to face outwards across the North Sea, then halted it in that position for a minute or so. It seemed as if the occupant was gazing out to sea and the contraption attracted no attention from passers-by. A newspaper delivery lad on a bike sailed past, a man dressed in painter's overalls also passed on a pedal cycle and did not halt or stare at it, and others ignored it. Eventually, it turned away from that viewpoint and began the return journey. It was an uneventful but important trip. The invalid carriage chugged slowly back to Sandside, renegotiating the group of fishermen in the process and vanished around the side of the cliff as it completed its final stretch of the trip.

It had taken fifty minutes this morning.

Then a voice said, 'Kilo Mobile to Control. Returned to base. No problems. Kilo Mobile out.'

'Received,' said Control.

'Stand by,' added Pemberton. 'Kilo One to all units. Remain at your posts, continue to observe the Promenade . . .'

Every police officer remained at his or her post for a further forty-five minutes, recording the presence of everyone who moved along the Promenade and then Pemberton dismissed them.

'Exercise Kilo concluded. Make your way back to Divisional Headquarters,' he said. 'Separately, not in groups. We will have a debriefing at nine in the Conference Room. The canteen is open for breakfast.'

The Sniper was pleased with his first jogging session along the Promenade. His earlier research had been proved correct – John Whittington in his invalid carriage did make a daily excursion along the Promenade beginning at six-thirty. And what a good idea, having his name on the back of his chair! People had recognised him and had waved in greeting – if only they had known who he was and what he'd done!

The only worry, from the Sniper's perspective, was that group of fishermen who had suddenly arrived. But they were fishermen, not undercover police, he decided. They were too small, scruffy and disinterested to be police officers. And, from his operational point of view, there was plenty of cover along the Promenade.

He noted lots of parked vehicles, places to wait out of sight like that restaurant complex, plenty of people moving about even at that time of day . . . yes, he could deal with Whittington here, very nicely. He saw no problem; in fact, it seemed ideal for his purpose. He'd do another test run tomorrow, just to check a few things. And then, after popping into a town centre gents to remove and pocket his auburn wig, he jogged back to Seaview for his breakfast.

He'd tell Mrs Crabtree that already he'd found some inspiration.

Pemberton and Tyndale jointly chaired the debriefing.

Tyndale began. 'I found it most encouraging that the dummy was accepted as a real person. I was quite surprised to find that regular passersby greeted it. That gives me tremendous confidence. I know the weather helped, but at least no-one decided to check whether the figure was alive! I thought the response was very reassuring and completely normal for an old person moving along in a covered wheelchair, doing the same trip every day. So, yes, I'm happy to continue with this plan.'

'Is it good enough to fool the Sniper, if he turns up?' Pemberton asked.

'I'm sure it is. If he watched today, he'd be convinced it was Whittington, I'm sure of that,' said Tyndale. 'If the regulars thought it was him, people who often see him chugging along there, then it must surely convince the Sniper. Having seen it in operation myself, it's good enough for me. Remember, all we have to do is draw him into the open, we're baiting the trap with the chair, no more than that.'

'Was he there, do you think, watching and planning?' was Pemberton's next question to the officers seated before him. 'He might have been there. We'd never know, would we? We need to check the videos and stills to see if we can spot him, but I must admit I didn't see anyone like his photo. Have we a local police officer here, someone who knows the routine hereabouts at this time of day?'

'Sir,' a young constable raised his hand. 'I often patrol that beat in the early morning. A lot of those people were regulars on that stretch of the Prom, the milkfloat, the window cleaner, fish lorries, dog walkers and so on. There were some strangers though, a jogger or two, some people walking, a cyclist, but that's the way it is here, being a holiday resort. There's always people about, especially in summer. If we film tomorrow, we'll catch most of them again. We can comb the pictures for strangers.'

'Right, we'll do that, we'll film it all again tomorrow. If he strikes, it means we'll catch him on film too. He does seem to like time to plan his moves. If we can

274

decide which are strangers to the town, we'll concentrate on those – remembering that one of them could be the sniper.'

'That bunch of fishermen were on holiday, I'm sure,' the constable told them. 'I've not seen them before. They arrived in an estate car, we've got the number, it's being checked. But I don't think we can suspect any of them.'

'We're looking for a loner. Any loners lurking about?' asked Pemberton. 'Hanging around with binoculars, or loitering near the nursing home, following the wheelchair, that sort of thing?'

Every officer present shook his or her head.

'No, no-one lingering or hiding, no-one looking suspicious,' said one of them. 'There were lots of joggers passing by but we always get them, day in and day out, locals and holidaymakers. Besides, a jogger can't hide a Kalashnikov in his vest and shorts!'

They discussed the people they'd seen; as they were on film, they could be further checked by policemen with local knowledge, all passing vehicles could be traced through their registration numbers and all non-suspects eliminated. The joggers captured on film would be compared with the pictures of Steele even though, at first sight, none resembled his photograph. Pemberton did remind them that if Steele was out and about, either on the Promenade during the early morning or in town, he would probably be in disguise – something as simple as spectacles and a baseball cap might suffice.

'Tomorrow, then?' said Pemberton when the discussions had concluded. 'Same time, same place, same routine. And we take lots of photographs, stills and videos.'

'Sir.'

Tyndale added, 'And don't forget our man might be in town. I want eyes peeled the whole time, I'll be giving those instructions to our town patrols. If he's in town, we must find him. He won't spend all his time on the Promenade or in his digs, wherever they are – and I have arranged for the Registers of all hotels and boarding establishments to be discreetly checked. Not that he'd use his real name!'

'It might be worth checking with fruit shops as well, to see if anyone's been buying large quantities of oranges!' smiled Pemberton. 'Or the supermarkets.'

Tyndale nodded. 'Yes, a good point. Be discreet though, we don't want some fruit shop proprietor telling his orange-buying customers that the police have been asking questions about orange eaters! That could scare him off! We want him here, we want him caught. By the way, the nursing home is fully protected by armed police, all day, every day until further notice. Whittington is safe there. He won't be allowed out, the staff will see to that.'

'What about his other outings, sir?' asked a sergeant.

'Whittington does not always go on those, he can be a bit of a loner, he mainly does the early morning run,' Pemberton said. 'His disease is a problem, so he's limited as to his freedom. He's best on a morning, so it seems. But if he does decide to change his habits, or forget that he's not supposed to be going out, Mrs Stockton, her staff or our resident police officer will stop him. We want him to appear to go only on that early morning trip. The sniper knows about that early outing. That's when he'll strike, if he's true to form.'

'Thanks.'

'And now I'd better ring the Incident Room at Roberthorpe, just a check call!'

The following morning, everyone was again in place at 4.45 a.m.; as with yesterday, the weather was poor, with

276

dampness in the air and a sea-fret threatening the town.

The remote-controlled wheelchair did its morning run at six-thirty, the regulars turned up as usual and some waved at the passing wheelchair. Joggers jogged, dog walkers walked, milkmen delivered and newspaper lads rode bikes. No-one took a shot at the passing invalid carriage, no-one stopped it to ask after the welfare of its occupant and so it returned to base without incident. Comparison of this morning's film and yesterday's showed a remarkable consistency, with the same people appearing at or very near the same time and in the same place; even the auburn-haired jogger in his orange jacket was on time, running with high steps and appearing to enjoy the brisk sea air even if the peak of his cap was rather low. The same joggers passed through, but there were two new ones, neither of which looked like Steele. One was too small and the other was a woman.

'No problems?' asked Pemberton at the debriefing.

'No, sir,' said his officers.

'Tomorrow, then, same time, same place,' and they all went home.

For the next four days, that was the pattern. There were no reports of anyone buying undue amounts of oranges and no sign of any suspicious person loitering upon the Promenade or apparently checking locations. Tests against the known pictures of Steele had not made any of the early-morning joggers appear to be suspicious; even though the auburn-haired high-stepper was prominent on the films, it had been confirmed none would be stopped and interviewed. It had been emphasised that entrapment of Steele was the priority here; Whittington was quite safe in his Home.

As time passed, the weather did improve slightly, but the invalid carriage continued to use the all-embracing plastic see-through hood and there were few changes to the personnel who were out and about at that time of day. The auburn-haired jogger in the bright orange jacket discarded that, now running in a yellow vest with 'Ferensby Gym' emblazoned on the back in black ink – that was a gym in Hull, well-known to some police officers – but the film sequences might have been a repeat of the earlier ones. So little change . . . no gunshots were aimed at the trundling wheelchair, no-one followed it and many of the regulars continued to wave at the wheelchair with their greetings, including the auburn-haired jogger.

'I'm beginning to think the Sniper never got here, I think the publicity might have made him go to ground,' commented Pemberton. 'There've been no sightings elsewhere though, no arrests of suspicious people, no reports from Ted Edwards or Jack Radcliffe, nothing from Wolverhampton or the railway police. My Incident Room is very quiet with no developments, and no-one in our seaside snaps has any resemblance to Steele. So where is he? Gone to ground? Done a vanishing trick or gone into hiding until all this has blown over? It's as if he's vanished from the face of the earth! And I must beware of the fact that some of our men – and the staff of the Home – might reduce their concentration – we need to keep them at the peak of alertness.'

'He's lulling you into a false sense of security,' warned Tyndale. 'You said he was cunning, you've said it all along. Don't let his absence convince you he's given up, Mark, you know better than that.'

'I accept we won't deter him, he could be somewhere else, planning another crime miles from here. But I can't justify all your men standing by like this, day after day, with nothing to show for it. He could have abandoned this project.'

'It'll be a week tomorrow since we started the exercise, Mark. Give it a whirl tomorrow, see what happens, Give it one more day.'

'And then we'll reappraise the whole thing, eh? We need to do that. We do know he was in Roberthorpe for a week before he struck, he might adopt the same tactics here, so yes, I'll agree to one more day! See you at four forty-five tomorrow morning then?'

And, so for the seventh day, the officers briefed by both Pemberton and Tyndale assembled at their prearranged points overlooking the Promenade. They occupied the points they had used since day one. The morning began as the other mornings had begun, with just a hint of mist over the sea although, on this occasion, the morning was drier than previously. The presence of early-morning mist promised a day of sunshine ahead, a bonus for the day-trippers and holidaymakers who would flock to Rainesbury if the sun remained visible long enough to attract them. When the sun shone, day-trippers were like moths flocking towards the light. They would come in their thousands, cars and slow-moving caravans to clog the roads, fill the car parks and frustrate the local residents. But that was life in Rainesbury – except at crack of dawn on the Promenade. By this seventh day, therefore, the routine had been well established.

All the officers, faithful to their duties, had slotted into their well-rehearsed and practised routine. They reported their presence by radio, they gazed upon the Promenade below them to observe the passing show and they awaited the regular morning ritual of milk floats, fishing lorries, dog walkers, joggers and newspaper boys. Their long wait would be alleviated by the appearance of a remote-controlled invalid carriage bearing a dummy in a white beret which might attract the bullets of a would-be assassin. So far, it had not done so.

279

There had been absolutely no suggestion of such a thing – the whole exercise was almost at the farcical stage. Nothing had happened, nothing looked like happening. There was a danger that the police on this special duty would become bored and careless. But if the Sniper did appear and fire his rifle, they would have to react, and react with speed. After a week of near immobility, they would have to become instantly active, they would have to contain him, disarm him and arrest him before he shot himself or anyone else. The signal to move would be a shot at the dummy unless he revealed himself earlier.

Then came the voice of Pemberton over the inter-linked radio. 'Kilo One to Control, is everyone in position?'

They acknowledged in numerical order, Kilo One, Kilo Two and so on until Kilo Two-Five when Pemberton confirmed, 'Action as usual. Observe Kilo Mobile, report any diversion from the normal, use initiative in the event of an attack.'

It was a well-practised if futile routine, but dutifully each officer made the appropriate acknowledgement and they would then while away their time until it was six-thirty. Then at six-thirty, Pemberton again set in motion the final sequence.

'Kilo Control, are you receiving?'

'Kilo Control receiving loud and clear.'

'Kilo Control we are all in position. Proceed.'

'Kilo Control. Kilo Mobile is proceeding,' came the response.

At Sandside, a nurse rushed into Mrs Stockton's office and said, 'Mrs Stockton, Mr Whittington's not in his room . . .'

'Find him!' she snapped. 'And tell that policeman . . .'
'Yes, Mrs Stockton.'

There was a slight delay as the remote-controlled invalid carriage made its way from the spare garage at the back of the building and chugged down through Sandside gardens to the main carriageway of the Promenade, and then it appeared in Pemberton's sight.

'Kilo One, target in view,' he said. 'No incidents to date. Maintain observations.'

As on every morning to date, the plastic hooded remote-controlled invalid carriage crossed the road to gain the wide pavement on the seaward side, and then it began to motor along the footpath, heading at a slow pace along the railings towards the distant circular restaurant at the far end of the run. As before, there was a slight mist over the sea and a touch of dampness in the air, but the figure in the chair with its familiar blue track-suit and white beret could be seen sitting firmly upright and staring straight ahead, as indeed he had done every day this week. This morning, there were no fishermen to negotiate, but there were the regulars – the paper boys, the joggers, the fish vans, the post office vans, the dog exercisers and more.

'The dummy's in the garage and I can't raise Pemberton,' shouted the constable in Sandside. 'All external radio links are closed during the exercise . . . and if I'm seen leaving here, it'll blow the whole thing . . .'

The wheelchair with its transparent plastic cover moved along the wide footpath towards the restaurant and no-one took any notice of the milk float which approached it. The milk float had appeared every morning this week; this was its regular run. It called at the restaurant to deliver countless bottles of milk and soft drinks before moving slowly along the Promenade, and its driver, the cheery and happy milkman, always waved at the wheelchair. This morning though, the milkman did not wave – perhaps he had become fed up of waving to the unresponsive old man in the chair? Or perhaps he had something else on his mind . . .

In fact, he had much on his mind this morning because, beyond the restaurant and out of sight of the police, a jogger with a backpack had hijacked the milk-float. He'd thrown down the remains of an uneaten orange, donned a white coat and told the driver to keep moving at risk of being shot dead. He must not divert from his path, he must not wave at anyone as the hijacker lay under the canvas cover in the rear with a fearsome looking gun . . . all the milkman had to do was to keep moving forwards, not looking behind, not stopping for anyone or anything . . . the instructions were very clear and very simple.

But this morning, the figure on the wheelchair waved at the milkfloat as it buzzed slowly towards him along the Promenade. Pemberton noticed the gesture and for the briefest of moments did not appreciate the significance of what he was seeing – then he realised.

'God, he's in there! Whittington's in that chair, he waved . . .' the truth dawned on him. The cunning old Whittington had outwitted those back at Sandside and managed to get aboard the buggie!

Pemberton cancelled the security switch and radioed Sandside Nursing Home. 'Kilo One. Check the dummy . . . I think Whittington is in the chair . . . check, check, check, now, now, now . . .'

'Sir, we know, we've been trying to raise you, he got into the garage . . .'

'God, what now!' cursed Pemberton as he focused his binoculars on the moving wheelchair, shouting to the

282

camera crews to do likewise. Then he was shouting into his radio, 'That is no dummy . . . he's there, Whittington is in that wheelchair . . . my God . . . he's letting the controller move it along . . . but he is there, a sitting target . . .'

Then, almost immediately, the wheelchair went temporarily out of sight as the milk float passed by, the milk float being on the road and the wheelchair on the wide pavement. No-one had taken any notice of the milk float as it had drawn closer to the invalid carriage because it had done so every morning this week.

Already, Pemberton was shouting into his radio. 'Abort, abort, abort . . .'

But he was too late because as the two vehicles passed, the tarpaulin in the rear of the milk float was moved aside just a fraction. The muzzle of a Kalashnikov appeared from beneath it and four or five shots shattered the silence of that morning. The man in the wheelchair slumped dead across the control handle with four bullets in his chest.

'Go, go, go,' shouted Pemberton.

As armed police officers tumbled out of vans and cars and bushes, a man leapt from the rear of the still-moving milk float and began to run towards the cars near the circular restaurant, but his escape bid was blocked by police officers armed with rifles. He could not go anywhere. He did not attempt to resist. He threw down his Kalashnikov, raised his hands and smiled in triumph. As some rushed to the aid of the man in the wheelchair, Steele waited until he was surrounded. Pemberton arrived moments later.

'Michael James Steele . . .' he began in a breathless voice rocked with emotion.

But Steele did not let him finish. 'You must be Pemberton. That was number four. Another good hit, eh? Four down, fourteen to go,' he said cheerfully and with pride in his voice. 'I didn't kill the ones I served time for, did you know that? I was innocent but I did eighteen years for it. Eighteen years, can you imagine that? I'm going for eighteen unconvicted killers, one for every year I should not have served. I said I was guilty so they'd let me out, I had to, to fulfil my mission but I wasn't guilty. I've got four so far, you've got me now but I'll be out in twelve years, won't I, if I plead guilty again? I've lots more killers to find, you see. When I get out again, that is. I'll keep hunting them down, you know that, don't you? I can easily get another gun. I'll come quietly now, I promise, I'll make a full statement. I'm looking forward to this trial . . . the newspapers will be there, won't they? I'll be famous. You know Whittington deserved to die, they all did . . .'

Pemberton, even now thinking of the disciplinary charge which would surely be levelled against himself and Tyndale for neglect of duty in allowing Whittington to die, interrupted the Sniper's non-stop flow of words and said, 'I am arresting you for the murder of Kenneth Bourne . . .'